HIGH NOON

ON COME ALONG SLOUGH

HIGH NOON
ON COME ALONG SLOUGH

BRUCE CAMPBELL

Illustrated by

Hilary Glass

Aristata Press

Library of Congress Control Number: 2024912050

Design & Layout: Anne McClard
Cover Art, Maps and Illustrations: Hilary Glass
Photo of the author: Nancy Henry

ISBN: 979-8-9906293-5-6 (hardcover)
ISBN: 979-8-9906293-3-2 (paperback)
ISBN: 979-8-9906293-4-9 (ebook)

All text, except where noted otherwise, is original to the author.

This book is a work of fiction. The places and characters are wholly
fabricated.

Aristata Press, Portland Oregon
www.aristatapress.com

For my Family

AUTHOR'S NOTE

ACCORDING TO THE GREEKS, allegory was the "description of one thing under the image of another." *High Noon on Come Along Slough* is an animal allegory—or book-length fable. The animal characters laugh and cry. They speak like humans. Human virtues and vices shape thoughts and govern actions. Most of all, this allegory/fable speculates on how a group of animals living on and around the waters of Come Along Slough responds to environmental emergencies. In writing my book, no real animals were injured or killed.

BIG RIVER
N
NW
NE
W
E
SW
SE
S
HOMELESS
CAMP
SLOUGH
KEY
DRY
GRASS
LAND
SOGGY
SLOUGH
GRASS
WATER
EDGES
SQUIB TOWN
COME ALONG SLOUGH

Because we are the rough beasts of the field, the Natural Law of Animals compels us to kill for a living. This hungry world has taught us no other way to survive.

KAWPHONIOUS THE GIANT RAVEN

In Long-Ago Time, a great flood drowned many of our ancestors, but Girl saved a few of us. She wasn't like the other Squibs. She was a good Squib.

AS TOLD BY MUSKRAT
(DESCENDANT OF GREAT MOTHER
MUSKRAT)

Four legs good! Two legs bad!

—*ANIMAL FARM*, GEORGE ORWELL

1 THE SLOUGH IS A VERY LARGE STOMACH

Muskrat crouched behind the cattails as three large Rats swam slowly past her. She dared not breathe. The Rats were hunting the Slough's muddy shoreline for Birds' eggs, Frogs, Ducklings, Goslings, Turtles, and newborn Nutrias. Muskrat knew she was also on the menu. One Rat lifted its whiskered snout, trying to catch a scent, slanting sunlight piercing the small black sac of its eyeball. Its nose twitched. Did the Rat see her? Muskrat almost bolted from cover, but she stayed put, trying to become one with the mud. The Rat lowered its head and moved on, its snaky tail creasing the surface of the water.

Soon after, Muskrat heard a high-pitched squeal. Then a thrashing sound. Then another squeal. Silence followed. Who had been killed? She released her breath slowly, waiting, unable to calm her heartbeat.

Finally, she eased herself out into open water. She saw no Rats, but since they could swim underwater, she didn't feel safe. She began to swim toward the far shore of the Slough. Algae and scraps of plastic flagged her small reddish-brown body. She stopped frequently to swivel around, looking for telltale ripples or bubbles. Shuddering, she imagined a Rat surfacing beneath her and ripping out her belly.

Chevrons of soupy green water marked her progress. Using her scaly black tail to change directions, she navigated around logs, lily pads, and the dark hulk of a half-submerged truck tire. She saw the approaching shoreline, its perimeter hackled with Slough grass. Pressing business awaited her there. As the recently elected secretary-general, it was her job to convene and preside over the United Slough of Animals. She hastened her pace. Not a good look for the boss to be late for an important meeting.

The animals called this body of water Come Along Slough. According to Owl, who claimed to know most everything, Kawphonious the Giant Raven had appeared in the Time-Before-Memory, commanding the first generation of creatures to "come along and see the Slough." The name stuck, but most simply called it the Slough. It was Muskrat's home, and she had known no other. Kawphonious had described the Slough as "a very large stomach." Muskrat agreed with this. At some point, the Slough swallowed everyone—even Coyote, who swallowed any animal he could get his jaws on. Muskrat wished the Slough would also swallow the Squibs. That wasn't likely, though. The Squibs did most of the swallowing—and it seemed that the more they swallowed, the hungrier they became. She feared they would soon consume the Slough and its community of animals.

Muskrat stopped swimming. The waning sunlight gave

the water a dusty gold glow. She sniffed the air. The Slough reeked of warm mud and rotting vegetation. A metallic object riddled with holes blocked her path. Squib Dog called it a refrigerator. What a strange word!

Fearing a Rat ambush, she detoured around the refrigerator and glided forward, her fur iridescent with tinges of motor oil. Rolling onto her back, she gazed up at a cloud of cattail fluff drifting overhead. Water coursed across her prominent rust-colored incisors. She sniffed again, this time catching the signature scents of skunk cabbage and bog rosemary, along with trace fragrances of goldenrod, pigweed, and nettleleaf horsemint. She smelled no Rats. Life was good.

Then a wave of sadness surged through her. For several mating seasons, all her litters had been born dead. Now most of the male Muskrats had mysteriously disappeared from the Slough. Had the Squibs trapped them? She wasn't sure, but she missed the old days when the males would cock their eyebrows and curl their tails, fighting for mating privileges. The nasal tease of active anal glands drove every Muskrat wild. Like any other fertile Muskrat, she courted the available males in turn, swimming amorous circles around them while squeaking her mating song. Now she had nothing to squeak about.

Muskrat shook off her sadness. She had to mentally prepare for the impending tasks of her high office. The first item of business on tonight's USA agenda was Elrod the Stoat. He'd committed another criminal transgression and needed to be punished. His filthy little mouth really aggravated her. Elrod's life had been rough, of course. His mother had shorted him on her milk, making him the runt of the litter, and then his beloved older brother had been smashed by a truck. Muskrat didn't care. Life on the Slough was full of sob stories, and she couldn't make exceptions for one miserable trash-talking Stoat. Elrod was a real jerk. For that matter, so was Coyote. Those two often ganged up to mock her authority and twist her words to their own advantage. In a recent USA meeting, Elrod had gone so far as to bare his fangs after she chided him for his snarky remarks.

"Don't take your mating frustrations out on me, sweetheart," he sneered. "Not my fault you keep getting the short end of the stick."

This got a quick laugh from Coyote. "She's a hot little Petunia," he said. "Shame nobody ever comes around to sample the goods."

Muskrat hated them both. But once the disagreeable Elrod business was over, she knew the USA would have to grapple with a much more serious matter: Rats. Hundreds of Rats had invaded Come Along Slough, claiming the territory as their own. The USA and its constituents now faced an existential threat. The Rats raided at night. They gobbled up Mama Mallard's eggs, slaughtered Robin's fledglings, and stole Squirrel's nuts. And it seemed that Rats savored the raw sewage that poured into the Slough. They clustered around the outflow pipe, frolicking in the gunk and snacking on the goodies. They squabbled, scratched, and hissed. They squealed and copulated, then snoozed. Disgusting! Many times, Muskrat had seen them swimming the Slough, the moonlight glinting in their hard black eyes. Each eye rotated independently of the other, bulging with malevolence. Crazy eyes. Nasty eyes. The USA had to act fast and shut down their whole bloody show.

Holding the office of secretary-general was tricky business, and dangerous. Two of her fiercest critics, Elrod and Coyote, sometimes threatened to eat her. Muskrat understood that she was a food source for any predator, but she kept hoping that her official position would exempt her from getting her head bitten off.

Muskrat craved pageantry and thunderous ovations, but being secretary-general came with scant prestige. She was mostly just a figurehead. Heavy with lowbrow protocol, the office lacked pomp and polish. She got more sneers than cheers. During any meeting, she was an easy target for potshots from the disgruntled. Slander and physical intimidation came at her from all sides. Holding a high office required her to tolerate mediocrity, sloth, and ridicule. The daily grind wore down her spirit—but she was no quitter. During each nerve-wracking meeting, she calmed herself by visualizing her comfort food: cattails. They fed both stomach and soul, and she could never get enough of them.

Muskrat refused to lie to herself, though; she didn't feel safe at any USA meeting. And it wasn't just because of Coyote and Elrod; she also feared Red-Tailed Hawk and Bald Eagle. Even worse, many feral Dogs roamed the Slough, castoffs of their Squib owners. If she set foot on dry land to search for food, the Dogs went after her. Sometimes they even splashed out into the water, snapping at her backside.

Her fear of a violent death was constant. If only she'd been born higher up on the food chain. Maybe then she could relax for a few moments and perhaps find a mate. In the meantime, she would strive to be the best Muskrat secretary-general possible, encouraging her fellow denizens of the Slough to be patient, kind, and humble as they squabbled about the scarcity of food and shelter. Yes, the pickings on the Slough were slim, but why be so ill-tempered about it?

2 A DUNG HEAP OF DO NOTHINGS

Seeing Muskrat's approach, Beaver emerged from a stand of cattails and slapped his tail on the water, calling the meeting to order. In the muddled light of early evening, a diverse quorum of creatures congregated beneath the trees, the overhanging branches crusty with dried moss and cobwebs. Elected by their peers, the USA delegates represented their respective species.

Muskrat stopped short of dry land, exposed her brow to public view, and spied Elrod standing close to Coyote. They both leered at her. The first sighting of those two predators always made her heart lurch. She took a deep breath and dug her paws into the mud, staying put. Returning to the open water wasn't a good option; with darkness approaching, even more Rats would swarm the Slough. She snapped off a cattail and munched on it, savoring the grassy smell, the fuzzy texture, and the strong honey-on-the tongue flavors offset with traces of bitterness. As she chewed, she mumbled to herself, "I won't let Elrod and Coyote intimidate me. No, no, no."

With daylight dwindling, cool air wafted up from the

Slough. She tightened her jaw, trying to focus upon the current issues that clamored for her attention. She always conducted business close to the water, keeping a wary eye mostly on Coyote. He liked to sneak up close and jangle her nerves, just to remind her that he was an apex predator. His unbalanced mental state was particularly unnerving. He often talked to himself, conducting one-sided conversations with a voice in his head he called Old Man Coyote. Coyote whispered, whined, growled, or even shouted. Everyone heard him, but ignored this disturbing behavior during USA meetings. Loose tongues could result in lost heads. Coyote didn't tolerate having his private business subjected to public comment.

Muskrat prepared to make a few opening remarks. Public speaking didn't come easily to her, especially since the other animals often interrupted her.

Something else also made her nervous. On occasion, bloodshed occurred during meetings whenever the ravenous need to feed asserted itself. Recently, Osprey had killed and eaten Carp.

"When that Fish flips me attitude," he explained, "it triggers my predatory instincts."

Everyone agreed that Carp had been asking for it, but Osprey's behavior was a flagrant violation of the USA's safe swim zone. It wasn't permissible to eat a USA delegate during a public meeting. But since it had only been Osprey's fifth infraction, the USA accepted his haughty apology and called it good after he'd pleaded *nolo contendere carpio* to involuntary Carp slaughter. Another Carp delegate had been quickly admitted to the USA, putting the whole unfortunate matter to rest.

Muskrat wholeheartedly wanted the USA to be a confederation of civic-minded species. But in practice, it was more a hotbed of malcontents, a fractious congress of rabble-rousers and shortsighted Slough Firsters. Some animals had been expelled from the USA. Skunk's inability to control his anal discharges had earned him a quick no-confidence vote. Opossum had played dead whenever the USA meetings became too rancorous, which annoyed the other delegates so much that they had removed him from office for "sleeping on the job." Afterward, the other Opossums boycotted the USA, accusing its members of "Possumism."

Coyote had successfully clamored for Garter Snake's expulsion. "Her forked tongue and slithery sarcasm riles-up the peaceful waters of consensus," he said. "If I try to give her constructive criticism, she gets all hiss-terical on me."

Muskrat scanned the assembled delegates. Above her, the Birds thronged in the cottonwood trees, twittering, chirping, and squawking. As usual, Crow made the most racket. Raccoon was lounging on a tangled mat of wild cucumbers, Squirrel was gnawing on a hazelnut, and above them on a dead cottonwood limb, Owl swiveled her head, fixing her sights on Field Mouse. Mole popped in and out of his hole, and Madame Rabbit hid herself in the blackberry brambles. Hummingbird whirred back and forth, impatient for the meeting to start. Closer to Muskrat, the water creatures congregated in the malodorous muck of the shoreline, situating themselves among the yellow flag irises, creeping buttercup, and clots of pond scum. Other than Beaver, she noted the presence of Carp, Western Pond Turtle, Heron, Kingfisher, Canada Goose, Nutria, and River Otter. She disliked many of the USA's delegates, but River Otter always had a kind word for her.

Muskrat guessed that Carpenter Ant and Dung Beetle were hunkered down beneath a rotting log. Their voices were too small to be heard, but they hardly ever missed a USA meeting. Brown Recluse was most likely lurking within the tangled downfall, feasting surreptitiously on Cricket. Muskrat felt a stab of fear, recalling how Brown Recluse's creepy six eyes always surveyed the assembly with icy curiosity.

Vast armies of very tiny animals lived in and around Come Along Slough. Muskrat had never bothered to learn the names of these itsy-bitsy creepy-crawlies who made their homes on land and water. Why should she? They were too small to matter. At best, they made a snack for Birds like Sparrow or Spotted Towhee.

A significant number of animals refused to associate with the USA. Gray Fox and Bobcat were the most outspoken critics, calling it "a dung heap of do nothings." Peregrine Falcon likewise dismissed the USA as "a gutless clutch of dumb clucks." Bullfrog labeled it "a mob of layabouts, loudmouths, and mud smackers." Bumblebee, Swallowtail Butterfly, and Grasshopper felt the USA was too "carnivore-centric."

These outliers considered the organization a Dog's breakfast of has-beens, ne'er-do-wells, and wannabes. The USA wasn't for the likes of them. As rugged individualists, they rejected government groupthink, clinging to the fundamental Founding Waters wisdom set forth by Kawphonious the Giant Raven in the Natural Law of Animals. Kawphonious had never mentioned any need for the USA. Only "the law of jaw, paw, and claw" carried any judiciary clout.

Muskrat wished more animals of quality would join the organization. Without a unified front, how could the USA ever beat back the dire threats besetting Come Along Slough? She had a favorite slogan: "Where we go one, we go all." Coyote ridiculed this. "Where you go one," he said, "we go none."

Squibs represented the greatest danger, of course. Only the necessary evil of Big Government could beat back this growing threat to the Slough's survival.

The USA's complex eat-and-be-eaten quota system kept starvation at bay. Everyone fostered the hope that the Squibs would someday vanish from the Slough, making it possible for the natural world to restore itself. Stories had been passed down from generation to generation, and according to Owl, the Slough had once been Squib-free. Hunger was rare then, and the water was clean. No animal feared getting trapped, shot, poisoned, or smashed on the highway. Every creature of the Slough yearned for the return of the long-overdue good old days.

Muskrat knew it was time to begin the meeting. As she struggled to call forth the appropriate words, her mind went blank. She hated Slough Speak, the official language of the USA. It was a mash-up of growls, snarls, hisses, quacks, chirps, gurgles, screeches, squawks, and squeaks. Slough Speak clogged up her throat like a mudball full of stones and sharp sticks. She much preferred squeaking—short squeaks and long squeaks, or an extra-loud squeal would suffice if she were terrified. She often wished the USA delegates weren't able to understand each other so well, though. Slough Speak made it easier for them to hurl insults like "scram," "you stink," "idiot," and "I will eat you." Any animal—even the secretary general—could be made into the butt of an inappropriate joke, drawing gales of rude laughter from the mob. Muskrat particularly disliked the crude body humor and smirking references to sex that sabotaged sober deliberations. Why couldn't everyone act like adults?

Muskrat glanced up at Owl, who was perched on a cottonwood branch, sleeping. She was a ginormous Great Horned Owl. Much larger than many others of her kind, she spent most days and nights sleeping and eating. Muskrat wished that Owl spent less time biting off the heads of Field Mice and more time being wise. This old Bird's legendary wisdom might help to curb the chaos of USA meetings.

Muskrat shivered. She couldn't procrastinate any longer. She signaled Beaver to slap his tail again, but louder. He did so with vigor, splashing water on her.

"Oops," he said, "sorry about that."

Beaver was always doing this. Was it his own private joke? At any rate, she was sick and tired of it. It seemed so disrespectful! Shaking the water off her head, she addressed the delegates in Slough Speak, spitting out every syllable.

"It's time to pledge allegiance," she announced.

Nobody responded. What was wrong? Was her Slough Speak all squeak and no squawk? She tried to muster an authoritative growl, speaking more from her diaphragm than her throat, but only produced a stuttering, strangulated squeak.

"I-I-IT'S T-TIME TO PLEDGE ALLEG-G-G-GIANCE!"

That worked. As the delegates recited in unison, Beaver slapped his tail to help everyone maintain the proper cadence.

> *I pledge allegiance to the United Slough of Animals,*
> *An alliance indivisible, dedicated to defending*

Our sacred home waters against Squibs
And all foreign threats, real or invisible,
So help me Kawphonious the Giant Raven.

Beaver's ending tail slap splashed Muskrat again. "Oops," he said. "Sorry about that."

3 MADAME RABBIT DEMANDS JUSTICE

Muskrat addressed the delegates. "Our first item of business is to hear a complaint from Madame Rabbit against Elrod the Stoat."

A plump Brush Rabbit hopped out from the brambles, her ears flat and her nose twitching furiously. To disguise her dislike of Madame Rabbit,  Muskrat pulled her facial muscles into a rictus of congeniality. Madame Rabbit's jittery nature got on her nerves. They were both easy prey and Muskrat didn't like being reminded of their shared vulnerability. But no matter. In principle, The USA's see-no-species policy gave equal weight to carnivores and herbivores, entitling the weak as well as the strong to the impartiality of blind justice.

"Please state your complaint," Muskrat said.

Madame Rabbit skipped any preamble. "Elrod the Stoat ate six of my newborn kits!" she wailed. "He murdered my babies! This is a flagrant violation of the predator-prey kill ratio, as established by the USA."

"Were you a witness to this alleged violation?" Muskrat asked.

"Yes," Madame Rabbit sobbed. "Elrod also tried to eat me, but I kicked him in his itsy-bitsy nuts."

The other USA delegates erupted in a cacophony of yipping, gabbling, quacking, croaking, splashing, cawing, and squealing.

Hummingbird hovered overhead. "It's very inappropriate for us to laugh at Elrod's nuts."

Muskrat voiced her agreement. She asked Beaver to slap his tail again, so the meeting could proceed forthwith. "Madame Rabbit," she said, "please let me extend to you the official sympathy of the United Slough of Animals. You have suffered a tragic loss."

"Your own babies were born dead," Madame Rabbit said, "so I'm sure you can relate to my loss."

"Please, Madame Rabbit, let's stay on topic."

"Elrod ate my babies! It's a fact. Now I gotta go find a willing buck and devote time to an unscheduled mating effort. As you may remember, mating can really tucker you out."

"We should hear Elrod's side of the story," said Muskrat.

"Why? So he can try to eat me again?"

"You have full immunity from predators here. But after our meeting concludes, it's advisable that you stay in an underground undisclosed location and focus on your mating effort."

Nutria, the sergeant at arms, ushered Elrod the Stoat to the edge of the Slough. Elrod had a chestnut-brown back and a creamy butterscotch belly. He wasn't very big, but his tight smirk concealed a set of sharp teeth.

"You heard Madame Rabbit's testimony," Muskrat said. "What say ye?"

He pointed one paw at Madame Rabbit. "She thumped me in the nuts. Why isn't she being charged with assault and battery?"

Muskrat winced. How could she ever put a stop to this coarse language? "Please stay on topic. Your injured . . . reproductive organs are irrelevant here. Did you eat her babies?"

Elrod shrugged and winked at Coyote. "I only ate five—not six. My cousin ran off with the last one."

"The USA forbids you from eating more than one male Rabbit between full moons," said Muskrat. "Did you eat males or females?"

Elrod shrugged again. "I don't do gender checks. They all taste the same."

"Surplus killing is strictly forbidden, Elrod. Consuming more than your allotted share of prey endangers the fragile eat-and-be-eaten ecology of our USA community."

"The USA's quota system blatantly discriminates against carnivores!" Elrod shouted.

"Don't change the subject. We're talking about your unauthorized consumption of Rabbits."

"Yeah, I ate a few," said Elrod. "What's the big deal? They were hardly even a mouthful. Five of them little meatballs don't add up to even one Bunny burger."

"Murderer!" Madame Rabbit screamed. "You ate my babies!"

Beaver slapped his tail.

"They tasted so good," said Elrod. "Couldn't stop with just one. Know what I'm saying?" He grinned at Muskrat, pointing at his teeth. "Look. Still got a wad of Bunny fur stuck between my choppers."

Muskrat heard Coyote guffawing, and from the branches above came the raucous laughter and whistling of the Raptors. Red-Tailed Hawk was the loudest. Muskrat feared losing control of the meeting.

"Let me remind everyone here," she said, raising the volume of her squeak, "that we represent the USA, a formidable multi-species force of beak, fin, fang, tail, claw, and talon. We must exercise moderation. No species has the right to overeat; that's what the Squibs do. We eat together, or we starve separately!"

"Eat together?" Elrod echoed dubiously. "Screw that! I never share my food … except when Coyote forces me to."

"Don't get your fur all ruffled up," said Muskrat. "I'm just trying to establish a point of parliamentary order."

"I accept your apology," said Elrod. His small pink tongue flicked out from between his lips. Then he brandished his sharp teeth.

Muskrat swallowed hard. Elrod could rip her into bite-sized bits. She wasn't much of a meat eater herself, though she occasionally snacked on Crayfish and Frogs, but she much preferred cattails, sedges, and duckweed. Elrod was a notorious Rabbit-killer. He liked to ride the back of an adult Rabbit and bite its neck until it collapsed and bled out. His victims died slowly.

Muskrat motioned toward Owl on the low cottonwood limb. "It's time for us to hear a legal opinion from the wisest delegate of the USA. She is our foremost expert on all judiciary matters relating to the fortunes of Come Along Slough."

"Old Four Chins can tell us our for-tunes?" asked Elrod.

This elicited a round of guffaws.

"The USA has a strict policy against body shaming," said Muskrat, "so please curb your tongue, Elrod."

Elrod stood on his hind legs, working himself into a lather. "Owl eats all the Field Mice she wants. But I snarf down a few extra Bunny Rabbits, and everybody yells at me. Call that fair? I call that a gross miscarriage of justice!"

"Owl eats extra Field Mice," said Muskrat, "because she

requires supplementary nourishment to sustain her great wisdom."

Owl knocked loose some bracket fungus and landed on the ground with a loud "oomph." She waddled forward, her ear tufts twitching, her wide yellow eyes sweeping the assembly. She had an enormous belly.

"Here comes the pudge!" Elrod cried. "Here comes the pudge!"

"This is your last warning, Elrod!" Muskrat squeaked.

At Owl's approach, Madame Rabbit scurried inside a root wad and peered out, her ears flattened.

Owl spat out a pellet full of bones and fur. She rotated her head, puffed out her chest, shifted her weight, and harrumphed. "We all must eat," she said, "or we will die. This is the Natural Law of Animals."

"The big humpalump has spoken wisely," said Elrod. "If I don't eat enough Rabbits, I'll starve."

Nutria farted loudly. It sounded like the croak of a Bullfrog. Coyote barked out a laugh.

"Sorry." Nutria swished his Ratlike tail. "Too many tubers. Won't happen again."

Muskrat resisted the urge to roll her eyes. "Please continue, Owl," she urged.

Owl harrumphed again. "All the creatures of Come Along Slough must obey the Natural Law of Animals. Only the Squibs flagrantly violate this law!"

"That's right!" Elrod shouted. "Why's everybody picking on me? Old squash-butt got it right for once. It's them killer Squibs we gotta worry about!"

Muskrat grimaced, annoyed that Owl had mentioned the Squibs. This wasn't the proper time to grandstand on an issue loaded with cheap emotional appeal. Officially, the USA referred to these dangerous creatures as "invasive bipeds," but everyone commonly called them Squibs, a term of contempt.

Muskrat noted the arrival of the half moon, which had crept above the eastern horizon. A breeze stirred the cottonwood leaves. She cleared her throat and interrupted Owl, who was working up more remarks.

"Thank you, Owl," Muskrat said. "As always, your pronouncements are … very enlightening. It's time for Elrod's defense now. The USA grants every criminal a public defender."

"I'm not a criminal!" Elrod shouted. "I'm a victim!"

Squib Dog came forward. He and Scratchit Cat were also USA delegates, both with nonvoting status, which required them to sit at the outer edges of the assembly. Unlike Squib Dog, Scratchit Cat rarely attended USA meetings, unless she was on the prowl for Birds. The USA had reluctantly admitted these domesticated creatures because of their useful insider knowledge about Squib behavior.

Muskrat wrinkled her snout. What had Squib Dog been rolling around in? Roadkill? He wasn't easy on the eyes, either. He had a square head, bristly brown fur, and bulging yellow eyes. His tongue hung long and wet, and his crooked tail testified to a previous tangle with Raccoon. Squib Dog also had a sizeable paunch. Obviously, he hadn't missed many meals.

"Look," Squib Dog began, "I get what Brother Elrod here is saying. Rabbits taste pretty darn good. No getting around that." He paused for effect. "But here on the Slough, we can't always eat what we want to eat. If Brother Elrod can't get his fill of Rabbits, I say he should dig himself up a fat little Mole."

"Objection!" shouted Mole, popping his head up from a dirt mound. "The topic of eating Rabbits bears no relation to eating me!"

Muskrat nodded. "Objection sustained. Elrod can't just gorge himself on Moles. The USA has clear guidelines on Mole consumption."

"Moles taste like dirt," said Elrod. "I don't eat dirt."

"Snarf down some Goose poop," Squib Dog advised. "That'll get the taste of dirt out of your mouth."

Elrod made a face. "Goose poop makes me gag."

"You're not helping your case here, Brother Elrod, but I get where you're coming from. Personally, I got a sweet tooth for Cat litter, but it always gives me the trots and squats."

"Go home, Squib Dog!" Madame Rabbit shouted from the shelter of her root wad. "Get! Stop wasting everybody's time!"

"Least I get two square meals a day," said Squib Dog. "Sometimes more, if I fetch a stick or beg for food."

"Go play dead for your owners," said Madame Rabbit, "and stay dead."

"She's making death threats!" Elrod shouted. "I don't feel safe!"

Wings flapped above, sending down a shower of feathers. Coyote yipped and scratched an ear with his hind leg. Nutria popped off another fart. River Otter floated on his back, snickering. Heron stood in the shallow water and squawked. Kingfisher chittered and flitted among the willows. Cormorant perched on a submerged log, spreading her wings wide to dry as she gazed across the water, searching for unwary prey.

Beaver slapped his tail again, and the assembly fell silent.

"We have deliberated wisely and fairly on this matter," said Muskrat. "Elrod has admitted to eating an excess number of Madame Rabbit's offspring, and now we will vote to confirm his guilt."

"No need for a stupid vote," Elrod said. "I'll just say I'm sorry, okay? Osprey apologized for eating Carp. Why can't I get the same sweetheart deal?"

"Your apologies are fake," said Muskrat. "You apologize, and then you go on another killing spree. You are in flagrant violation of the USA's guidelines for eating quotas."

"Here's a word to the wise," Elrod warned. "Any of you vote against me, I'll light a forest fire up your ass."

"I don't got no vote," said Squib Dog, "so don't set fire to *my* ass."

"Elrod ate my babies!" Madame Rabbit wailed. "Let's skin the bastard alive!"

"The USA has a long-standing policy against vigilante justice," said Muskrat. "We will punish him according to the dictates of USA law."

Elrod snarled at Muskrat. "Whatever happened to 'innocent until proven guilty'?"

Raccoon swished her tail. "You were born guilty, Elrod," she said. "That's why your mother refused to suckle you."

"You leave my mother out of this!" Elrod growled. "She said I was the pick of the litter!"

"I feel sorry for Elrod," said Squirrel. "Everyone calls him a rotten-egg-sucking no-account, but his daddy ran off with another Weasel, and his older brother got squashed out on the highway. And he's always suffered from Short Stoat Syndrome. No wonder he's so screwed up. Why pick on him? It's kinda mean."

"Let's stifle the chitchat," said Muskrat. "Time to vote, so we can enter Elrod's conviction into the official record."

"As a USA duly-elected delegate," Elrod said, "I have immunity from prosecution."

Muskrat ignored him. "Now ... show me some wings, paws, and fins. Who thinks Elrod is guilty as charged?"

Elrod was found guilty, unanimously. Even Squirrel voted for his conviction.

Elrod crouched low to the ground and growled. "You suckers are really gonna regret this." He swiveled his head toward Coyote. "Why did you vote against me? I thought we were pals!"

"We are pals, but you cheated me out of my share of baby Rabbits," Coyote explained. "I wanted to teach you a lesson about loyalty to your betters."

Crow squawked for attention. As the self-proclaimed poet laureate of the Slough, he often spoke in rhymes, hoping to impress female Crows. It never worked; after hearing his overblown verses, they detested him. The males also hated his poetry, considering it a high crime against all Crows. Though an elected USA representative, Crow held no prestige with anyone. His own kind had elected him a USA delegate just to get him out of their feathers. He was an outcast—and a frustrated poet.

"Elrod the butt wad," Crow recited, "with your bad Rabbit habit, you ram it and jam it, but dammit, you just can't can it, can you? On Hare meat you're hooked, and now your bloody Goose is cooked."

Scrub Jay hopped down from his branch and squawked in Elrod's face. "Even for a Weasel, you have too much Rabbit blood on your paws!"

"But you snatched Robin's hatchlings!" Elrod shouted. "I saw you! You also violate the eating quotas!"

"You Rat fink!" Scrub Jay shouted back. "Keep your filthy trap shut!"

Once more, Beaver slapped his tail.

"Elrod," Muskrat said, "you have been judged by your peers and found guilty of high crimes. As secretary-general, it is my solemn duty to pass judgment on you."

Elrod showed his fangs. "So, do I get a slap on the paw or something?"

"It's too late for that. Because of the severity of your crimes, you are hereby banished from Come Along Slough."

Elrod perked up. "Didja say I'm famished?"

"No. *Banished.*"

"Banished? What does that mean?"

"You are expelled from the USA."

"But I'm . . . irreplaceable. No other Stoat can do this job the way I can."

"Don't worry. We're in no hurry to replace you."

"A Stoat-free USA sounds great me," said Mole.

Raccoon shuffled up to Elrod and released a squishy rope of greenish dung. "All Stoats are terrorists."

Elrod ignored these insults. "How long am I banished for? A day? Two days?"

"Forever," said Muskrat.

"You can't banish me! As a duly elected USA delegate, I represent the natural right of every Stoat to act like a Stoat." He twisted his head toward Madame Rabbit and licked his snout. "You go hump yourself up a fresh batch of Bunny tots, okay? I'll be along shortly to pay my respects."

"If you come near me or my babies," cried Madame Rabbit, "I'll kick you so hard, you'll have balls for brains!"

Red-Winged Blackbird swooped down and pecked Elrod's head, then Carp splashed water at him. Nutria waddled forward and tried to hustle Elrod out of the meeting, but he broke free and faced his accusers.

"The Slough is rotten with Rabbits!" he screamed. "I performed a public service!"

"Give Slug a big hug for me," said Crow. "Do the crime, you get the slime."

"Be careful out there, Elrod," Coyote cautioned. "Your brother got smashed by a truck. So could you. What runs in the family stays in the family."

"Adios," said Scrub Jay. "Been nice knowing you … Not."

"As a True-Born Son of the Slough, I demand a retrial!" Elrod wailed. "Squib Dog is an incompetent fool!"

"I didja a solid," Squib Dog said. "Nobody else wanted the job."

"Remove Elrod from Come Along Slough!" Muskrat commanded.

Elrod stood his ground. "All of you have slandered my good character, but if you agree to forget this unpleasant business, I promise not to violently retaliate against the guilty parties."

Nutria and Raccoon sandwiched him between them so tightly that he couldn't free himself. Then they marched him off. His protests echoed across the Slough.

Muskrat closed her eyes and smiled.

4 A DECLARATION OF WAR

Muskrat called for order. "Rats have invaded the western end of the Slough," she announced. "We have a zero-tolerance policy for these abominable creatures. To protect our sacred territory, we must declare a war on the Rats. Before we agree to this, minimal public input is customary."

"Who needs input?" asked Coyote. "Let's just whack the Rats."

"What's a war, exactly?" asked Nutria.

"A war gives us official permission to kill Rats," Raccoon explained. "As many as we can."

Nutria looked confused. "So … I gotta kill Rats? Why?"

"Because they're Rats," said Raccoon. "The only good Rat is a Dead Rat."

"I think I got it now," said Nutria. "Kill Rats. Kill 'em 'til they're dead."

Muskrat addressed Owl. "Do you have an opinion on this matter, oh wise one?"

Owl had been dozing, but at the sound of Muskrat's squeak, she awoke with a jolt. "The Rats are like Squibs," she said, "except with longer tails."

"Not so easy to kill Rats," said Squib Dog. "Fight one Rat, you end up fighting a hundred."

"You sound scared," Coyote jibed. "You scared?"

"You bet your sweet patootie I'm scared," said Squib Dog. "Rats don't fight fair. They mob you and bite like crazy. It really hurts."

"If you help us fight the Rats," said Coyote, "perhaps the USA will give you the right to vote."

"Really?"

Coyote yawned. "We'll see. But first, you must distinguish yourself in combat. Everyone loves a war hero."

"Our war on the Rats will be a just and noble war," said Muskrat. "It will be a war to end all wars. We will have peace in our time."

"Rats are horrible," said Raccoon. "They kill their

victims and collect trophy tails. No self-respecting Raccoon wants to lose their tail."

"Rats stink up the Slough," said Western Pond Turtle.

"The Slough stinks already," said Heron. "Stinks bad."

"I agree," said Kingfisher. "Heron is correct. He's absolutely correct."

"Rats are really mean to flowers," Hummingbird noted. "They don't sniff 'em. They just bite 'em and smush 'em all up. It's awful!"

"Rats violate the Natural Law of Animals," said Owl. "They are shameless gluttons! We must make the Slough safe for finding food."

"I'll build a big dam to trap them," said Beaver. "Then I'll drown them!"

"I regret that I have only one life to lose for my Slough," said Carp.

"I'll tunnel beneath the Rat Army and undermine their morale," said Mole."

"There will be blood," said Osprey. "Rat blood."

"Damn the Rats, and full speed ahead!" squawked Scrub Jay.

"My Slough, right or wrong!" Coyote cried, then yawned.

"KILL THE RATS!" the animals shouted. "KILL THEM ALL!"

Nutria kept farting.

Muskrat was very pleased that everyone was in accord. "Thank you for your unanimous support," she squeaked. "We are now officially in a state of all-out war with the Rats!"

"Say it in Slough Speak," said Coyote. "Not everyone here understands Muskrat squeaky-weaky."

Muskrat took a deep breath and repeated her statement in the USA's lingua franca. She appointed a war council with the right mix of carnivores and herbivores. Nutria was tasked with delivering the official declaration of war to the Rats.

"Fighting the USA will terrify those Rats!" shouted Raccoon. "They'll flee the Slough like they're escaping a sinking log!"

A short distance away, Elrod crouched on a moldering cottonwood stump, listening to the USA's war cries echoing across the Slough. It was time to make nice with the Rats. He turned and ran toward a Squib garbage dump. He had a slight acquaintance with General Flavius Chopper, the supreme commander of the Grand Rat Army. They both appreciated the taste of Rabbit. Maybe some kind of mutually beneficial arrangement could be worked out whereby Elrod could exact fitting revenge on the USA.

5 THE WAR AGAINST THE RATS

The war on Rats didn't go well. By day, most Rat fighters slept in their underground nests, where the USA's allied forces couldn't attack them. At night, the Rats advanced guerilla-style through the underbrush, ambushing military outposts and plundering valuable resources. They stole eggs, attacked the burrows of Raccoon and Mole, and scrambled into the trees to slaughter hatchlings and fledglings. Rat assassin squads eliminated many USA field commanders. Even worse, Elrod the Stoat was now one of the Grand Rat Army's top field generals.

"I know the Slough inside and out," Elrod had bragged

to General Flavius Chopper. "And I'm an expert at sneak attacks."

"Just make sure you don't screw anything up," General Chopper said, "or I'll eat your eyeballs."

Elrod remained calm, though General Chopper was very large—at least three times the size of an average Rat. "Not to worry," Elrod mumbled. "I'm a top-notch military strategist."

General Chopper brandished his long, curving incisors. "I suppose you expect a reward for betraying the USA?"

"Perhaps an unlimited supply of Rabbits? You'll get your share, of course."

The supreme Rat commander scowled. "What else do you want?"

Elrod hesitated before speaking. "Well, I'm a general, but your Rat soldiers sneer at me. They don't want a Weasel giving them orders. Make me an honorary Rat, so I'll get some respect."

"Respect for you is a big ask, but I'll grant you honorary Rat status."

"I only ask for what I justly deserve."

General Flavius chuckled. "Don't worry, General Elrod. You will certainly get that."

General Elrod persuaded the Starlings to fight for the Rats. Soon, the Starling Air Force attacked the USA, giving no quarter to either defenders or the defenseless. The Starlings and the Rats both traveled in groups, made unnerving screeching sounds, and attacked en masse. In payment for their support, the Rats awarded the Starlings exclusive access to a prime Squib garbage dump.

General Elrod then expanded the war to daylight hours, instructing the Rats to hide beneath floating logs. As the logs drifted toward the USA encampments, the Rats surfaced and attacked, inflicting severe losses upon the defenders.

Muskrat had no aptitude for tactics or strategy.

Declaring war on the Rats had been easy; winning a war wasn't. The slaughter of her friends and neighbors sickened her.

"All this blood and bedlam really befuddles me," she confessed to the USA's war council.

"Perhaps it's time for you to step aside, so we can put somebody more competent in charge," Coyote suggested. "After we win the war, we'll put you back in office—if you're still alive."

"But who would replace me?"

"Owl. Only her wisdom will lead us to victory."

So, the USA made Owl both secretary-general and supreme commander of military operations. Since Owl couldn't see very well by day, she established her headquarters inside a hollowed-out cottonwood tree, where the sunlight wouldn't blind her. She conferred often with Coyote about overall strategy. Sparrow and Bushtit relayed Owl's orders, and Flicker tapped out secret codes to surviving USA field commanders. Turtle Dove cooed approval for all of Owl's decisions, and Crow perched on a high cottonwood branch spying on the enemy movements while cawing poetry.

"The Slough is blood red," he cried, "and soon we'll all be dead!"

Hummingbird hovered close to Owl, providing updates on the war effort. "The Rats have annihilated entire platoons of honeysuckle, fleabane, and wild mint," she sobbed, "and trampled sturdy ranks of hollyhocks and foxglove. They've befouled wildflowers and Slough grass. The bugleweed will fall next. We must send help immediately!"

Owl sucked in her belly and coughed up a Field Mouse pellet. "Our forces are stretched pretty thin right now."

Coyote volunteered to help with the war effort. "I will sneak behind enemy lines and dig up valuable intelligence."

"Dig up some Field Mice," said Owl. "My stomach growls so loud I can't focus on military strategy."

"Your wish is my command."

Coyote collected a few Field Mice for Owl, but he also met clandestinely with General Elrod. While dining on freshly killed Rabbits, they exchanged military secrets. Since neither side had any secrets worth knowing, the two of them made up whatever came into their heads, embellishing their falsehoods with enough credible details to pass muster. It was wicked fun.

"We will only tell big lies," said Coyote. "They're more believable than little ones."

"I hope this crazy-ass war lasts forever," Elrod said. "I'm putting on weight, but who's complaining? By the way, I forgot to thank you."

"For doing all your thinking for you?"

"No. You voted to banish me from the USA."

"You're not mad at me?"

"You kidding? Getting kicked out of the USA gave me a real boost! I used to be your shadow. Nobody took me seriously. Now I'm a general in the Grand Rat Army. I'm admired and feared."

"I hope General Chopper doesn't get wind that you're a two-timing traitor with an expanding waistline."

Elrod snickered. "Well, as one two-timing traitor to another, a little war should never curb our appetites. Ready to snarf down more Rabbit?"

"As we consume the spoils of war," said Coyote, "never forget, I always get the biggest share."

The war continued up and down the Slough. The USA mounted a massive counteroffensive. Using Scrub Jay for air support, the Crows dropped walnuts on the Rat combatants. Red-Winged Blackbird fighters harassed the Starlings. Aerial combat was close and bloody. Dead and wounded Birds rained from the sky, littering the ground with feathers and body parts. Blinded Birds crowded the shoreline.

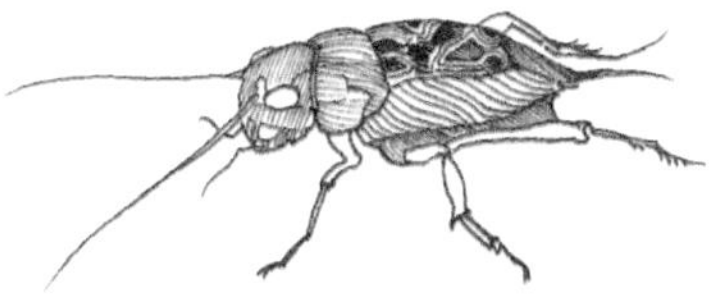

Next, the Duck and Canada Goose Navy created a blockade. Beaver, Nutria, Muskrat, Carp, and River Otter provided underwater surveillance. Cricket set up an early warning chirrup system for impending attacks. Heron and Kingfisher acted as forward observers, though they grumbled about coordinating with Osprey and Red-Tailed Hawk.

"I don't trust those raptors any further than I can spit a fingerling," said Heron.

"Heron is right," Kingfisher said. "Heron's absolutely right."

The Rabbit Thumper Brigades and Racoon Raiders swarmed the enemy positions, but the Rats beat back every assault. They chewed off the ears of the Rabbits and the tails of Raccoons, festooning tree limbs with their war trophies. The Rats gained more and more territory. Owl called an emergency war council, but only a few animals attended. The USA's ranks were decimated. Beaver didn't even bother to slap his tail on the water.

"The Rats stole a whole winter's worth of hazelnuts from me," said Squirrel.

"The Slough is chockful of Rat crap," Carp complained. "My eyes are turning brown."

"They violate the flowers," said Hummingbird. "Larkspur and lupine languish prostrate in the fields, nectar streaming from their open wounds."

Raccoon licked her Rat-mangled tail. "Squib Dog warned us. Kill one Rat, and twenty more pop up."

"Let's face it," said Muskrat. "We're losing the Slough to the Rats."

"Glad we fired you," said Coyote. "You sound like a defeatist."

"I wasn't *fired*," she sputtered indignantly. "I resigned. Temporarily."

Owl spat up a Field Mouse pellet. "We must continue to punish the Rats. They have flagrantly violated the Natural Law of Animals."

"Where's Madame Rabbit?" asked Squirrel. "Shouldn't she be here doing her part in losing this war?"

"She's hiding from General Elrod," said Raccoon. "He and a Rat hit squad are on the hunt for her. He wants to make an example of her."

Muskrat flopped onto the mud and sighed. "Coyote," she asked, "isn't it time for you to give your latest intelligence report?"

"What's an intelligence report?" asked Nutria.

"I'm the secretary-general now," Owl told Muskrat sternly, then turned to address Coyote. "Isn't it time for you to give your latest intelligence report?"

Coyote settled onto his haunches and belched. "Sure, why not? As you all know, I've been squeezing military secrets from General Elrod's itsy-bitsy brain."

"You mean Elrod the Traitor," said Muskrat.

"Point taken, but you did banish him."

"It wasn't just me. Everyone banished him."

"Did you squeeze any secrets from General Elrod's brain?" asked Owl.

Coyote puffed up his chest, tail erect. "The Rats are sick and tired of the war and want a truce between belligerents. General Elrod feels confident that we can draw up a peace treaty that benefits all parties."

Squirrel chittered loudly. "For starters, the Rats better return the nuts they stole!"

"Here's the whole poop," said Coyote. "The Rats will divide the Slough in half. They get the biggest half, 'cause they kicked our butts fair and square. The Rats will join the USA, but they insist upon majority representation."

"Outrageous!" Muskrat squeaked. "That's not a peace treaty, that's cowardly capitulation!"

"Oh, and one more thing," said Coyote. "General Elrod wants the USA to apologize publicly for banishing a True-Born Son of the Slough."

"We have nothing to apologize for!" Muskrat shouted.

"Actually, General Elrod wants *you* to apologize personally. He's pretty sore about how you gave him the bum-rush."

"Just apologize unofficially," suggested Mole. "Not officially."

Coyote yawned. "Elrod insists upon full exemption from the USA's kill quotas. He wants to eat his fill of Rabbits without anyone passing judgment on him."

"Well," said Raccoon, "we do have an overpopulation of Rabbits."

"Elrod's cocking his leg on the USA," said Muskrat. "He hates everything we stand for."

Coyote barked out a laugh. "Blah, blah, blah. You hurt Elrod's pride. Do you expect him to blow cattail fuzz at you?"

She flashed her incisors. "Are you on his side—or ours?"

"Why do you keep forgetting your proper place, Muskrat?"

"My proper place?"

"On the food chain."

The animals debated the peace proposal. Squirrel scurried up and down the cottonwood, Hummingbird flitted between the branches, Carp thrashed around in shallow water, and Owl dug out Lice from her chest feathers. Raccoon gently probed her lacerated tail.

Finally, Coyote yawned, stretching his jaws so wide that his eyes scrunched shut. "I know how to whack the Rats," he announced.

The other USA members stared at him.

"Whack the Rats?" Squirrel asked. "This another one of your Coyote tricks?"

"Tricking you is beneath me."

"You always trick us," said Muskrat. "It's how you entertain yourself."

Mole popped his head out of his hole. "How do we whack them Rats, Coyote?"

Coyote grinned. "We'll reconvene tomorrow, and I'll tell you all about it."

"Why not now?" asked Muskrat.

"My two experts on modern warfare aren't here yet."

"What's modern warfare?"

"Don't worry your little head with big words, Muskrat. All you need to know is that modern warfare will kill every last Rat."

6 MODERN WARFARE

THE NEXT AFTERNOON, Coyote addressed the war council. "As promised, I have invited my two experts on modern warfare—with Owl's approval, of course."

Squib Dog and Scratchit Cat appeared at the edge of the clearing.

"These house pets aren't trustworthy," said Owl.

"Just give us a quick listen, will 'ya?" said Coyote, "and pay attention."

Squib Dog ambled forward, grinning companionably, and sat next to Raccoon. Scratchit Cat followed at a leisurely pace, her tail twitching. She had tufted ears, glossy yellow fur, and one blind eye. Her puckered socket made it seem she was always winking. Sunlight glittered in her good green eye. She regarded the other animals before fixing her attention on Hummingbird.

"Yum! Scrumptious, simply scrumptious."

Hummingbird retreated to a higher branch.

"Brother Coyote asked me and Sister Scratchit to drop by for a parley about modern warfare," said Squib Dog.

Coyote yipped for attention. "Squib Dog and Scratchit will help us destroy the Rats."

"These house pets aren't trustworthy." said Owl, "Squibs provide them food and shelter. They live outside the Natural Law of Animals."

"Don't get your tail feathers in a twist, Sister Owl," said Squib Dog. "Just give us a quick listen, will'ya?"

Scratchit sauntered forward. "The USA's military strategy sucks. It's all fat and no fang."

Owl blinked. "All fat and no fang? How so?"

"It's also all blubber and no beak," said Scratchit.

"What Scratchit is trying to say," Squib Dog interjected, "is that modern warfare will smash Rats fast."

"The Squibs hate the Rats even more than we do," said Coyote. "Given our present predicament, the enemy of our enemy is our friend."

The other animals in the war council didn't look happy.

"Collaborate with Squibs?" asked Muskrat. "We haven't sunk that low."

Scratchit stepped forward. "The Squibs will be our puppets. I'll jerk their strings and make 'em march to my meow."

"Don't go hogging all the credit, Miss Pussy," said Squib Dog. "They can march to your meow, but I'll make 'em hearken to my barkin'."

"It was my plan, not yours. I had to explain it to you several times before you understood it."

Squib Dog shouldered her aside. "Here's the deal: the Squibs will fight for us without knowing it. All we gotta do is lay low and watch the Rats drop dead."

Scratchit slid in front of Squib Dog. "For starters, we'll sneak a dozen dead Rats into our Squibs' house."

Squib Dog leaned over Scratchit, drooling onto her

back. "We'll drop some of them stinky punks into the toilet."

Scratchit Cat shook dog spit off her fur. "And we'll deposit a dead Rat in the baby's crib. The Squibs will freak out and wipe out every Rat around Come Along Slough. A perfect plan, no?"

"How will dropping dead Rats in a toilet help us win the war?" asked Squirrel.

"Poison," said Scratchit. "The Squibs use it to kill Rats."

"According to the Natural Law of Animals," said Owl, "the proper way to kill Rats is to rip them into bloody shreds."

Scratchit's good eye glittered. "Don't be such a fuddy-duddy. Poison will make your Rat problem go away."

"If the Squibs poison the Rats," said Muskrat, "won't we also be poisoned?"

"Collateral damage is regrettable, but unavoidable," said Scratchit.

"Collateral damage? Is that part of modern warfare?"

"I'm so confused," said Nutria.

Scratchit raked her claws across a log. "We can't kill the Rats without also causing a little collateral damage."

"The way I understand it," said Squib Dog, "collateral damage means killing accidentally on purpose."

"I don't want to kill our friends and neighbors accidentally—or on purpose!" cried Muskrat.

"Admittedly, the use of Squib poison is problematic," said Coyote. "That's why the USA will adopt a policy of plausible deniability. We will vigorously deny any involvement in this manner and blame the mass deaths entirely on the Squibs."

"If we go with this cockeyed plan," said Muskrat, "we'd have to alert all the other animals about the poison and give them time to relocate."

Coyote shook his head. "If we alert them, we alert the Rats."

"But that's not … right. I thought we were better than that."

"This is why you aren't secretary-general anymore, Muskrat. During a time of crisis, a pipsqueak with moral scruples is useless."

"Let's stay on topic here," said Scratchit. "Our expert advice on modern warfare doesn't come for free."

Squib Dog nodded. "As members of the USA, we want the right to vote. Coyote agrees with us."

"Please, please," said Coyote, "no need to give me so much credit."

Scratchit Cat arched her back. "I don't care about any stinking vote. I only want more opportunities to shred Sparrow or Turtle Dove without anyone bitching about it."

"Half the Birds you kill, you don't even eat," Muskrat snapped.

"I identify as Cat. Cats kill Birds. If it pleases me, I eat them."

"You torture little animals for fun before you kill them," said Hummingbird. "You tortured Gold Finch—even Field Mouse. You're a heartless monster!"

"Get over it, Flowerface. I'm a natural-born killer."

"If the Squibs didn't feed you Kitty kibble, you'd starve to death!"

Raccoon groaned. "Let's not get lost in the weeds, okay? Like Muskrat, I have my moral scruples, but I can forget about them if this poison makes every Rat die in agony."

"What's your opinion, Owl?" asked Muskrat. "You're the secretary-general—not Coyote."

Owl was perched on a sagging cottonwood branch, her eyes closed. "Somebody say something?" she asked.

"Modern warfare will poison all the animals," Muskrat

said. "It will kill the Rats—and us. If everyone's dead, nobody wins."

"It's like . . . mutually assured destruction," said Hummingbird.

Owl fluffed up her feathers. "Kawphonious sympathizes with our moral quandary, but if poison makes the Slough Rat-free, he will look the other way."

"Then it's a done deal," said Coyote. "Let's poison the Rats!"

Without further debate, the war council approved the use of Rat poison. It wasn't unanimous, though; Hummingbird and Muskrat voted no. A resolution was passed, declaring that Squib Dog and Scratchit received full voting rights—but only if the Rats were vanquished.

"I got the vote!" Squib Dog barked. He flopped onto his side and licked the spot where his testicles used to be.

"You got the vote," said Coyote, "but I got it for you. Don't ever forget that."

Owl spread her wings and made an impromptu speech. "WE SHALL POISON THE RATS ON THE LAND! WE SHALL POISON THE RATS IN THE AIR AND IN THE WATER! WE SHALL…"

7 DREGS OF VICTORY

THE SURVIVING members of the USA gathered on the muddy shoreline and surveyed the carnage. Hundreds of shriveled and twisted Rat corpses littered the Slough. Some bobbed and drifted beneath the overhanging cedar boughs or were wedged in stands of yellow flag irises. The smell of death clung to water and land. The USA had won the war.

The fierce battles between the opposing armies had been devastating, yet collateral damage had inflicted greater losses. Many animals living on or around Come Along Slough had been killed or sickened.

"Aaaaargh!" Owl cried. "Hot diggity Dog! Go flog a Pollywog! So sad! So sad!"

"Suffer, suffer, suffer. It's always the same for us," Madame Rabbit moaned. "Especially me."

Muskrat gestured at Crow, who was perched on a willow branch above her, preparing to recite his commemorative poem. "We have innocent blood on our paws," she said, her voice quavering. "Please mention that in your poem."

"I have talons," he snapped. "Not paws."

Coyote bumped into Muskrat, knocking her off balance. "Excuse you," he said, "for blocking my path."

Muskrat edged away. "You're usually not so clumsy. Did you accidentally swallow Rat poison?"

Coyote grinned. "You need to change your name."

"Why should I do that?"

"Everyone's licking their war wounds. You won't win any friends calling yourself Musk-*Rat*. Get what I'm saying?"

Crow squawked and began to recite his poem.

> *Hooray! Hooray!*
> *Oh, what fun! What fun!*
> *We won! We won!*
> *With the greatest of ease,*
> *We brought them to their knees*
> *Like double amputees!*
> *Ratta-tatta-tat, those dratted Rats*
> *Failed, wailed, turned tail,*
> *And retreated on the run!*
> *On that fateful day of reckoning*
> *We weren't iffy or squiffy*
> *When doom was beckoning!*
> *We never wallowed in woe*
> *But swallowed our foe,*
> *Using methods impure*
> *To make ourselves secure.*
> *Oh, how those blasted Rats*
> *Gagged and sagged,*
> *Puffed and chuffed,*
> *Squeaked and shrieked,*
> *Crawled and bawled!*

> *We were gratified to see*
> *Such widespread scenes*
> *Of gruesome genocide.*
> *How we sighed with pride*
> *As those wild-eyed Rats*
> *Sniveled and shriveled*
> *And upchucked*
> *Mud and black blood*
> *Then died dumbstruck,*
> *Their victory denied.*

Coyote snarled at Crow. "Time for you to shut up."

"But I have not yet begun to versify," Crow protested.

"Scram!"

Crow clamped his beak and flew up into the treetops.

"That poem really choked me up," said Carp.

"It's the bad water that choked you up," said Squirrel. "The Slough is filthier than ever now. How can you swim there?"

"I keep my mouth closed as much as possible."

"Dead Rats taint the flower nectar," Hummingbird complained. "Yuck! And since that bloody-minded Cat got the vote, she thinks she has the right to stalk me."

"Squib Dog and Scratchit Cat got the vote," said Mole, "and all we got were piles of stinking dead Rats. And all this collateral damage."

Raccoon eyeballed Coyote. "You put us up to this. We got played."

"If you feel your delicate sensibilities have been violated," said Coyote, "I advise you to register a complaint with the proper authorities."

Raccoon didn't back down. "I heard rumors that Elrod isn't dead. Didja warn your little butt-buddy about the Squib poison?"

Coyote glared at her. "What makes you think General

Elrod is alive? Are you still collaborating with enemy agents?"

"Don't try that stupid crap on me, Coyote. I'm not a collaborator. I'm a wounded warrior. My Rat-chewed tail proves it."

"I doubt Rats chewed your tail. Most likely, your wound is self-inflicted."

"Hey, I heard Elrod plans to raise an army of dead Rats," said Carp.

Raccoon laughed. "A dead Stoat and his gang of cadaverous cutthroats don't scare me."

"Why do we always pick on Elrod?" asked Squirrel.

Madame Rabbit thumped the ground. "You soft on Stoats?"

"Well, maybe he was damaged goods, but he had some positive traits."

"A mass murderer has positive traits?"

Hummingbird's shrill cry startled the gathering. She pointed one quivering wing at the Slough. "Nasty, nasty, nasty. Oh, so nasty!"

The animals peered at a large black lump floating a short distance away. Carp swam out to investigate and returned quickly.

"Just another dead Rat," said Carp. "But it's a big one. Pee-yew!"

Coyote trotted closer to the shoreline and squinted at the corpse. "It's General Flavius Chopper," he announced, "the supreme commander of the Grand Rat Army."

"We gotta sink that big stink before he befouls the Slough," said Raccoon.

Carp spat some brown water. "I will Rat-ify that."

"Then let's get busy and haul away the dead Rats," said Muskrat.

Beaver slapped his tail on the water. "Should I call the USA to order?"

Muskrat stood on her hind legs. "At ease, Beaver. We'll clean up this mess, and after we're done, I propose we blast away the blues with a Come Along Slough victory party."

"Who put you in charge, Musk-*Rat*?" asked Coyote. "As an ex-secretary-general, you have no authority to propose anything."

She lowered herself to all fours. "Okay, what does Owl propose?"

Owl stared blindly at General Chopper's corpse, which had floated closer to shore. "Blast away the blues," she muttered. "Capital idea! I think a party would… Uh, what was I saying?"

"Can't we party first and do the clean-up later?" asked Squirrel. "I need to shake my booty."

"Shake your booty by dragging dead Rats from the Slough," said Coyote.

"Party pooper," Squirrel grumbled.

"I will supervise this operation," said Coyote. "Everyone will follow my exact instructions."

"Who made you the boss?" asked Raccoon.

"Owl put me in charge of this cadaver detail. Right, Owl?"

Owl blinked at him.

Coyote grinned at the group. "After we dispose of the dead Rats properly, perhaps Owl will authorize a victory party."

On the far side of the Slough, Elrod the Stoat crouched within the blackberry brambles. He was hot, tired, thirsty, and hungry. The voices of the USA drifted across the water. At first, the words weren't comprehensible. Then his little ears stiffened, and a low growl gurgled deep in his throat. He heard one word clearly: "party." His body quivered, and he began to pant, his tongue protruding. A party! Elrod loved to dance. His Weasel Wakadoodle always cleared the floor. He was the best body-slammer in Come Along Slough.

Maybe Coyote could snag him an invitation to the party. Without even consulting him, Coyote had hatched a plan to poison the Rats. Elrod felt double-crossed. While dining on Rabbits during the war, they'd agreed to stoke the fires of the conflict, thus satiating their ravenous appetites. Coyote had broken that agreement. Without explaining his reasons, he had helped slaughter the Grand Army of the Rats.

"You disrespected me," he told Coyote shortly after this catastrophe. "I thought we were pals."

"You're an honorary Rat, but I'm still your pal—the only one you'll ever have. If I hadn't warned you about the poison, you'd be dead, just like your comrades-in-arms. You don't sound very grateful, General Elrod."

"I am grateful ... sorta."

"Suck it up, little buddy," Coyote told him, "and stop sweating the small stuff."

"But now I'm the general of ... nobody."

"Hang with me, General Nobody, and you'll never go hungry. Trust me on this."

"Trust you? Like I got a choice?"

He and Coyote planned to meet that evening for a dinner of cold Rabbit leftovers. Elrod would voice his desire to attend the USA's victory party. Coyote was a born conniver, a trickster beyond compare. Elrod didn't want to be a Stoat without a Slough. Coyote could easily sneak a Weasel non grata back to his home turf. Then Elrod could get back to the business of eliminating the Slough's surviving Rabbit population. Besides, it was high time for a True-Born Son of the Slough to claim his due and magnanimously accept apologies from all those who had cocked a leg on his reputation.

Elrod grimaced as he clawed cockleburs and foxtails

from his fur. With his teeth, he plucked out a blackberry thorn from his butt.

8 CADAVER DETAIL

REMOVING all the corpses was a miserable task. Dead Rats clogged the whole Slough, including the large network of marshy canals and side channels that fed into the larger body of water. The reek of death permeated the air, prompting some animals to plug their noses with algae and mud.

Standing upwind of the stench, Owl and Coyote supervised the cadaver detail.

"Haul them a good distance from the shoreline," Coyote ordered. "Don't dump them too close to where the Squibs live. If they see dead Rats, they'll put out more poison."

Crow perched on an alder branch, reciting motivational poetry to the workers. "As we stand here squawking and gawking," he began, "let's get with it! Don't fear it! Don't doubt it! Don't pout about it! Get the spirit! Be proud about it! No ifs, ands, or buts—let's bury those goopy Rat guts like Squirrel nuts!"

Coyote barked at Crow. "Stop yakking and get to work!"

Crow flew off.

Owl sighed. "I'm hungry for more White Field Mice. Do you have any?"

"When I have a moment to catch my breath, I'll scrounge some up," said Coyote.

"During the war, you really got me addicted to those tasty little critters."

Coyote grinned. "I was just doing my part to help the war effort."

Owl belched. "Strange. The more White Mice I eat, the more I crave them."

They both watched as Beaver, Nutria, Mama Mallard, and Muskrat nosed Rat corpses onto the muddy shore. With the assistance of many other animals, they dragged them inland. Osprey and Red-Tailed Hawk scouted out a good burial location among the cottonwoods, cedars, alders, and ash trees that fringed a small swampy meadow thick with skunk cabbage and scouring rush. Mole, Raccoon, Squirrel, and Squib Dog dug up the vegetation and pushed the dead Rats into the burial pit.

"This meadow isn't large enough for all these squishy corpses," said Squib Dog. "If we want to bury a big lug like General Flavius Chopper, we'll need lots more space."

Mole spat dirt. "Coyote claims if we smash the Rats flat, we'll have more room to pack them in."

"Screw Coyote," said Raccoon. "It's time that layabout did some honest work himself."

"Go tell him that," said Squirrel. "He values … feedback."

Hummingbird soon discovered another burial location. It looked like a hill but was a Squib garbage dump mounded over with many layers of fill dirt. Thorny ramparts of blackberries encircled its boundaries, and ailanthus and scrub oak populated the steep slopes. Tentacles of English ivy and bindweed strangled the trees and overtopped the canopy. The animals cleared the ground at the base of the hill and dug a wide cavern through a jumbled barrier of broken glass, plastic debris, and scraps of metal. They hauled General Chopper and the other dead Rats into the cavity and plugged it with rocks and loose dirt. Afterward, they sat around panting and groaning from exhaustion.

Owl and Coyote ambled over to inspect the completed work.

Squib Dog cozied up to Coyote. "How's it hanging, Brother Coyote?"

"Get away from me," said Coyote, "and stop smelling my butt."

"Then stop sticking up your tail, Boss Dog. It's driving my nose nuts."

Coyote yawned. "I suppose you all earned your victory party."

"We can't party here," said Hummingbird. "The Slough is a stink hole."

"I'll task Muskrat with finding us a stink-free party spot," said Coyote.

"Why me?" asked Muskrat.

"Because I volunteered you," said Coyote. "Report back to me ASAP."

Owl waddled forward to speak. A Mouse bone lodged in her throat gave her voice an otherworldly warble. "We must honor the heroes who perished defending our homeland," she said. "Therefore, at daybreak tomorrow we will observe a moratorium on eating until the following sunrise. No exceptions. Even the plant eaters will observe this moratorium."

"What about the itsy-bitsy nobodies that crawl underground?" asked Raccoon. "Will they also observe this moratorium?"

"Let them eat dirt," said Mole.

"Owl's moratorium is a noble idea," said Coyote, "but perhaps we should observe its restrictions only within the hallowed boundaries of Come Along Slough."

"I don't getcha, Coyote," said Squib Dog. "You're making me itch, but I don't got no idea where to scratch."

"As is fitting and proper," Coyote explained, "we won't eat our own neighbors on the Slough. Instead, we'll eat our non-Slough neighbors. In that manner, we will observe the moratorium in spirit, if not in practice."

"That might cause another war," Squirrel observed.

"I don't want to make this about me," said Coyote, "but I can't go an entire day without red meat. Besides, our non-Slough neighbors deserve to get eaten. They didn't help us fight the Rats."

Owl cleared her throat. "As my trusted advisor, Coyote speaks wisely. We will only eat our non-Slough neighbors." She fixed her large eyes on Coyote. "Keep those White Field Mice coming, but in observance of the moratorium, make sure none come from the Slough. Are we clear on that?"

Coyote bowed his head. "Your wish is my command."

"Don't wander too far from home," cautioned Nutria. "I saw Elrod chewing cattails. He has a dangerous look in his eye."

"Coyote claimed Elrod's dead," said Muskrat. "But he's alive?"

"He's half-starved but alive."

"Poor Elrod has gone vegetarian," said Squirrel. "Chewing on cattails is as bad as it gets."

"Some of us love cattails," Muskrat pointed out.

Madame Rabbit moaned. "I don't feel safe!"

"Don't worry," said Mole. "The USA will keep you safe."

"Let's hunt down Elrod," shouted Raccoon, "and drown that slippery little bastard!"

Coyote glared at Nutria. "Are you sure you saw Elrod?"

Nutria glanced toward the Slough. "Uh, pretty sure."

"But you're not *absolutely* sure, are you? Perhaps you only saw a miserable Musk-*Rat*."

Nutria blinked, thinking it over. "Well, maybe, but…"

Coyote wheeled around and addressed the group. "Nutria means well, but eating tubers gives him bad gas, causing him to fart out falsehoods."

The animals laughed. Nutria was easy to poke fun at.

"The stink of gossip can suck the air from our lungs," said Coyote. "In these perilous times, we must fact-check everything we see and hear and never bear false witness against our neighbors."

"With all that fancy language of yours," said Squib Dog, "you must have political ambitions."

9 PARTY TIME ON THE SLOUGH

Following Coyote's orders, Muskrat found an isolated section of the Slough that dead Rats hadn't befouled too badly. It would suffice for a victory party. During her search, a pack of stray Dogs had chased her into the Slough.

She complained to Squib Dog. "Can you please tell those Dogs to stay away so they don't wreck our victory party."

"I'll call in a few favors," he promised.

Coyote inspected the party location. "I guess it'll do," he told Muskrat. "For once, you have met minimum expectations."

Muskrat took a deep breath. "Now that the war is over, it's time for me to shoulder my former responsibilities."

Coyote wrinkled his nose. "What responsibilities?"

"During the war, I stepped aside from my office temporarily. Owl took my place."

"As I recall, you couldn't stand the sight of blood."

"I'm ready to reassume my position as secretary-general."

"No need to be so hasty. I think Owl is doing an excellent job. Anyway, you need more time to grow a backbone. Don't you agree?"

Muskrat kept quiet. If she pressed the issue, he might find a way to shut her up permanently.

A few days later, the USA gathered along the Slough's grassy mudflats. The party got off to a good start. Flicker and friends provided a background beat, rapping steadily on cottonwood trunks. In the high branches, Red-Winged Blackbird, Gold Finch, Warbler, Turtle Dove, and Thrush provided a cheerful, spirit-lifting chorus of Birdsong. Mama Mallard, Canada Goose, and Crow joined in, but it was clear they couldn't carry a tune. Crow was the worst of all.

Heron stood in shallow water, not moving. "I hate parties," he told Kingfisher, who was perched on an adjacent willow branch. "All that noise scares away the Fish."

"You're right," said Kingfisher. "Absolutely right."

Raccoon and Squirrel crooned a catchy tune, first sung in the time of Kawphonious the Giant Raven:

"Whatzat hullabaloo
Whatzat happy humming
Coming from Come Along Slough?
Whatzat summer-long yoo-hoo

Callin' howdy do only to you?
No time to piddle or diddle
With life's little riddles!
Why be weary and teary
Your days dark and dreary
From insults and assaults
You relive but can't forgive
When the sweet swampy place
Gives you a full body embrace.

Beaver slapped his tail in time as the animals danced the Slough Shuffle, the Hump and Hustle, the Shag and Bag, and the River Quiver. The castanet clicks of Crawdad's claws elicited huzzahs and approving nods. Nutria and Muskrat spat cattail fuzz. Tree Frog performed a riveting set of backflips. Madame Rabbit was furiously thumping a hollow log. River Otter juggled Carp while balancing Freshwater Mussels on his nose.

Above the Slough, Eagle, Osprey, Red-Tailed Hawk, and Swift entertained onlookers with feats of aerial acrobatics. Eagle and Osprey dived toward the water, aiming for Ring-Necked Duck, who pretended to be a sitting duck. Each time the raptors got close, though, Ring-Necked Duck dove beneath the surface. Eagle and Osprey would try again and again, with the same results. "Synchronized ducking" was a great hit.

Scratchit Cat stood apart from the other animals, licking her paws. She trained her good eye on Hummingbird, who sat safely on an overhead cottonwood branch.

"I have vivid recurring dreams about you," she told Hummingbird. "Do you ever dream of me?"

"Yes," Hummingbird replied. "I dream about pecking out your remaining eye."

Squib Dog trotted up to Scratchit and squatted next to her. "Hey, hey, USA all the way! Squib Dog and Scratchit Cat saved the day!"

"Calm down," said Scratchit Cat. "You sound like a fool."

"Sheesh. Who rubbed your fur the wrong way? I'm proud and loud and not afraid to let everybody know it. We got the vote! We got the vote!"

Crow hopped close. "It's time for Crow to end your show. You two suck-ups make me wanna upchuck."

"Ah," purred Scratchit Cat, "so many birds, so little time."

"I ate a dead Crow once," said Squib Dog. "Tasted like Chicken."

Crow flew off.

Beaver waddled up next to Squib Dog and flashed his reddish incisors. "Congratulations on getting the vote."

"Why, thank you, Brother Beaver."

"Coyote's taking all the credit for your idea of getting rid of the Rats, but you're the one who came up with it. Brilliant, just brilliant."

"What about me?" asked Scratchit. "Where are my congratulations?"

Beaver ignored her. "That Rat poison trick of yours saved our tails, Squib Dog."

Squib Dog ducked his head and rolled one eye up at Beaver. "I showed them Rats who's their daddy, didn't I? We hit a few rough patches, but we come out on top. Hey, hey, USA all the way!"

"Hush," said Scratchit. "You're so embarrassing."

"We won the war!" Squib Dog shouted.

"Yes, yes, we won the war," said Beaver. "And we survive, but don't thrive."

Squib Dog gave him a puzzled look. "Don't quite catch your drift, Brother Beaver."

"The Slough is too small. Small stinks."

"I like stink. At least, most of it."

"We gotta think outside the stink, Squib Dog, and think big. Our future is about being big, not small."

Squib Dog shook his head. "On the Slough, the future ain't what it used to be, is it?"

"The future belongs to the big dreamers," said Beaver. "I'm a big dreamer. So are you."

"Let's scram," said Scratchit, "before we catch a bad case of Beaver fever."

"The Slough needs dams," said Beaver. "Big dams. Lots of them."

"What are dams?" asked Squib Dog.

"They make big water."

"How come you wanna make big water?"

Beaver glanced around and waddled closer. "The Rats are dead, you see. Now the USA has an excellent opportunity to expand its territory. If we build dams, the Slough will become huge. More room for me, more room for you."

"Big water might drown the Squibs," said Scratchit.

Beaver glanced at her, exposing his incisors. "The war on Rats taught us that progress never comes without a little collateral damage."

"I would never call the war on Rats progress," said Scratchit. "And now you want to drown the Squibs? You sound like a real bonehead."

"Let's not get lost in the cattails," said Beaver. "It's time to make the Slough great again."

Squib Dog shook his head. "Great *again*? I'm not so sure it was *ever* great."

"You're probably right," Beaver agreed, "but a few flattering fibs help to disguise ugly facts. At the next USA meeting, I will present my dam-building plan. I'm hoping both of you will support me with your votes. Can I count on you?"

"I'm not your Cat's paw," said Scratchit.

"Hey, you got my vote, Brother Beaver," said Squib Dog.

"Don't know exactly what a dam is, but I'm for anything that will improve the neighborhood."

10 OWL AND COYOTE CONFER

Coyote and Owl left the party and strolled along the shoreline, making parallel tracks in the mud. To match Owl's tottering pace, Coyote had to walk slower than he preferred. He stopped so the secretary-general could catch her breath. They gazed across the water, tracking the drifting clouds of cottonwood fluff.

Owl sneezed. "My allergies," she wheezed, rotating her massive head toward Coyote. "By the way, kudos to you for those scrumptious White Field Mice. They pamper my palate dreadfully. Every bite brings me to a happy state of full salivation. Where do you find those juicy bad boys?"

"Oh, here and there," said Coyote vaguely.

"Well, keep them coming. I hunger for more."

"The heavy responsibilities of being secretary-general weigh you down. I wish to lighten your burdens of office."

Owl gave him a stern look. "I get your drift, Coyote. No need to lay it on so thick."

"My apologies."

But Coyote was never apologetic about anything. He enjoyed having fun at her expense. The clueless secretary-general obviously didn't know the difference between a

White Field Mouse and a White Rat. During the war, Coyote had prowled at night far beyond the Slough, searching for additional sources of food. A large building had piqued his curiosity. Peering through a lower window, he had seen Squibs in white coats fussing over scores of caged White Rats. Every Rat had its fur shaved from belly, back, and skull. The Squibs inserted transparent tubes into the Rats' necks and groins. A gray liquid glowed inside the tubes.

Owl sneezed again. "These White Field Mice are most peculiar. You say they have pink eyes? What color is pink, anyway? I can't see the same colors as you. My eyes are built for night hunting, not for the blinding blast of daylight."

"Trust me, they have pink eyes."

Coyote felt thankful that Owl was too thick-witted to realize he was pulling another fast one. In truth, his ability to perceive different colors had its own limitations. The word "pink" had plopped unbidden into his head, like water dripping onto a rock: "pink, pink, pink." What did it mean? "Pink, pink, pink." It was Old Man Coyote again. He was always sounding off inside Coyote's head, shouting nonsense words such as "sputum," "amuse-bouche," "in flagrante delicto," and "Leck mich am Arsch." At any rate, Owl had swallowed the whole story about pink-eyed White Mice. Good thing this doddering old dimwit didn't know about the loud voice in his head. If she ever suspected that OMC had masterminded this ruse, she might stick her beak into his business.

"The pink eyes," he told Owl, "indicate my products are freshly-killed."

Owl mulled this over for a moment before commenting.

"Some have bald heads, and other parts of their bodies also lack fur. Do they suffer from mange?"

"No worries," Coyote assured her. "Premature baldness is a distinctive feature of White Field Mouse. It marks their superior flavor profile."

"Fur plugs up my bowels dreadfully. These bald Rodents are so slick, they slide right on through to the end of the line. Yet I have detected a curious burnt taste. Did a thunderbolt strike them, giving the meat a swarthy aftertaste?"

Coyote stifled his laughter. He'd watched the Squibs attach wires to these White Rats. Then the Rats convulsed and screeched, their mouths and anuses oozing a dark substance. Sparks flew from their fur. Smoke curled from ears. Some Rats had caught fire. "They weren't struck by lightning," he assured Owl. "They got themselves a bad case of sunburn."

"Ah, that makes sense."

Coyote had watched Squibs tossing cartons of dead Rats out into a drainage ditch. When it was safe, he trotted over, sampled the goods, and vomited.

Old Man Coyote had urged him to deliver a White Rat to Owl. *"She's getting too old and lazy to hunt for her own food."*

"Those Rats are full of bad stuff," replied Coyote. "Eating them might kill her."

OMC wasn't concerned. *"You're the carnivore king of the Slough. Every animal is subject to your will. One and all must bow down to your spoor. If they don't, you can kill them."*

Coyote liked the sound of that. To encourage Owl to eat suspect food, he had ginned up a plausible story. "Every top-tier carnivore craves this species of Field Mouse. It's a very rare kind of 'white meat.'"

The secretary-general had snapped down the white meat and was soon hooked on it. She suffered no apparent bad effects. In fact, the White Rats had spiked her appetite.

As they continued to take in the view next to the Slough,

Owl furrowed her brow. "These White Field Mice are very fattening."

"All the better for your Owlish figure."

"You're quick with the compliments, Coyote. I appreciate that, even if you're not sincere. The other members of the USA aren't so forthcoming with perfunctory praise. They make hurtful jokes about how much I eat. To feed my brain, I must first feed my belly."

"The contents of your brain," said Coyote, "must never be judged by the contents of your stomach."

"Eating so much of this white meat does make me feel a little . . . light in the talons."

"For you, light is good."

Owl pivoted and waddled back toward the party. "Let's get down to bare bones and pellets, shall we? You said you have something important to discuss. So, out with it."

Coyote fell into step with her. "It's time to resolve the Elrod issue."

"He's still alive?"

"A trusted source informs me that Elrod's still kicking."

"A trusted source? You mean Old Man Coyote?"

Coyote stumbled as if clubbed over the head. Owl knew about Old Man Coyote? How? OMC wasn't visible. Nobody could hear him except Coyote, but Owl's sharp ears had obviously picked up some chatter. Maybe it was time to put this gluttonous Bird on a Rat-free diet and teach her a lesson about violating privacy.

"I wasn't trying to eavesdrop on you," Owl assured Coyote, "but everybody hears you talking to yourself. Sometimes you howl. Who is Old Man Coyote?"

Coyote growled. "This isn't about me. It's about Elrod."

Owl blinked. "As you wish. Please proceed."

Flattening his ears, Coyote struggled to assume a submissive look. "Elrod is a True-Born Son of the Slough. He deeply regrets his ill-considered actions and begs to be rehabilitated. He has a fierce desire to become a model citizen of the USA again."

Owl shook her head. "Impossible. The USA delegates would never stand for it. To them—and to me—he will always be a traitor. Worst of all, General Flavius Chopper made Elrod an honorary Rat. Why would we want an honorary Rat in the USA?"

"Public opinion is a fickle thing," said Coyote. "A clever leader could play that to personal advantage."

"Pray tell, how's it to my advantage to invite a lawless Rabbit-killer back to the Slough?"

"I hesitate to divulge this," said Coyote, "but Elrod is working on your behalf. He helps me collect White Field Mice."

"Elrod? Rubbish!"

"Elrod wishes to curry your favor, but the White Field Mice population is dwindling."

"Why?"

"Squibs have destroyed their natural habitat."

"Should I be worried?"

"Very worried. The White Mice are now an endangered species. They are very scarce, but you can count on Elrod to deliver the goods."

"That criminal really wants to become a model citizen of the USA?"

"He dreams about it day and night."

Owl fell into a sneezing fit. Finally, she spoke. "You've put me in a difficult position, Coyote, but I will ponder this matter and get back to you."

"Don't ponder too long," said Coyote, "or else your supply of White Field Mice might dry-up sooner than you fear."

Coyote's eye caught distant movement. He stiffened, his senses on full alert. He squinted, trying to focus better, and spied a Squib. A young female Squib with long black hair!

She was on the far side of the Slough. She was floating on some object and using a wood pole to move herself across water. He saw her turn toward a side channel. The tall shore grass soon enveloped her body.

Coyote dismissed the Squib sighting as inconsequential. Then he heard Old Man Coyote inside his head. *"Pay attention to her, goober smooch! She's gonna save your sorry ass!"*

"Save my sorry ass?" asked Coyote. "What do you mean?"

OMC didn't answer.

Owl stopped and pivoted toward Coyote. "Were you talking to me, or to that invisible friend of yours?"

11 THE PARTY CRASHER

As Coyote and Owl returned to the victory party, they saw Squib Dog racing toward them. He skidded to a stop, panting hard. Nearby, the others had grouped like herd animals next to a stand of willows, appearing anxious. Scrub Jay hopped and flapped his wings but didn't squawk. Raccoon was chewing on her tail. The smell of death pervaded the air.

"We … been waiting … for you," Squib Dog gasped.

"Gak!" Owl cried. "You stink!"

"It's not my … stink. It's…"

Squib Dog pointed a paw toward the water. Near the shoreline, a small creature with patchy gray fur humped along like a Caterpillar, its bloody haunches wriggling with Maggots. Owl covered her beak with both wings. Coyote gobbled some grass, then puked. Squib Dog whined.

The creature raised its head, its eyes clotted over with blood and pus, and veered toward Madame Rabbit. Its ghastly appearance had silenced the other animals. They watched as the creature crept Caterpillar-slow toward Madame Rabbit, who appeared unaware of any threat. She sat grinning, eyes closed, head bobbing, her ears flopping.

One foot thumped a hollow cottonwood log with a steady beat: *da-da-da-dum-da-da-da-dum.*

Owl kept her wings over her beak. "I fear for Madame Rabbit. That malodorous monstrosity has set its sights on her."

"Madame Rabbit is a witless twit," said Coyote. "She's in la-la land. Just look at that goofy grin plastered on her puss. Do you see it? She's been hooking up with a big buck. Now her brain's on the blink."

"If Madame Rabbit gets killed," said Squib Dog, "it'll spoil our victory party. We must save her!"

"Don't move," said Coyote.

Squib Dog looked confounded. "Why?"

"Stay!" Coyote commanded.

Squib Dog lowered his head and sighed. "Sheesh, you sound like my Squib when I done something bad."

Coyote growled. "Now get!"

"You just told me to stay."

"Do what you're told!"

"Okay, okay. Heard you the first time." Squib Dog slunk off and joined Scratchit Cat, who sat a short distance away, licking her paws.

"We gotta rescue Madame Rabbit," Squib Dog told her.

Scratchit trained her good eye on him, a wisp of a red feather clinging to her whiskers. "Hush. I'm digesting my meal."

Squib Dog dropped to the ground, clamping his paws over his ears. "You ate Hummingbird, didn't you?"

As if to answer his question, Hummingbird appeared, hovering overhead. "That half-blind Cat keeps trying," she said, "but she's way too old and slow."

Scratchit leapt for Hummingbird but missed.

"Old and slow! Old and slow!" Hummingbird taunted her.

Nearby, Coyote watched them, contempt creasing his

snout. Then he spoke to Owl. "We will not save Madame Rabbit."

"But this foul-smelling foreigner has trespassed into USA territory!" Owl protested.

"Foreigner?" Coyote scoffed. "Hardly. You don't recognize that little piece of worm meat?" Coyote pointed a paw at the creature, which had nearly reached Madame Rabbit. He lowered his voice. "It's Elrod. He's disguised himself with the rotten remains of General Flavius Chopper."

Owl clacked her beak. "A Rat cadaver is a little ripe, even for the likes of Elrod. Is this your doing, Coyote? Did you concoct this hare-brained scheme?"

"Look up, Owl. Look up and learn."

Owl looked up. It was evening, so her eyesight was excellent. "I see only a black speck."

"Keep looking."

Owl gasped. "I see a Bird! A Raptor! A … Sharp-Shinned Hawk! A non-USA Sharp-Shinned Hawk! It has violated our airspace! We must alert our air defenses!"

"Calm down," said Coyote. "No need to get hysterical. I know that Hawk. She's one of my … assistants."

The Sharp-Shinned Hawk streaked down from the sky toward Madame Rabbit. At the same moment, Elrod shucked his Rat carcass and charged Madame Rabbit.

Knocking her flat, he used his body to shield her from the aerial attack. Sharp-Shinned Hawk caromed off the log and rolled beak-over-tail into the muck. The Raptor squawked, shook her head, and winged her way up into the trees. Songbirds scattered, chirping out alarms.

Elrod sprawled spread-eagle on Madame Rabbit's soft belly. Raising his head, he smirked at the stunned congregation of animals.

"A Stoat in time stops the crime," he said.

"Baby killer!" Madame Rabbit screamed. "Get off me!"

Elrod snuffled her fur. "Hey, I just saved your life, sweet cheeks. Show me a little love, okay?

"A True-Born Son of the Slough has returned from the dead!" Coyote shouted.

The other animals stared at Elrod and Madame Rabbit.

Owl whispered to Coyote. "So, you staged this whole preposterous show?"

Coyote also whispered. "Nobody else needs to know, right?"

"Somebody help me!" Madame Rabbit screamed. "Elrod is murdering me!"

The animals edged closer to gawk at Elrod.

Coyote raised his voice. "Elrod saved Madame Rabbit's life!" he cried. "Hooray for Elrod the Hero!"

Silence followed.

Coyote growled. It was a menacing growl—the one he used to persuade other animals to see things his way. "Let's hear a little more enthusiasm, okay? Let's give it up for Elrod! Hooray for Elrod the Hero!"

The animals gave a half-hearted cheer. Coyote growled for them to show more enthusiasm.

"Elrod is a hero!" Mole squealed. "He saved Madame Rabbit! I think."

"My next hatchling will be named Elrod!" quacked

Mama Mallard. "But only if he promises to never raid my nest."

"Can we do anything for you?" asked Squirrel. "You look like something the Cat dragged in."

Elrod crawled off Madame Rabbit's belly. "I hurt all over. I want somebody to give me a head-to-toe tongue bath and lick away all my pain. That's what a hero like me deserves."

"You're no hero!" Madame Rabbit shrieked. "You're a Rabbit killer!"

"Curb your tongue," Coyote warned. "You can't slander a True-Born Son of the Slough."

"But Elrod has been banned forever from the Slough," said Madame Rabbit. "That's what Muskrat told us."

Coyote fixed her with a menacing stare. "Owl is secretary-general now. She's in charge—not Muskrat. Why are you digging up old history, Madame Rabbit?"

She glanced timidly at the other animals for support, but they all looked away. "Everyone fell for Elrod's cheap little trick" she muttered. "Now you have thrown me to the Dogs." Flattening her ears against her back, she gave the log a light thump and hopped away into the brush.

The animals watched her leave. Then they mobbed Elrod and chanted in unison. "Elrod the Stoat! Elrod the Stoat!"

"At your service," said Elrod.

Raccoon sniffed his fur. "You smell like a dead Rat. An honorary dead Rat."

Crow flew down from a branch and joined the group. "Great blood and pain you caused," he said, "as the Slough you set aflame, yet now your acclaim scrubs off the stain of your shame."

Squib Dog trotted up to Elrod, his tongue flopping out. "Saving Madame Rabbit took some real balls."

"Too bad you don't have any yourself," said Elrod.

The animals laughed at this old joke. Reminding Squib Dog that he was castrated invoked a spirit of camaraderie among USA members, reinforcing their feelings of superiority over domesticated animals.

Coyote whispered to Owl. "It's the secretary-general's duty to officially welcome Elrod back to the Slough. If you choose your words wisely, perhaps an extra White Field Mouse will be in your future."

Owl scowled, waddled over to Elrod, and cleared her throat. The other animals fell silent. Elrod stood on his hind legs, rubbed his front paws together, and grinned, exposing two upper fangs.

"Your heroic act of saving a life has erased your disgrace," Owl began. "Braving bodily harm, you protected Madame Rabbit, a creature whose great reproductive capabilities help maintain the USA's eating quotas. Elrod the Stoat, welcome home!"

Elrod kept grinning and rubbing his paws together. "Thanks for those high-falutin' words, Fatty Boom-Boom."

"Swear to me that you will never again eat more than your USA-prescribed allotment of Rabbits," Owl demanded.

Elrod rolled his eyes. "Yes, yes, my huffy Buffarilla, I swear."

"You almost sound sincere," said Squirrel.

"It's foolish to think," said Crow, "that a Skunk will give up its stink."

Coyote nudged Owl, ushering her to a spot on the shoreline out of earshot. "Wise words heal many wounds," he told her.

Owl didn't look happy. "This was a sloppy show from start to finish, Coyote. Sharp-Shinned Hawk doesn't attack from high in the sky like other Hawks, and it's much too small to successfully attack Madame Rabbit. The whole thing was an obvious sham."

"Have you contracted a bad case of the scruples?"

Owl looked flustered. "I'm hungry."

"I'll tell Elrod to fetch some White Field Mice right away."

"Do it sooner than right away."

Coyote trotted over and separated Elrod from his throng of admirers. They moved off to speak privately.

"Ready for some fun?" he asked.

"I was born ready," said Elrod.

"Owl's hungry. Go fetch her a White Rat. But wash first. You reek."

"Thanks to General Chopper's carcass, I won't ever smell like a Stoat again."

"Just keep Owl fat and happy, my little stinkeroo, and we'll go on a Rabbit raid—just the two of us."

Elrod's nose twitched. "Let's start with Madame Rabbit."

Independence is all very well, but we animals never allow friends to make fools of themselves beyond a certain limit.

—*THE WIND IN THE WILLOWS*
KENNETH GRAHAME

12 SHARP-SHINNED HAWK LOSES HER HEAD

THE NEXT MORNING, Coyote ordered Elrod to duck down in the weeds while he visited Sharp-Shinned Hawk.

"She's really grouchy," said Elrod. "She's even rude to the other Hawks."

"She has a prickly personality," Coyote agreed, "but I must pay her for services rendered."

Standing beneath her nest, he saw her perched on a cedar branch, glowering down at him in the haughty manner of her kind. He glowered back. She held the superior position, but he wasn't intimidated.

"Why are you here?" she screeched.

"I always pay my bills on time."

"Pay me. Then scram."

"Your aerial acrobatics have earned you a bonus."

"Cut the crap! Deliver the goods!"

Coyote spat out a slimy wad of something he'd been carrying inside his jaws.

Sharp-Shinned Hawk hopped down to a lower perch, craning her neck to get a better view of the bloody clump. "Are you sick?"

"I have brought you a pair of Rabbit ears. You only earned one, but I'm giving you two. Consider it a bonus."

Sharp-Shinned Hawk screeched again. "That's what I get for risking my life?"

"These ears are slightly chewed, yet they are still fresh and juicy."

"I sprained my wing doing your stupid stunt!"

"I had no idea you were such a klutz."

"You tricked me into doing your dirty work, Coyote!"

"I didn't trick you. Despite your obvious lack of qualifications, you got the job. I wanted to hire Red-Tailed Hawk, but he snubbed my offer."

She glared at him. "I demand two whole baby Rabbits! If I don't get them, I'll inform the USA that you and your crazy-ass Stoat played them for fools!"

Coyote sighed. "I can only blame myself for hiring somebody too old and feeble to perform unskilled labor."

"I'm not old and feeble! I was born only two winters ago."

"Have you experienced dizzy spells? Bouts of fatigue? Any loss of memory?"

"I'm warning you, Coyote! Do *not* mock me!"

"Do you suffer constipation? If so, Rabbit ears are great stool softeners."

"I don't like how you're disrespecting me. I want four baby Rabbits now!"

"My, my, you're such a shrewd negotiator. Okay, my feathery friend, you got me. Four baby Rabbits it is."

"Deliver them today!"

Coyote winced. "I have a bad crick in my neck from looking up at you. Come down closer to me so we can flesh out the details."

"Do you think I'm an idiot?"

"How about five baby Rabbits?"

"Didja say five?"

"I hope you're not growing deaf. Yes, five."

Sharp-Shinned Hawk glided down and perched on a lower branch at eye level with Coyote. "Here's the deal. I want five baby Rabbits—every week!"

"Five a week, eh? Extortion isn't an effective way to build trust."

"Nobody trusts you. Why should I?"

Coyote mumbled something.

Sharp-Shinned Hawk leaned closer. "Huh? Speak up! I can't hear you."

Coyote mumbled louder. "Ear today, gone tomorrow."

"Why are you talking nonsense?

Coyote yawned. "Sorry, but you're boring me." He yawned wider—and in one lightning-quick motion, he bit off Sharp-Shinned Hawk's head.

Decapitating Sharp-Shinned Hawk was Old Man Coyote's idea. *"Kill that snitch before she squeals on you!"* he had commanded.

13 RABBIT FOR THREE

Coyote, Elrod, and Skunk lounged on a bloodstained grassy knoll not far from Come Along Slough, their bellies bulging from the scores of Rabbits they'd just devoured. Dead Rabbits were scattered every which way, as if flung about by a whirlwind.

"I got dibs on that fat one," said Coyote.

"I can't stop pigging out," said Skunk.

"Oink, oink," grunted Elrod. A wad of Rabbit fur tickled his snout, and he sneezed.

Coyote stopped gnawing on a leg bone and grinned. "Hope you're not Rabbit intolerant."

Skunk giggled and rolled on the ground. "Ha! Elrod? Rabbit intolerant? Good one, Coyote!"

Elrod sneezed again. "What can I say? I love Rabbit, and Rabbit loves me."

"You need to exercise portion control before your gut explodes," said Coyote.

Skunk kept giggling.

Elrod raked his claws through the grass, cleaning off the blood, and squinted at Coyote. "You only go around once, so you gotta grab all the Rabbits you can."

"You saved Madame Rabbit—and then you ate her."

"When I'm motivated, I pack a wallop."

Skunk chewed on Rabbit liver. "Thanks for the good grub, Coyote. You and Elrod did all the hard work. I feel guilty living off the juicy fruits of your labor."

"I always eat first, then Elrod eats. You get whatever's left."

Skunk spat out a mouthful of liver, looking stricken. "Sorry. Did I eat out of turn?"

"I'll let it go this time."

Skunk didn't socialize much. He was a loner. Long ago, he'd been expelled from the USA; accidental discharges from his anal glands had disrupted too many meetings. His discharges occurred whenever anything startled him, and Skunk startled easily, releasing a suffocating stink that cleared the Slough in seconds. Skunk now lived a hermit-like existence beneath a rusted-out truck near one of the Squib garbage dumps. He had few visitors, but lately, Coyote had chosen to hang out with him. Skunk felt flattered. Why would such a powerful carnivore want to associate with a Skunk?

"My diet sucks," Skunk told Coyote. "Earthworms, Crickets, and Duck eggs. Standard stuff, very boring. Sometimes I'll snack on a dead Possum, but nothing puts me back in the pink like Rabbit."

"Meat is good," said Coyote.

Skunk ogled the bloody chunk of Rabbit in Coyote's jaws. "I visit Squib Dog sometimes. He never shares his food. He attacked me when I ate his leftovers. I sprayed him good."

"Don't spray us," said Elrod. "We're on your side."

"I only spray as a last resort. Then I empty my whole load."

"Wish I had a weapon like yours," said Elrod. "I'd use it to blast everyone I hate."

"I can't waste my spray. Takes days for me to recharge my anal glands. A stink-free Skunk is soon a dead Skunk."

Coyote farted. It was a wet one. "This Rabbit is full of fat," he said.

"Phew!" Skunk gasped, moving away. "You sure you're not part Skunk?"

Elrod laughed. "Don't stand too close to Coyote. When he drops his mud, it's an avalanche."

Skunk faced Coyote, putting on a deferential look. "You offered me a free lunch. You've never done that before. What do you expect in return?"

Coyote swallowed a glob of gristle. "Only the pleasure of your company."

"Nobody ever wants the pleasure of my company."

"When I need a favor from you, Skunk, I'll let you know. In the meantime, just eat, swallow, and be merry, for tomorrow you might choke to death on a Rabbit bone."

"Too bad you didn't get invited to the victory party," Elrod told Skunk. "You would've loved it."

"I never get invited to any parties. I heard some animals talking, though. They said you saved Madame Rabbit from Sharp-Shinned Hawk. Is that true?"

Elrod paused before answering. "She got greedy, and everybody knows greed kills."

Drowsy from their feast, they soon dozed off.

Coyote woke first. He glared at his companions. Skunk was still sleeping, his dusky nose wedged into a Gopher hole, and with every wheeze, he stirred up clouds of dust. Elrod was grunting as he chewed furiously on a Rabbit foot. Coyote leaned over and nipped the bushy black tip of Elrod's tail.

"Ouch!"

"You're making too much noise."

"Skunk's making the racket, not me."

"You're chewing with your mouth open. Didn't your mother teach you anything?"

"When you're bored, you always lash out at me."

"I'm not bored, Elrod. Just concerned … for your welfare. You're in a sticky spot right now. The USA won't forgive your transgressions this time. You've gone on way too many killing sprees."

"But you put me up to them, Coyote. I didn't act alone. You egged me on from the start!"

Elrod was right: all the mayhem had been Coyote's idea. After the victory party on the Slough, he and Elrod had gone on the hunt, killing whatever they wanted. Elrod squirmed down narrow holes and flushed prey out into Coyote's waiting jaws. They'd eaten Field Mouse, Mole, and Garter Snake. They had raided Mama Mallard's nest. Then they slaughtered Madame Rabbit and dozens of other Rabbits in her warren. These extrajudicial killings would outrage the USA, but Coyote wasn't worried about being blamed for them. Old Man Coyote was always coaching him on how to cover his tracks.

"Lie! Lie! Lie! Never stop lying!" he repeatedly shouted from inside Coyote's head. *"Lying is your secret power!"*

OMC had urged him to supply Owl with the White Rats. Some tainted substance in them was obviously scrambling the old Bird's brains, turning her into a hapless turnspit. Bending Owl to his will was now easier than ever.

"You're the king of connivers," Elrod told him, "but you've never done me dirt. Well, almost never."

"I always play to win."

Elrod sighed. "The USA probably wants my head on a stump."

"Don't ever let your fears stop you from filling your belly, Elrod. The USA is a society of slackers and freeloaders. Why should the government feed the laggards who lack the backbone to do an honest day's killing for their food? Prey-predator ratios? Kill quotas? Meat for the meek? Ridiculous! Only trickle-down gastronomics work for us. What we don't eat can trickle on down to the deadbeats and layabouts. How else can carnivores like us get ahead in an eating game that's rigged against those higher up on the food chain?"

"I kinda get you," said Elrod, "but if we keep eating too much, there'll be nothing left to eat—even for us. Isn't that what the Natural Law of Animals is all about—not eating ourselves out of house and home?"

"We are the only law that counts."

Coyote was lying; he knew their flagrant overconsumption couldn't last forever. The Squibs had stripped resources from the Slough, befouling land and water. Food was scarce. The animals struggled to feed themselves while coping with their ever-shrinking habitat. If things got too bad, Coyote planned to lope off in search of another predator-friendly habitat. Hopefully, OMC would guide him to such a place. But until it was time to leave, he'd eat his fill.

Elrod couldn't shake off his worries. "If the USA lowers the boom on me, don't ditch me."

"Have I ever ditched you, Elrod?"

"Well … you voted to banish me from the Slough."

"Don't be such a has-been Bird."

"What's that?"

"It's a Bird that flies backwards. It only sees where it has been, never where's it's going. That's why it keeps crashing into things."

"I'm not a has-been Bird—or even a has-been Stoat."

"Good to hear. Therefore, we must fabricate a plausible falsehood that explains your urge to slaughter helpless animals."

"I kill Rabbits and eat them. What else is there to explain?"

"Your PTSD."

"PT say what?"

"Post-traumatic slaughter disorder. A terrible affliction. PTSD means you're not responsible for your criminal actions."

"Where are you going with this?"

"Elrod, you're a war veteran. Your rendezvous with death inflicted deep emotional wounds."

"But I loved that war! Until our side got poisoned."

"Sadly, the savagery of up-close combat caused irreversible psychological damage."

"I was a general. I always led from the rear."

"That's true, but you're still an emotional wreck. The chirrup of a Spotted Towhee may trigger your war-related trauma, sending you off on a bloody rampage."

"I'm a Stoat, Coyote. Stoats go on bloody rampages."

"And you suffer hallucinations. You talk to your dead brother."

"Hey, will ya get off it? You talk to Old Man Coyote—constantly. Even in your sleep. What's that about? Maybe *you're* the one with PTSD."

Coyote showed his fangs. "It's your ass we're trying to save—not mine."

Elrod swallowed hard. "You really think this PTSD bit might help me beat a bum rap?"

Coyote cocked an eyebrow. "You can bet your life on it. The USA already knows you're a high-strung Stoat with poor impulse control. Convince them that the war on Rats tipped you over the edge."

"I should pretend I'm crazy?"

"You won't have to pretend very hard, little buddy."

"Other than humiliating myself, what else should I do?"

"Scratch your anus 'til it bleeds. It'll convince everyone you've reached the end of your wits."

14 THE RATS OF SQUIB FLATS

Coyote, Elrod, and Skunk decided to walk off their Rabbit. At the edge of a Squib junkyard, they followed a narrow path between heaps of gutted, rusted-out vehicles.

Skunk stepped over a crevice oozing a thick black liquid. "We're close to Squib Flats," he said.

"You live here?" asked Elrod.

"You kidding? My junkyard is much nicer than this."

"Get down!" Coyote cried. "Male Squib!"

A skinny Squib sat on the sagging doorstep of an old tumbledown house, one hand hanging slack across his kneecap. His head rocked slowly, as if he were nodding off. The animals hid behind a thick clump of thistles and peered out.

"A male Squib?" Elrod asked Coyote. "How can you tell?"

"The males smell like a Chicken three days dead."

The Squib brought a tubular object to his lips and sucked on it. Clouds of smoke enveloped his head.

Elrod squinted at the Squib. "What's he doing with that thing?"

"Smoking a Fry Daddy," said Coyote.

"What?"

"Squib Dog claims his owners smoke them day and night."

"Hey," said Skunk, "I recognize that house. It's where Squib Dog lives. The poor slob."

"Don't feel sorry for him," said Coyote. "He deserves what he gets."

"He gets free food," said Elrod. "He doesn't have to make an honest living like us."

Coyote stiffened. At the far edge of the junkyard, two Rats hopped and twisted in the dust, biting, scratching, and screeching. Elrod and Skunk also saw them.

"I wonder what they're fighting about," said Skunk.

Elrod snickered. "They're not fighting—they're screwing. I saw them doing that during the war on Rats. Even in the heat of battle, they screwed their brains out. It was like they wanted to murder each other."

"Didn't the Squibs poison all the Rats?" asked Skunk.

Elrod shook his head. "Some escaped." He studied the Rats a few moments. "Let's kill 'em while they're busy. They'll die happy. We'll be performing a public service."

Skunk shook his head. "Count me out. My best offense is a good defense."

"Watching them go at it like that," said Elrod, "is giving me a big stiffy."

"You're a sick bastard, Elrod. You know that?"

Coyote gave Elrod a light nip on the ear. "I never see you with any female Stoats. How come?"

Elrod's tail twitched. "The females call me Elrod the Ramrod. They swoon over my spoor and come back for more."

"So, females don't scare you?"

Skunk chuckled. "It's more likely he scares females."

Elrod looked indignant. "I don't bother with the older ones. They're grouchy and give me too much lip."

"You prefer the younger ones?" asked Skunk.

"I like them right out of the hatch."

"Uh, I'm not sure what you mean."

"When the kits are born blind, deaf, and hairless, I get the pick of the litter."

"You make me wanna puke," said Skunk.

Suddenly, they heard a loud crack. The topmost Rat flipped into the air and landed on its back, legs twitching, its head blown off. The other Rat scurried beneath a jumble of car parts.

"Gunshot," said Coyote. "Keep your heads down."

Skunk released his full load. The sound had startled him.

"Gak!" Elrod gasped, clasping his paws over his nose. "Gak! Gak! Gak!"

"Couldn't help it," said Skunk. "Sorry."

Coyote sprang to his feet and bolted at full speed away from Squib Flats.

Elrod staggered after him. "Help me, Coyote," he moaned. "I'm dying ... from post-traumatic stink disorder!"

15 COYOTE CONTACTS HIS INVISIBLE FRIEND

Coyote ran hard through several Squib neighborhoods, trying to shake off the smell of Skunk. Cutting across backyards, he flushed out a few Cats, but didn't give chase. A Squib yelled at him. He dashed across a highway. Cars swerved around him or screeched to a stop. He kept running, skirting rows of enormous buildings where hundreds of Squibs worked. Stopping to catch his breath, he scrunched down into the bushes and watched the Squibs scurry in and out of a building. Sweating and grunting, they performed their baffling tasks, waving their arms and shouting at each other. Coyote heard nerve-wracking noises: *KABOOM! CHUGGA-CHUGGA! CLANG! RATTA-TAT-TAT-TAT! BEEP BEEP! WOOP WOOP! BRIIIIIIIIIIING!*

He trotted off, sticking to the late afternoon shadows. If he were spotted, the Squibs might try to shoot him. It had happened before. *Bang! Bang! Bang!* Once, a fat Squib with a pink face had climbed into a big machine and chased him overland. Coyote had raced down into a drainage ditch. The machine had followed, flipped over, and burst into flames.

As he slunk through whatever cover he could find, he felt

carved out and a tad depressed, which puzzled him. He'd gotten more than enough to eat. Elrod and Skunk had fawned over him, vying for his favor and lavishing praise upon him. He'd even watched two Rats having sex. All in all, a pretty good day. So, what was his problem?

Maybe talking to Old Man Coyote would revive his spirits. They hadn't chatted for several moons. Talking to OMC was never easy; it was like getting brained with a rock. Trotting over into the cover of some cottonwoods, he stretched out in a patch of ragweed.

"Hello?" he whispered, squeezing his eyes closed. "Are you there? It's me. Is this a good time to talk?"

A short cackle echoed inside his skull. He heard a scratchy sound, like an animal clawing the ground. Next came the sound of two stones scraping against each other. Coyote shivered, his heart racing.

"OMC? You there?"

A raspy voice answered. *"I was napping. What the hell do you want now?"*

"Uh, I have a question."

"Ask it. Then bug off!"

Coyote took a deep breath. "Can I come visit you? You're in my head, but I'm sure you also exist outside of me. Wherever that is, I want to meet you face-to-face. Like real Coyotes."

Silence. Had OMC fallen back to sleep? Coyote kept talking. "Right now, you're just a loud voice that echoes inside my skull."

More silence. OMC wasn't holding up his end of the conversation. Maybe he was hard of hearing. Coyote started to raise his volume but thought better of it. Shouting back at OMC wasn't advisable. OMC was an alpha male who didn't tolerate any challenge to his authority. Coyote decided to try a different approach.

"It's kinda awkward to talk about," he blurted out. "I

just saw two Rats going at it. Can you give me some advice about my own . . . situation. A top predator like me should never have to go without."

No response. Coyote took a deep breath and tried again. "It isn't just about sex, of course. I want to pair-bond with a special someone, but I can't find any available females to mate with. I'm very lonely."

OMC spoke, harshly. *"You had a mate before, fungus face, and five pups—but the Squibs killed them! You couldn't protect them, could you?"*

OMC wasn't being fair. Yes, he'd once had a mate—and five pups. A poisoned Deer carcass had killed his mate. His pups were shot in their den. Coyote had escaped, but took a bullet in the ribs. He'd hidden out behind a dumpster, feverish, dehydrated, and leaking blood. The bullet hugged his lungs. Every breath hurt. He scrounged for food scraps, but feral Dogs attacked him and chased him off.

Eventually, his wound had healed enough that he was able to limp his way to Come Along Slough. Not a great place, but preferable to living on the streets. Anti-Coyote sentiment was strong on the Slough, but using charm and trickery, he quickly insinuated himself into the USA's inner circle, discovering that many of these long-winded, vainglorious animals were gullible—or just plain stupid. Everyone soon learned that crossing a carnivore wasn't a wise move.

Unfortunately, he was the only Coyote on Come Along Slough. His social life was in the dumps, forcing him to hang out with animals of a lesser sort. It brought out his mean streak. He wanted another mate—one who would give him more pups and make him a proud papa again. Neighboring communities had small Coyote populations, but every desirable female was already paired up with a hypervigilant male. He'd fought with a few of them, attempting to steal their mates, but he always lost. His battle scars confirmed he was a frustrated lover, not an accomplished fighter.

As he brooded over his predicament, he winced from the sharp pain of the bullet still in his ribs. Then he heard OMC's voice.

"Visit if you must, but you will regret it."

A wave of joy swept through Coyote. "I'll leave immediately. Just tell me where you live."

"I don't give out my address to strangers."

"Where should I start looking for you? Just give me a hint about how we can develop a closer relationship. Please."

Once more, Coyote heard an animal clawing the ground. Then a short cackle followed by an explosive splutter. OMC spoke.

"If you want a closer relationship with me, empty your bowels!"

"What? Empty my bowels?

Silence.

Coyote curled up into a tight ball, his tail warming his nose. Hoping to find some facsimile of OMC, he would empty his bowels until he was hollowed-out. He suspected OMC was only testing his mettle. No doubt, he was a wily but kindhearted grandfather—one who would offer him a helping paw, wise counsel, and a generous helping of Fawn haunch. This grandfather lived somewhere in the wider world, but before Coyote beat the bushes for him, he first had to tease out from his feces any clues about this elusive creature's exact location.

16 THE BIG BADA BOOM

By evening, Coyote had the runs. He kept squatting, blasting out the last of Rabbit. He tried contacting Old Man Coyote. "Hello, it's me again. Are you there?" His feces didn't respond.

Now he was hungry again. He wanted to hunt, but he reeked of Skunk, which would scare off any prey. He cut a path toward the far western end of the Slough. Squib Dog had told him about the easy pickings at the new Squib homeless camp there, and now Coyote dropped by regularly to cadge food scraps.

"Lots of Dogs live in the camp," Squib Dog had explained. "Some of them want to fight me, but I'm on good butt-sniffing terms with most."

Coyote splashed across a shallow, trash-clogged canal and arrived at the fringes of the camp. Big and little Squibs lived here in tents and makeshift shelters. Some slept out in the open. At night, the adult Squibs sat around bonfires, eating, drinking, laughing, weeping, and screaming. If they saw Coyote lurking at the edge of the firelight, hoping for a handout, they called out to him or whistled, urging him to come closer, but he always kept his distance. He didn't trust Squibs.

Coyote saw Squib Dog nosing through a pile of tin cans. Wishing to stay unseen, he veered off toward a dead cottonwood. No doubt Squib Dog expected to be thanked for revealing the camp's easy pickings. But Coyote wasn't beholden to anyone. As he crouched behind the dead cottonwood, Squib Dog spotted him and trotted over. Coyote came out of cover, putting on a nonchalant "fancy meeting you here" look. Squib Dog had a companion: a small Dog with kinky white fur, a bald tail, and bulging green eyes.

Squib Dog greeted Coyote and introduced Larry.

"Smartest Dog I ever met," he said. "If you come up short of brains, Larry can give you some of his. He's got plenty to spare."

Larry stepped forward. "Welcome to our tribe. Care to share a meal with us?"

"No," said Coyote, noting Larry's fluent Slough Speak. "I'm on the hunt for small game, my preferred repast."

"Hunting isn't so easy these days. Good thing Squib Dog keeps you posted about the free chow here."

"I knew about this dump before he did. Anyway, I'm not too keen on handouts. I prefer to work for a living."

"Well, if you're ever in need, Squib Dog is a friend indeed."

Coyote bristled. "I meet my needs without anyone's help."

"A Dog can be a Coyote's best friend."

"My best friends are me, myself, and I."

"Sounds like misery loves company."

Squib Dog barked out a laugh. "Oh, Larry, you're not just the smartest Dog I ever met, you're also the funniest!"

Coyote scowled. Little Larry had a big mouth on him.

Coyote would have to do something about that. Maybe later when no witnesses were around.

"Me and Larry got a ham bone," said Squib Dog. "You wanna share some of it with us?"

Coyote's stomach gurgled. A ham bone was a real prize, a high-value food that he wanted only for himself. Maybe he could snatch it and run off with it.

"You hate handouts," said Larry, "but a ham bone might tide you over 'til you obtain food more to your liking."

"Is it large enough to be worth my while?"

"It's a pretty piece of meat for three hungry fellows like us."

"We buried it," said Squib Dog. "It's nice and ripe now. Let's go dig it up."

"Lead the way," said Coyote, "and I will decide whether to partake."

As they walked through mustard weed and reed grass, Squib Dog spoke to Coyote privately. "Go easy on Larry, okay? He gets the fits. Bites his tongue and foams at the mouth."

"Is he rabid?"

"He calls it 'the seizures.' His eyes go real crazy. A long time ago, his Squibs beat him bad and broke his head bone. Hasn't been right since."

"Sounds like the perfect friend for you."

"Don't say nothing. Okay? He's very sensitive about his condition."

"My jaws are sealed."

They arrived at a stunted scrub oak, and Squib Dog and Larry dug up a hefty ham bone packed with meat and fat. Coyote wanted it all, but the bone was too big and greasy for him to carry off at top speed. Feeling thwarted, he crouched down with the two Dogs and devoured most of the goodies, including the marrow, and the meal was soon over.

The three animals lounged beneath the scrub oak, licking globs of fat off the grass, their eyes glassy with satisfaction.

"Hope you didn't spoil your appetite," Larry said to Coyote.

"I ate very lightly."

Squib Dog sniffed Coyote's fur. "Didn't want to say nothing earlier, but how come you smell like Skunk?"

Coyote shot him a nasty look before addressing Larry. "The Squibs here don't live in regular houses like other Squibs. What's up with that?"

Larry rolled onto his back and snapped at a Horsefly. "They got nowhere else to live."

"This dump of yours is even worse than Squib Flats."

"Hey, don't cock your leg on my digs," said Squib Dog. "Maybe it ain't easy on the eyes, but me and Scratchit like it just fine."

Coyote growled. "Don't interrupt when I'm talking to Larry."

"Living here is hard," Larry continued. "A full stomach can't always fix a broken heart—or broken spirit."

"How come you're so chummy with these Squibs? Do they pat your head and rub your belly?"

"Nothing like that. I just listen to them. I know how they feel about things because I understand their words."

Coyote gave Larry a sharp look. "Nobody understands Squib talk except Squibs."

"That just ain't true," said Squib Dog. "I get told to sit, stay, play dead, and I understand perfectly. But Larry understands Squib talk much better. He's small in body, but big in brains."

Coyote growled for silence, but Squib Dog had more to say.

"Larry's a Squib expert. He's been learning me about … about…"

"The economy," Larry interjected.

"Thanks, Larry. Them big words you plant in my brain don't always take root."

"What's the economy?" Coyote demanded.

"It's…" said Squib Dog. "It's…"

"Some kind of animal?"

"I suppose you could call the economy an animal," said Larry. "It's an invisible beast that haunts us day and night. You can't run away from it, it's always hungry, and it eats your body and soul."

Coyote glanced back over his shoulder. "Will it try to eat me?"

"It prefers Squibs."

"Fine by me. Hope it eats up every last Squib."

"The economy eats Squibs, but at the same time, it gives them money."

"Huh?"

"The economy runs on money," Larry explained. "And Squibs can't obtain shelter and food without it. The ones here in this camp are flat broke."

"How come?"

"A few greedy Squibs grab most of the money for themselves and refuse to share it with anyone else."

Coyote laughed. "Hey, those are *my* kind of Squibs."

"Larry says the economy is what he calls a 'zero sum game,'" said Squib Dog. "That's because the economy is based on … uh, what's that word?"

"Capitalism," said Larry.

"Larry will smarten you up," Squib Dog told Coyote. "Before I met him, I was all bark and no brains. Stick with Larry and he'll give your brain a big boost."

Coyote controlled his temper. Hanging out with this fancy-talking Dog had made Squib Dog a bit too cheeky. He fixed his attention on Larry. "If I catch your drift, this economy is a real trickster."

"I'm sure you can relate," said Larry. "From what I hear, you're also an accomplished trickster."

Coyote understood that Larry was throwing him a compliment, but he wasn't going to acknowledge it. "Unlike you, I don't swap spit with the Squibs. This economy baloney really goofs with my head. Why can't you explain it to me . . . more intelligently?"

Larry nodded at Squib Dog. "Perhaps my star pupil can do that for you."

Squib Dog scrunched-up his brow, drool bearding his jaw. "I'll give it my best shot."

"Keep it simple," said Larry.

Squib Dog stared intently at Coyote. "The economy is so bad right now, my Squibs can't even afford Dog food. That's as bad as it gets."

"They can't afford Dog food 'cause they blow their money on Fry Daddies," said Coyote.

"No need to get snarky," said Larry.

"I'm not getting snarky," Coyote growled. "Are *you* getting snarky?"

Squib Dog groaned. "Poor Coyote's on overload, Larry. Don't tell 'em about the Big Bada Boom or he'll blow his lid."

Coyote shook his head as if stung by a Wasp. "We're talking about the economy. Why are you changing the subject, fool?"

"Bada bing, bada boom," said Squib Dog, "scares the crap out of me."

"He's jangled-up," said Larry. "The Big Bada Boom is a real game changer."

Coyote stood slowly. "First the economy. Then this Big whatever-you-call-it.   I'm   hearing   nothing   but gobbledygook."

No need to feel stupid." said Larry. "Not everybody's science smart about the Big Bada Boom."

"I don't feel stupid, Little Larry, but I do feel like throwing a big fit and foaming at the mouth."

"Coyote!" Squib Dog cried. "I toldja not to say anything!"

"What's the big deal? You said Little Larry's sick in the head."

Squib Dog growled. "You talk out loud to Old Man Coyote. That's as sick in the head as it gets."

Larry barked for attention. "Let's take a deep breath, okay? We're all civilized carnivores here. Coyote seems confused about the Big Bada Boom. Fair enough. He deserves a good explanation. Squib Dog, will you do the honors again?"

Squib dog let out a soft whine. "Coyote's giving me bad performance anxiety."

"Just channel your inner Canine."

"Okay, Here's the dope, Coyote. The Squibs call the Big Bada Boom 'climate change.' They get naming rights, 'cause they're the ones who are changing the climate."

"Climate change is a tame name. It doesn't cut the mustard," said Larry. "Climate collapse is more to the point. It's very bad news for the Squibs—and for us."

"What's the big deal?" Coyote scoffed. "The climate changes all the time. The wind blows, the sun shines, it rains, it snows, but the climate never collapses."

"You're confusing climate with weather," said Larry. "It's a common mistake, so once again, you shouldn't feel stupid."

"Stupid is when some double-talking Squib-licker disrespects me."

"Then let me give it to you straight and simple. The Big Bada Boom is a world-wrecker. Floods, droughts, diseases, windstorms, heat waves, frigid temperatures, widespread starvation. Mass die-offs of plants and animals. No more me, no more you."

"When Larry has his fits," said Squib Dog, "he has … visions. He can see the future."

"He can't see *my* future," said Coyote.

"You're standing on a molehill, but Larry's standing on a mountaintop. He sees the big picture."

Coyote stifled an urge to rip out both their throats, but Larry probably had friends within barking distance. Tangling with a pack of snarling brutes was a lousy way to end the day.

"Somebody else also knows about this coming catastrophe," said Larry. "A Girl lives here in camp. She can't talk or hear, but she sees what I see."

"I haven't met her yet," said Squib Dog, "but she and Larry see the future like it was yesterday."

Coyote suspected that this Girl might be one he had recently glimpsed on the Slough during his victory party walk with Owl. "I thought I was getting a free lunch today," he said, "but I had to pay through the ass for a crummy ham bone. I can stomach your crazy talk. It amuses me, but this blather about some Squib Girl makes me blow chunks."

"Well, you best listen up to Larry about the Big Bada Boom," said Squib Dog. "He says a huge flood will wipe us out real soon."

"I'm not scared of water. I can swim like a Fish."

"You may swim like a Fish," said Larry, "but you will soon *flounder*."

"Oh, Larry," Squib Dog said, "you're killing me with the jokes! You get it, Coyote? Flounder? It's a Fish Larry told me about."

Without a word, Coyote trotted off to search for Elrod, confident this little weasel would never dare to trifle with the apex predator of Come Along Slough.

17 HUMMINGBIRD MAKES A NEW FRIEND

Hummingbird saw a strange-looking Bird flitting from tree to tree. She guessed it was about twelve of her own wingspans in size. The bird had a large red beak, bright blue head, scarlet-and-yellow chest, and dazzling grass-colored wings.

Deciding to investigate, Hummingbird hovered in front of the stranger, her wings whirring. "Hello. Who are you?"

The Bird fixed its spooky red eyes on Hummingbird. "I'm Maggie."

"Very pleased to meet you. I'm Hummingbird. Are you new to the Slough?"

"I'm dreadfully lost," said the Bird.

"I'm so sorry. What kind of Bird are you?"

"I'm a Lorikeet. A Rainbow Lorikeet."

"What should I call you?"

"Maggie the Parrot is fine. Or just Maggie."

"How do you know Slough Speak?"

"I learned it from migrating Birds. I speak many different languages."

Hummingbird perched on a willow branch to inspect Maggie more closely. She was gorgeous. Just looking at her sent the best kind of shivers down Hummingbird's backbone. "Are you a foreigner?"

"I'm very far from home. Call me a foreigner if you wish, but I'd much prefer to be called a friend."

"Owl hates foreigners. She's the secretary-general of the USA—the United Slough of Animals—and outsiders make her very grouchy."

"That's okay. Birds like me get pigeonholed a lot. 'Rolling stone,' 'tramp,' 'drifter,' 'vagrant,' 'bag Birdie'… I've heard them all, but I'm just a Bird of passage trying to find her way back home."

"Sounds like you've been through a lot."

"Very true. I was a freeborn Lorikeet until some Squibs caught me. I did hard time in a cage. My life has been very topsy-turvy. I was in a zoo for a while. I even worked as an emotional support animal, 'til my Squib traded me in for a Peacock. Right now, I'm working as a life coach. I cope with my troubles by helping others to cope with theirs."

"How does a life coach do something that complicated?"

"Positivity is the tool of my trade."

"Positivity?"

"It's the only known cure for negativity."

"Is negativity a disease?"

"A disease of mind and spirit."

Hummingbird sighed. "I think it's infected a few of the animals on Come Along Slough. Maybe a good strong dose of positivity would cure them."

"Sounds like Come Along Slough needs a good life coach."

"Probably a whole army of life coaches."

Maggie laughed. "I'm curious. Is Hummingbird your entire name?"

"It's a plain name, isn't it? A few of the other animals here get more glamorous names, but not I. Nobody calls me Anna's Hummingbird, which sounds more exotic."

"Hummingbird sounds beautiful to me. I love your green feathers, and that darling spot of red on your throat."

Hummingbird whirred her wings, embarrassed. Nobody had ever complimented her name or the color of her feathers. "Thank you. Maggie is also a beautiful name. The double G rolls off my tongue like . . . like a drop of honeysuckle nectar."

"Alas, Maggie is a Squib name. I used to have a proper Lorikeet name, but I can't remember it. Blame it on early-Lorikeet trauma, I guess,"

"Where is your home?"

"Australia. Despite all my travels, I'm still an Aussie at heart."

"Is Australia near the Slough?"

"It's at the bottom of the world. For short, we Aussies call it 'the Down Under.'"

Hummingbird knew about the bottom of the Slough, but knew nothing about the bottom of the world. Many Birds migrated seasonally, particularly during winter and spring, and Hummingbird had listened to their entrancing tales about faraway places.

"All migrating Birds are shameless liars," Owl had warned her. "Canada Goose, in particular, is a repeat prevaricator, but Tanager is the worst of all. Take this Bird twaddle with a particle of pollen, Hummingbird."

Still perched on the willow branch, Hummingbird stared up at Maggie. "What's bottom-of-the-world Down Under Australia like?"

"I don't remember much," she said. "I was just a fledgling in my eucalyptus nest when I was stolen away from my mother."

"Oh, how awful. Squibs are so mean."

"I miss my mother."

"I'm sure you'll see her again."

"She's probably dead by now, but I plan to wing my way back to Australia and finish out my days feasting on low-hanging tropical fruit."

"Is Australia far away?"

"Very far away, but I wish to return there before I die."

"You don't look old enough to die."

"Lorikeets don't show their age, but I have lived fifteen winters. I'll be fortunate to live even five winters longer."

"Fifteen winters! Gosh, that's terrific. I'll be lucky to live even seven winters."

"That can't be true," said Maggie. "You're the quintessence of longevity."

Hummingbird's heart beat furiously. "Why thank you, Maggie! I'm not sure what that means, but you are very kind. I bet you're a wonderful life coach."

"I'm hungry," said Maggie. "Is there anything around here to eat?"

"I'm sure we can find something suitable."

Maggie enjoyed snacking on pollen and nectar. Hummingbird was delighted. As they investigated a flowery meadow, they compared tongues. Maggie had a brushy tip to her tongue. Hummingbird had a forked tongue with nectar grooves.

"I also love fruit," said Maggie. "My Squib captors fed me mangos and papayas. All that fiber kept me regular."

"I also crave fiber in my diet," said Hummingbird, "so I occasionally snatch up Insects. Once, a big Hornet got stuck on my beak."

"Did it sting you?"

"No, it just vibrated my tailbone. Felt kinda good. Know what I mean?"

"I sometimes eat seeds," said Maggie, "but Lorikeets have weak gizzards, so we prefer softer food. You know, squishy stuff."

The word "squishy" made Hummingbird giggle. Maggie giggled also.

"I can tell we're already fast friends," Maggie said.

Hummingbird agreed. "I feel as if we've known each other forever."

"Perhaps you would like to come to Australia with me?"

"You're really inviting me?"

"You'd be a wonderful traveling companion."

Hummingbird was in a complete tizzy. She'd never traveled outside the Slough before. The thought of going to Australia terrified her, but she trusted Maggie—even though she'd only known her a very short time.

"I … don't know what to think," said Hummingbird.

"Don't think about it for too long," said Maggie. "The Bird of Time is always on the wing."

"I could use a life coach to help me with a problem," said Hummingbird. "Scratchit Cat keeps stalking me. I'm a nervous wreck."

"You probably suffer from Pussyphobia," Maggie said, "Fear of Felines. I also suffer from it. Cats terrify me."

"But you're so … large. I'm sure you could fight off a Cat."

"Once a Cat bites your neck, it's lights out."

Hummingbird trembled. "Is Pussyphobia curable?"

"Only if you stand your ground and never allow a Cat to subjugate your Birdhood."

"If I stand my ground, Scratchit will swallow me in one bite—unless she decides to torture me first."

"You must master your fear, Hummingbird. I will be your life coach."

"Wow. I've never had a life coach before. I'm so excited!"

"We have a lot of work to do, so let's get cracking."

18 MUSHROOM MAGGIE

Hummingbird brought Maggie to the next USA meeting and waited impatiently for the stragglers to appear. Beaver, Nutria, and Muskrat had arrived earlier, but for many representatives, punctuality wasn't a core value. Squirrel, Raccoon, and Scrub Jay took their time arriving. Then Squib Dog trotted into sight next, his tongue lolling out. Nervously, Hummingbird looked around for Scratchit Cat. Where was she lurking?

Elrod the Stoat didn't dare show his face; he'd killed and eaten Madame Rabbit, along with her friends and family. Public opinion had hardened against Elrod, but using Owl's authority as cover, Coyote had lobbied the USA to once again forgive the little Weasel's transgressions. Coyote blamed Elrod's recent killing spree on PTSD: post-traumatic slaughter disorder.

"He can't stop scratching his ass," he explained. "That's a surefire symptom of PTSD."

Attendance had flagged recently. The war had decimated the Slough population and the hard business of living left little time for civic responsibilities. Hummingbird was pleased to see Black-Capped Chickadee, Nuthatch, Sparrow, and Bushtit. Since Scratchit had become a delegate with voting rights, these Birds had boycotted USA meetings, refusing to associate with this serial Bird-killer.

She heard Squirrel and Scrub Jay teasing Crow as he recited a poem to anyone within earshot.

"Crow causes tears to flow like the waters of woe," said Squirrel, "yet he thinks his sappy rhymes make us happy and snappy."

Scrub Jay hopped back and forth. "That cutesy Crow thinks it ain't too cool how you drool doggerel while playing footsie like he's your sweetheart tootsie."

Squirrel swished his tail in the dirt. "Alas and alack! You have insulted our bard in black! Don't speak of his pretense, expecting him to turn the other cheek! He will sense this offense immense and bite off your brazen beak!"

"Excusez-moi, but your bliss I must dismiss," Scrub Jay squawked, "because your rhymes drizzle out like Crow's shizzle."

Crow silenced them with a cold stare. "Shut your traps and can the crap," he cawed, "or I'll rip you both a new ass crack!"

Other USA representatives soon arrived: Carp, River Otter, Blue Heron, Kingfisher, and Flicker. Osprey, Bald Eagle, and Red-Tailed Hawk showed their haughty faces, perching high above the fray on the uppermost branches of a cottonwood. Hummingbird also spied Carpenter Ant, Yellow Jacket, Dung Beetle, Banana Slug, and Earthworm. She couldn't see them, but she heard Cricket's chirrup, and Tree Frog's rivet-rivet.

Hummingbird hoped the usual blabbermouths didn't disrupt the meeting. She wanted things to go well for Maggie. She hovered close to where the Lorikeet was perched on a rotting cottonwood log. "Some members of the USA are real jerks," she whispered. "Please don't take anything they say personally."

Maggie cracked open a hazelnut and prized out the meat. "A life coach doesn't take anything personally."

She finished off the hazelnut and closed her eyes. Was she dozing, or meditating? Hummingbird wasn't sure. Maggie had tried teaching her how to meditate, but she couldn't slow her heartbeat enough to get into what Maggie called "the zone of mindfulness."

Hummingbird fidgeted on the log and reflected on her new friendship. She'd grown quite fond of her life coach. Maggie had patiently unpacked all Hummingbird's fears, tossing them off like bits of deadwood. Maggie had a sharp mind. She was a good listener and a wonderful conversationalist. But Hummingbird hadn't yet decided about flying off to Australia. Going so far from the Slough terrified her. Maggie assured her that many "handsome hummers" lived at the bottom of the world. Hummingbird had never felt the urge to mate; she had always rejected every male that came courting. Perhaps the male Hummingbirds in Australia were more appealing than the ones on the Slough, but she doubted it. Males were all the same. Who needed them?

During their life coaching sessions, Maggie worked tirelessly to expand Hummingbird's mind beyond its Slough-bound limitations.

"You have a United Slough of Animals," Maggie said one day, "but not a United Slough of Flowers. Why?"

Hummingbird whirred her wings, trying to organize her thoughts. "Well, I absolutely love flowers, but I couldn't imagine a coalition of honeysuckle, penstemon, and bleeding hearts voting for a dandelion as their secretary-general."

Maggie cocked her head. "When a dandelion says hello to me, do you know how I respond?"

"How?"

"Achoo!"

Her life coach liked to joke around. Humor helped Hummingbird loosen up and open her mind. Maggie spoke often about the Be Here Not World.

"It overlaps this world," Maggie explained. "We live in it and don't live in it at the same time."

Hummingbird pondered this puzzlement. "So … I'm in two places at once, while I'm not in two places at once?"

"It's a paradox."

"Pair of what?"

Maggie laughed. "A paradox is any idea that contradicts itself. For example, we live simultaneously in the local world and a nonlocal world. These two worlds are one world. It's a real brain-twister."

Hummingbird couldn't get her wings around the Be Here Not World. Living in the Be Here Now World was more than enough for her. Two worlds crowding the same space sounded like big trouble.

As she waited for the meeting to start, Hummingbird felt tense. She yearned for a taste of foxglove pollen to calm her nerves. Or maybe a quick flutter among the come-hither red of bee balm and coral bells would tranquilize her anxiety. She glanced at Maggie. The hollyhock red of the Lorikeet's beak slowed the staccato of her heart.

She heard Beaver slapping his tail. Coyote growled for attention. The USA meeting was starting. Maggie kept her eyes closed. Perhaps she was daydreaming about Australia.

"The secretary-general has asked me to fill in for her," Coyote announced. "She's currently preoccupied with weighty matters of state."

Muskrat squeaked derisively and pointed at the sagging cottonwood limb where Owl perched, snoring loudly. "In other words, she's sleeping off another whopping meal of those White Field Mice you provided her. Thanks to you, she's doubled down on dumb. Now she's your personal paw puppet."

The air whooshed from Hummingbird's tiny lungs. Things were getting off to a bad start. Trying to heal the USA's emotional wounds was a fool's errand. She was ready to fly off to Australia. She'd miss Come Along Slough, of course, but it was time for her to experience something new.

"We will ignore the hostile remark from our *former* secretary-general," said Coyote. "Hummingbird? You're at the top of the agenda."

"Hey!" Beaver protested, slapping his tail in the water. "I'm at the top of the agenda!"

"I made an executive decision," said Coyote. "You're up next. Don't slap your tail again unless I order you to do so." He turned back to Hummingbird. "I understand you wish to introduce some …vagrant?"

Hummingbird took a quick breath. "Vagabond—not vagrant. Maggie is a Rainbow Lorikeet. She's from way down under the world in the land of Kangaroos and Kookaburras."

"She lives underground?" Mole asked. "I like her already."

Maggie's eyes opened. She wagged her grass-colored wings and puffed out her scarlet chest. "I thank the USA for inviting me here today and giving me the opportunity to make new friends."

"Maggie is my life coach," said Hummingbird.

Coyote gave her a sour look. "A life coach, you say?"

"Maggie provides emotional support for animals," she explained, "and helps them discover the path to self-fulfillment."

Coyote's paw patted his belly. "For the moment, I have all the self-fulfillment I need."

A few animals gasped at this rude remark, but from the treetops, the raptors screeched laughter.

"But I *do* like the looks of Maggie," he added. "I bet there's lots of tasty meat down under her fancy feathers."

"Maggie's here to feed your mind," Hummingbird snapped. "Not your belly."

"I don't need a life coach to feed my mind," Coyote scoffed.

"My professional services are pro bono," said Maggie, "but if you throw some fruits and nuts my way, I won't complain."

The other animals badgered Maggie with questions about the wide world beyond Come Along Slough. Her showy plumage attracted many compliments, which rankled Crow.

"Yakety-yak," he said, "go full black, or get the hell back."

"Scat!" said Coyote.

Crow flew up to a high cottonwood branch. Red-Tailed Hawk screeched at him for trespassing on a raptors-only perch.

Owl snapped open her eyes and swiveled her head, the cottonwood branch creaking. "We will fight them in the air!" she screeched. "We will fight them in the—"

"The war on Rats is over," said Scrub Jay. "Get a grip."

Owl blinked. "I'm hungry. Coyote, where are you?"

Coyote winced. "Right here, Madame Secretary-General."

Owl kept blinking. "Fetch me another White Field Mouse, will you?"

"After the meeting, okay?"

"Everything is so bright," said Owl. "Can somebody please dim the lights?"

"We'll dim them after the sun goes down," said Raccoon.

Scrub Jay flew up to Owl's branch. "We have a special visitor. A Rainbow Lorikeet named Maggie. A real peeperpleaser, she is, and her feathers are beautimagnifis-crumptious."

"Maggie," Hummingbird asked, "will you please introduce yourself to Owl?"

Maggie flew closer to the base of the cottonwood. "I'm honored to meet you, Owl," said Maggie, gazing upward. "You are truly a Great Horned Owl . . . of impressive proportions."

"This foreigner," Coyote growled, "slipped across our borders without official permission."

"Calling her a foreigner, said Hummingbird, "represents a microaggression on her Birdhood."

"Take it from me," said Raccoon, "Coyote only does macroaggression."

Hummingbird flew from her log and hovered close to Owl. "Maggie's helping us out from the kindness of her Aussie heart."

"Where's my White Field Mouse?" Owl squawked.

Coyote trotted closer to Owl. "Patience," he said in a low voice. "Elrod's working on it." He faced Maggie. "Just get on with it," he said. "Then I'll escort you safely from the Slough. You never know. A rogue carnivore might be lurking in the shadows."

Squirrel scurried up to Maggie. "Is Come Along Slough the biggest place in the world?"

"The Slough is just a tiny bubble on a very large lake," she said.

Owl made a harsh noise, as if choking on a bone.

"Uh-oh, Maggie," said Hummingbird. "You popped her bubble."

Owl cleared her throat. "Kawphonious the Giant Raven would beg to differ with you on this matter."

Maggie cocked her head. "Uh, Cawphony the Giant Raven, you say?"

Owl's branch broke. She grunted as she hit the ground

belly-first. Picking herself up, she waddled toward Maggie. "Kawphonious wisely warned us," she said, "that falsehoods are facts gone rotten."

"I apologize if I've offended you," said Maggie.

Owl clacked her beak. "We will not dither away our day with hogwash and frippery! Flights of fakery will go down in flames!"

Mole popped his head up from the dirt. "I got a question for Maggie."

"Ask away," she said, flying closer.

Mole squinted at her. "Squibs dig up the ground and wreck my tunnels. They trash my Earthworm stash. Is there anywhere that's safe from Squibs?"

Maggie shook her head. "They own the world."

Raccoon groaned. "What a bummer."

Hummingbird gazed at all the sad faces. The other animals looked as if the air had left their lungs. "The Squibs treated Maggie really mean," she said, "yet she doesn't have a negative bone in her body. She's a very positive Lorikeet."

"Me and Maggie swing the same way," said Squib Dog. "We keep our negativity on a choke chain."

"Please put Scratchit on a choke chain," said Hummingbird. "Maggie's coaching me on how to cope with my Pussyphobia, but Scratchit still gives me nightmares. "

"No worries," said Squib Dog. "She's Catnapping at home. Get it? *Cat*-napping?"

Coyote sneered at him. "Ha ha. Stop it, Poop Dog, you're busting my gut."

Squib Dog ignored this put-down. "I still want to hear about them Kangaroos and Kookaburras."

"Maybe later," said Maggie. "Right now, let's try a trust-building activity. How does that sound?"

"Sounds terrible," said Raccoon. "I trust nobody."

"Coyote!" Owl screeched. "Why haven't you brought me a White Field Mouse?"

"To start our trust-building activity off on the right foot," said Maggie, "let's take a therapeutic stroll beneath the trees. Forest bathing is very relaxing."

"I prefer water bathing!" Carp interjected.

Maggie laughed. "If you swim close to shore, you will benefit from both kinds of bathing."

"It's not always safe wandering away from home," said Muskrat.

"We won't go far. We'll stop at a hollowed-out cottonwood where I spotted some Mouse Dicks growing. If everyone's willing, I want us to pick some and eat them."

Coyote leered at the other animals. "Eating Mouse Dicks builds trust?"

Maggie waited for the laughter to die down. "Mouse Dicks are edible tiny mushrooms. They are also *magic* mushrooms. Ingesting them is a way to grow group trust."

"Mushrooms are vegetables," said Coyote. "I eat vegetarians, not vegetables."

"Mouse Dicks have other colorful names," Maggie explained. "Some call them Dirt Squirts, Kangaroo Jacks, or Silly Willies. I prefer Mouse Dicks because they're small, pink, and fuzzy. Best of all, they spew their spores like mushrooms twenty times their size."

"What does a Mouse Dick taste like?" demanded Squirrel.

"It's very tasty," said Maggie, "and has the moist, complex minerality of Slough mud and leaf rot."

"What's so 'magic' about Slough mud and leaf rot?" asked Muskrat.

"My anus aches from sitting so much," Squib Dog complained. "I say we put our mouths where the mushrooms are and let the magic do its stuff."

"Follow me," said Maggie, "and the magic will find you."

"Count me out," said Coyote. "I'll stay here with Owl and observe the magic from a safe distance."

Maggie flew off. Hummingbird didn't follow immediately. Instead, she hung back in the leafy cover of a low cottonwood branch and spied on Coyote. She didn't trust him for a second.

She saw him trotting off into a stand of cattails to empty his bowels. Then he leaned his snout close to his steaming excrement, mumbling words that Hummingbird couldn't hear.

Beaver poked his head up from the shallows. "Don't do that!" he shouted at Coyote. "I don't take a squat in *your* home, do I?"

Coyote recovered from his surprise quickly. "How come you didn't run off with Marvelous Maggie and her Merry Band of Mouse Dick munchers?"

"Munching trees is more my style."

"You look kinda downcast. Somebody lick the musk off your Beaver mound?"

"I didn't get the chance to present my ideas about building dams on the Slough."

"Don't blame me. Blame Hummingbird and her Kookaburra-crazy life coach."

"Everyone was very eager to hear about my dam plans. Even Scratchit Cat seemed interested."

"Then why didn't she attend today's meeting?"

"Oh, she's here. Very close, in fact. She's slinking through the woods. Probably on the hunt."

"Hmmm," said Coyote. "I'd better go see what she's up to."

Scratchit's unsuspected proximity alarmed Hummingbird. She flew away immediately, fearful that this stealthy Bird-killer was stalking her. She caught up with the other animals. Maggie was fluttering from tree branch to shrub, sunlight and shadow dappling her plumage.

"Breathe deeply!" she cried to the other animals. "Aerate your brains!"

Feeling the safety of numbers now, Hummingbird performed a series of exuberant J-shaped dives before hovering close to her life coach. The two Birds touched beaks briefly, their feathers a smolder of greens, yellows, and reds.

Something caught Hummingbird's eye. In the underbrush, a swatch of yellow appeared. A green eye glittered.

Then Scratchit struck.

19 SAVE OUR SLOUGH

IT WAS A HOT DAY, and low water exposed a spongy shoulder of mud along the Slough shoreline. Heron and Kingfisher lingered in a shallow pool, squawking complaints about their poor fishing prospects. Carp and Western Pond Turtle listened to the conversation from a safe distance. Carp sheltered next to a half-submerged log, while Western Pond Turtle basked on top, the noonday sun baking the mud onto her shell.

"It's an absolute disgrace," said Heron, who thought most everything was a disgrace.

"I agree absolutely," Kingfisher chittered. Kingfisher had forgotten what she was agreeing to, but she generally agreed with Heron about everything. The largeness of him and his gruff personality never put her off. Kingfisher often flitted around him, complimenting his statuesque physique and the magisterial S shape of his neck. Sometimes she fetched a silvery Minnow to curry his favor or harried a Snowy Egret homing in on their fishing territory. Heron paid her no more attention than he would a Mosquito, but since her unflagging adulation confirmed his high opinion of himself, he tolerated her compliments.

"The water goes up," said Heron, "and then it goes down. Lately, it goes down more than up."

"I absolutely agree absolutely," said Kingfisher.

River Otter joined them. "When the water gets too low," he said, "I just vamoose over to the Big River and hang with my pals. Gotta go with the flow, you know, and make every day a good day."

"You socialize with your own sort," said Heron, "whereas I do not. I savor solitude. Only during mating season does the Natural Law of Animals compel me to couple up with those of the same feather."

"You're so grumpy," said River Otter. "Don't you ever get tired of yourself?"

"Grumpy is good."

"Grumpy is good," echoed Kingfisher. "Absolutely."

"Why not lighten up and laugh more?" asked Otter. "Go play with the other Herons. Give it a try. You might like it."

"Your sunny disposition really annoys me."

"Who wants to be gloomy? Not me. I'm a born optimist."

"And a born escapist. If things get tough, you run away. Your optimism shelters you from the hard facts of life."

"What's wrong with that? Why complain about how bad things are on the Slough? Why not focus on the good?"

"The good? Give me one example of something good about the Slough."

"Well … we're alive. I feel very good about that. And grateful."

Heron gave a derisive squawk. "You sound like Maggie —and look what happened to her. You see the Slough as you wish it to be, not as it is. This low water reduces the available food, making it hard for me to maintain my standard of living."

"Like I toldja, Heron, go with the flow and maybe you won't sound like such a curmudgeon."

"There's no flow to go with," said Heron, inclining his long beak toward the mudflats. "The water is stagnant and full of Squib garbage. It's a disgrace!"

"It's a disgrace!" Kingfisher cried. "Absolutely!"

"Okay, I'm done here," said River Otter. "All this trash talk wears me out." He spun around off his back and swam away, barely creasing the water.

"River Otter's smiley face hides a deep frown of foreboding," said Heron. "Anyway, enough chatter. I will try my fishing luck elsewhere—alone."

Kingfisher looked hurt. "Alone. Absolutely."

They went their separate ways. For Heron, two was always a crowd.

Feeling more secure now, Carp surfaced and began conversing with Western Pond Turtle. "This low water makes my blood boil," he complained. "Literally."

"I love the mud," said Western Pond Turtle, "but shallow water makes me easy pickings for Heron."

"Hard to hide now," said Carp. "Heron hunts me. So do Osprey and Bald Eagle. What am I to do?"

"Mama Mallard can't protect her nest," said Western Pond Turtle. "She builds it close to the waterline, and the next day, everything's high and dry."

Carp flapped his tail in agreement. "Then Elrod thieves her eggs."

"Elrod's a cutthroat," said Western Pond Turtle. "Why doesn't the USA squash that egg-sucking scofflaw? He keeps getting away with murder."

"Coyote claims he suffers from PTSD, whatever that is. And the USA buys his load of hooey, no questions asked. Coyote's got them under his paw."

"I think PTSD means 'psycho-terrorist spreading death.'"

"Owl has surrendered her authority to Coyote. Everyone in the USA lacks backbone. Even the invertebrates are spineless."

Western Pond Turtle craned out her neck, bringing her head closer to Carp. "I'm glad some of us are making a principled protest and boycotting the USA meetings. I just wish Owl hadn't lost her brains. We could use a smidgen of her wisdom."

"Owl knew Maggie was bad news for the Slough," said Carp. "She tried telling us that foreign Birds and mushrooms don't mix, but we didn't listen."

Western Pond Turtle nodded. "No fungus among us is my motto now."

"Maggie was very charismatic," admitted Carp. "Those Mouse Dicks of hers got me excited. I was ready to take a swim on the wild side."

They broke off their conversation as Muskrat and Nutria swam over to them, sludge plastering their pelts.

"The Squibs are stealing more of our water," Muskrat told them.

Nutria coughed and spat out a wad of algae. "Me and Muskrat saw them. They're sucking us dry. Let's go tell them to stop it."

"You can talk to Squibs?" asked Carp.

"Uh, I talk with my eyes. I just stare hard and give them the old Nutria stink eye."

The other animals didn't hold Nutria to account for being so slow-witted. Brains weren't his strong suit. A cheerful sort, he had the bulk and shape of Beaver, but instead of having a flat tail, his was Ratlike. Homely and flatulent, he minded his own business and never threatened others, asking little from life except to eat his fill of tubers, willows, and cattails.

"We must fight for our water," said Muskrat. "If necessary, there will be blood."

"Blood scares you," Western Pond Turtle teased. "Even Dragonfly's shadow makes you dive for cover."

"The Slough belongs to us," said Muskrat, striving to sound resolute, "not the Squibs. They violate the Natural Law of Animals, whereas we—"

"Oh, stop using your squeaky secretary-general voice on us," Carp interrupted. "We aren't Elrod or Coyote. We're your friends."

"Sorry. All this Squib talk makes me testy, I guess."

Muskrat disliked whiling away her days nibbling sedge and cattails while gossiping with the likes of Nutria. She still wanted her old job back. She hated the constant character assassination that came with being secretary-general, but waking up to face the void of another day was much worse.

Western Pond Turtle clambered to the high end of his log. "If we beat the Rats, we can beat the Squibs."

"We didn't beat the Rats," said Carp. "The Squibs beat the Rats for us. They poisoned them."

"Lest we forget," said Muskrat, "they also poisoned us."

The water animals fell silent. Nothing had changed. They couldn't do anything about the Squibs.

Beaver swam over and slapped his tail on the water. Usually, he avoided the heat of the day, but he obviously had something to say that couldn't wait.

"You haven't attended the USA meetings lately," he said.

"Drama fatigue," said Muskrat.

"But you are required to represent the special interests of your respective species. Not attending is dereliction of duty."

"What's the use of being there," asked Carp, "and arguing about things we can't change?"

Western Pond Turtle chimed in. "My constituency considers the USA irrelevant, obsolete, and dysfunctional."

Beaver wasn't deterred. "You gotta attend tonight's USA meeting. It's very important. We're gonna gather beneath the cottonwood—the one that's half dead."

"Half-dead cottonwood?" asked Carp. "Please be more specific. If you've seen one half-dead cottonwood, you've seen them all."

Cottonwoods grew like weeds on Come Along Slough, but they quickly died and collapsed. Their trunks made commodious habitats and perches. Riddled with Insects, the wood provided feasts for Flicker and other Woodpeckers. Squirrel stored nuts in the cracks. Crow, Osprey, Eagle, and Red-Tailed Hawk used the highest limbs for strategic advantage.

"It's the one with the heart completely rotted out," said Beaver. "Raccoon likes to snooze and canoodle inside."

"I know that cottonwood," said Muskrat. "It's where Maggie …"

"Poor old Mushroom Maggie," said Nutria.

"Hummingbird's heartbroken," said Western Pond Turtle. "She had a Honeybee in her beak for Maggie."

"The poor little thing's still grieving hard," said Muskrat.

"Maggie wasn't subject to the USA's eating quota," said Western Pond Turtle. "I suppose Scratchit killed her fair and square. Coyote stole what was rightfully hers."

"Hummingbird disagreed," said Carp. "She served up swift justice to Scratchit."

Beaver exposed his buckteeth. "Hummingbird's swift justice was also blind justice."

"Good one, Beaver," said Muskrat.

"I don't get it," said Nutria. "Justice is blind?"

"Hummingbird pecked out Scratchit's good eye," said Carp.

Nutria looked even more puzzled. "So, justice and Scratchit are both blind?"

"She's blind and very cranky," said Beaver. "Can't go nowhere without Squib Dog's help. He's her personal seeing-eye Dog now."

"She's blind as a Bat," said Carp.

Nutria looked exasperated. "Bats are blind, too?"

"Don't overthink it," Carp advised.

"Come to tonight's USA meeting," said Beaver, preparing to swim away. "I'm notifying everyone."

"Why should we bother to attend?" asked Muskrat. "Coyote runs the whole flimflam show."

Beaver turned. "Here's the skinny, Muskrat. I need votes for my Save Our Slough project. Coyote promised to put my SOS proposal at the top of the agenda. Again."

"Save Our Slough?" asked Western Pond Turtle. "Isn't it way too late for that?"

"Not on your life," said Beaver. "We must declare a war on low water and build dams. Big Dams."

"A war on low water?" asked Muskrat. "Has Owl thrown her weight behind your SOS proposal?"

"Haven't you heard? We have a new secretary-general now."

"We do?"

"Raccoon just got voted in. Nobody claims she's the sharpest stick in the wood pile, but at least she's pro-dam."

"Raccoon lacks the chops for high office," said Carp. "She's more worried about grooming her tail than attending to business."

"Only seven animals showed up at the last meeting," said Beaver. "Coyote ordered them to vote for Raccoon, and they did without any objections."

"Why do the strong always rule the weak?" Western Pond Turtle bemoaned.

Carp thrashed about, splashing water on everyone. "I'm not weak. My motto is *carp-e diem.*"

"Seven animals aren't a USA majority," said Muskrat. "Raccoon's election isn't legitimate."

"Coyote says it is," said Beaver. "Nobody's gonna argue with a carnivore."

"But Raccoon has no qualifications."

"Qualifications? She just needs to be a punching bag. You should know that better than anyone else."

Muskrat ignored this jibe. "Did Owl object to being replaced as secretary-general?"

Beaver snorted. "She just sits on her branch and hoots about White Field Mice. Her body's here but her brain flew off into the wild blue yonder."

"Her brain flew away?" asked Nutria. "It has wings?"

"Owl was never wise," said Muskrat, "but we always pretended she was. Now we can't even pretend. Those White Field Mice Coyote feeds her have nibbled holes in her brain."

"Just come to the meeting and cast a vote for my SOS proposal, will ya?" asked Beaver. "The Slough needs dams —lots of them. If we work together as a team, we can defeat this low water and make the Slough great again."

After all is said and done, more is said than done.

—*AESOP'S FABLES*

20 THE WHITE FIELD MICE

Owl couldn't stop hallucinating. Right now, as she perched on a cottonwood branch, she hallucinated a mob of Cricket-sized White Field Mice. They had shaved heads, each bald pate a pinprick of bright pink. The tiny White Field Mice were climbing her flanks. She felt the steady scrabbling of tiny claws. Owl shook her tail feathers, but the White Field Mice scaled her breast. Then her head. A snowy ringlet of Rodents crowned her skull. She heard them break into song, their voices shrill and insistent. Her ear tufts twitched.

Our sweet old non-aerobatic Owl,
Our uncharismatic, autocratic fowl,
Our problematic, phlegmatic pal,
Our zillion-in-one Chosen One!

The White Mice scurried back down her body and lined up on the limb as if preparing to march off. She saw their furry faces, their shining pink eyes. In unison, the White Field Mice squeaked: *"OWL IS THE CHOSEN ONE!"*

A shiver of joy shot up her spine. The chosen one? What

a nice compliment! Apparently, these little Doodlebugs worshiped the ground she waddled on. Her throat tightened. These mini-Rodents looked so vulnerable. Perhaps they needed her protection.

"Mama is a bit under the weather right now," she murmured, "but don't you be frightened my little cuddle cakes. Mama won't eat you until you grow into bite-sized White Field Mice."

With these words came a sharp pang of hunger. One talon seized a dead branch. She bit down on it, snapping it off.

The White Field Mice were singing again.

Through thick and thin
We'll live within your skin,
Becoming your kith and kin,
Keeping you near, giving you cheer
While you wheeze
And by slow degrees
Lose your cheese.

The White Field Mice chanted: "Chosen One! Chosen One! Chosen One!" Then recommenced their choral performance:

As you regurgitate and defecate
We will meditate
Upon your overweight state.
Tending to your impending ending,
We'll put you at ease
With your eating disease
And never make one mean squeak
About your non-sleek physique
And non-existent mystique.

Owl didn't like what she was hearing. Now she wanted to gobble down every one of these little squeakers. She opened her beak. Her prey had vanished. Blinking rapidly, she squawked. She was very hungry. Where was Coyote?

Wasn't it time for him to deliver more of those jumbo White Field Mice?

Every hallucination gave her a wicked headache. She had one now, and trying to ignore the pain, she lapsed into a bittersweet reverie. In her younger days, she had been a prolific procreator. Broods of winter-born owlets had populated her stick-and-twig nest, its crusty layers redolent of dried blood and rancid meat. High in the treetops, she'd tucked her little snuga-bugs next to her, keeping them safe from predators, their eager beaks gaping for Mama's tasty treats. On cold nights, she shed the feathers on her underside, the warmth of her bald belly preventing her babies from freezing to death.

Then everything had changed. More Squibs crowded in around the Slough. They scraped the land down to its bones, built roads, erected buildings, and dumped filth into the water. Owl's clutches began to fail. Her owlets rose malformed from pools of bloody sludge. They flapped their stunted wings. Their brittle beaks crumbled like dried clay. She could do nothing for her babies. She watched them die, bracing herself for the lonely days that lay ahead.

"Oooh, oooh, oooh, oooh," she wailed, the descending pitch of her grief-stricken cries announcing that a sorrow had turned her heart into a cold stone.

21 BEAVER MAKES BIG WATER

EVERY ANIMAL HEARD the cottonwoods cracking and splashing down into the Slough. The war on low water had been declared, the resolution winning by only one vote. Coyote had tricked Squib Dog into casting the tie-breaker. This turn of events had upset Muskrat, but since she wasn't the secretary-general any longer, she had no bully pulpit to decry the folly of this unnecessary war.

Now Beaver and his buddies were leading the charge. They had already built several dams and plugged drainage culverts and side channels with logs and woody debris. The Slough had risen enough to flood nearby Squib houses, roads, and worksites.

This war was mostly a spectator war. Beavers were the only animals on the front lines. To avoid getting hit by a falling cottonwood, everyone else watched from a safe distance as Beaver and his buddies built more dams. Despite her negative feelings about this ridiculous spectacle, Muskrat also watched. The crash and splash of large trees was mesmerizing. She couldn't help admiring Beaver's engineering ingenuity. He really knew how to build dams.

In her role as the new secretary-general, Raccoon had depended upon Coyote's carnivore charisma to shore up her authority. One look from him could silence anybody. She also used Owl's proximity to her advantage. Owl clung to the limb of a dead cottonwood close to her empty nest, dumbstruck and vacant-eyed. The old Bird presided over each meeting like a statue, her frozen, impassive countenance confirming that all was well with the USA.

"Even if Owl's brain has become a shriveled-up apple," Raccoon said, "the silence of her sizable self undoubtedly militates for us to declare war on low water!"

When it came to Rats, Muskrat had been passionately pro-war, but this war on low water seemed suicidal. She kept reminding the USA members that every animal regularly drank water. Many bathed and swam in it. Waterfowl depended upon it for food and shelter.

"Even if the water is too low," she said, "why declare war on something so essential to daily survival?"

Coyote growled at her. "The USA doesn't need any Nervous Nellies second-guessing our secretary-general. Raccoon's voice is Owl's voice."

Hearing this, Muskrat had curled her lip. "After this war," she asked, "what's next? Do we declare war on rocks and trees? Or the clouds? Rocks cause us to stumble and fall. Trees drop dead leaves on us. Clouds block the sun. While we're at it, why don't we wage war on the entire natural world?"

The animals had debated this issue for several days.

"What if the water fights back and drowns us?" asked Nutria.

"If it tries doing that," said Raccoon, "we'll swim to shore and mount a counterattack."

Nutria wrinkled his snout. "But I thought the water was too low to swim in."

"You got tubers on the brain? asked Squirrel. "Low water doesn't stand a spitting chance against Beaver and his buddies. It will immediately sue for peace."

Mama Mallard poked her head out from the cattails and quacked. "If Beaver uses the few trees we have left to make his dams, we will lose our shade. The water will get so hot it'll boil my eggs."

"We learned from fighting the Rats," Coyote explained, "that collateral damage is regrettable, but unavoidable."

"Don't fret, Mama Mallard," said Raccoon. "Before Beaver fells too many trees, the Squibs will surrender uncon-ditionally."

"I'm really confused," said Nutria. "I thought the water had to surrender—not the Squibs."

Muskrat squeaked for atten-tion. "If Beaver builds these 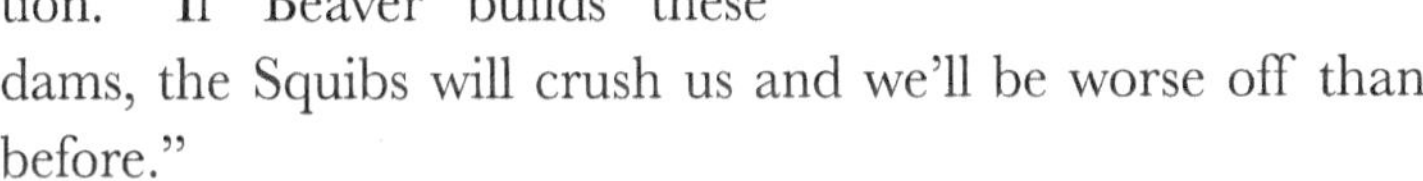 dams, the Squibs will crush us and we'll be worse off than before."

"I hope you're not one of those cut-and-run fraidy-Cats, Musk-RAT," said Coyote.

"You care only about yourself—and causing trouble," Muskrat squeaked. "You want to destroy the USA—just for your own amusement!"

Crow hopped up to Muskrat. "Your absurd words fall like wet turds. If you don't curb your speech you'll end up south of Coyote's mouth like a rotten peach!"

Squirrel whispered into Muskrat's ear. "A word to the wise. Go along to get along. Animals like us can't fight the food chain."

Seeing that Coyote was giving her a menacing look, Muskrat had clammed up, but she still fumed about how he had tricked the USA into voting for the war resolution. Paws and wings had been counted. The vote was deadlocked.

At this point, Squib Dog had trotted into the meeting. "Sorry I'm so late," he muttered. "I had to help Scratchit find her litter box."

"You haven't voted yet," said Coyote. "Are you in favor of SOS?"

"Huh?"

"Saving Our Slough."

Uh, I guess so. Isn't everybody?"

"Then say yes."

"Say yes?"

"That settles it," said Coyote. "The resolution has passed. We have declared war on low water."

"Hold on!" Muskrat squeaked.

Coyote held up a paw. "Silence, Musk-RAT! Beaver wishes to make an important statement."

Before speaking, Beaver slapped his tail in a shallow pool of muddy water next to the shoreline. "We will make the Slough great again!" he shouted. He'd repeated this phrase a lot lately, hoping it would catch on as a rallying cry for his casus belli.

The war on low water hadn't gone as planned, though. It dragged on and on. The Squibs removed the Beaver dams. Beaver and his buddies harvested more trees and built new dams. The Squibs destroyed them. The Slough seesawed between high water and low water. Much of the shoreline was soon deforested.

One afternoon, Carp spoke to Western Pond Turtle and Muskrat about this dismal situation. "Can't Beaver and his buddies at least keep the Slough at a Fish-friendly level? Or a Turtle-friendly or Muskrat-friendly level? Why must we suffer all the collateral damage?"

"You were right about this war," Western Pond Turtle told Muskrat. "Coyote bullied us into it. What does he hope to gain from stirring up so much trouble?"

"Chaos," said Muskrat, nibbling on the cattails. "He thrives on it. This war has antagonized the Squibs. Like I toldja before, Coyote doesn't care a whit about us. "

"Well, at least he hasn't eaten us. Yet."

Muskrat spat out some fuzz. "We must force Raccoon from office and replace her with somebody who isn't Coyote's mouthpiece."

"Force Raccoon from office?" asked Carp. "Are you advocating mob violence?"

"In these dire times, restoring the democratic traditions of the USA requires radical action."

"Wish Owl hadn't lost her walnuts," said Western Pond Turtle. "We need a real war hero to crack a few heads."

"Being secretary-general is a no-win proposition," said Carp. "You get blamed for every Sparrow fart. Heck, we might as well elect a hapless sap like Elrod. He'd be perfect for the job. Everyone hates him already."

Western Pond Turtle snorted. "Elrod's PTSD certainly qualifies him for high office, doesn't it?"

The animals shared a huge laugh about this.

"Post-traumatic Stoat disorder," Muskrat quipped.

More laughter.

Muskrat blew water out her snout. "Poor Owl perches day and night on her limb like a moonstruck nincompoop. She can't tell the difference between a cottonwood and a cocklebur. Those White Rats Coyote feeds her have scrambled her brains."

"White Rats?" asked Carp. "I thought they were White Field Mice."

"That's what Coyote told her, but it was another one of his tricks. He's been feeding her White Rats."

"Ugh. How do you know that?"

"I was nibbling cattails and overheard Coyote and Elrod talking. They were laughing their butts off about it. Those vicious, self-serving carnivores aren't our friends. We must install a new secretary-general who isn't under Coyote's paw."

"Who would replace Raccoon?" asked Carp.

Muskrat took a deep breath. "I'm certain a highly qualified candidate is just waiting to be nominated."

They saw Nutria swimming rapidly toward them. He stopped a short distance away, his long Ratlike tail curling over his back.

"Horrible news," he panted. "Just horrible!"

"What happened?" asked Muskrat.

"It's Beaver. The Squibs murdered him—and his Buddies!"

"Murdered?" Carp asked. "I just saw Beaver last night. He was busy building the biggest dam ever."

"The Squibs set traps and caught them all," said Nutria. "Clubbed their brains out and skinned them naked. It was horrible, horrible! Raccoon has called an emergency USA meeting."

22 KAWPHONIOUS KIDNAPS OWL

MORE HALLUCINATIONS HAUNTED HER. Now a gargantuan Bird had spirited Owl up into the clouds. Perching on the Bird's spacious back, she fought for balance, an icy wind whistling through her feathers, the world around her gray and frigid. In one blink, Come Along Slough had become a gone away world.

She squawked at her abductor. "Enough bunkum and Possum piffle! Do you hear me? You have stolen the secretary-general of the USA! If I'm returned unharmed, things will go easier for you."

Compared to the size of this Bird, Owl was just a speck of Gnat scat. Her body rocked as the Bird's enormous wings beat the air, fanning the stench of carrion into her face. She gagged.

A massive black head pivoted toward her. Owl saw cold boulder-sized eyes and the cruel curve of a beak. It was . . . Kawphonious the Giant Raven! Who else could it be? But why had he kidnapped her?

Hearing screeching laughter, Owl wrapped her wings around her ears. "Stop it and put me on the ground before I puke!"

She dug her talons into a musty mat of feathers, fighting for balance. Heights terrified Owl. Even standing on a log gave her the jitters. She'd never told anybody this, but it was true—and embarrassing. In contrast to her younger days, flying now made her dizzy. Taking to the air could end with a crash landing, resulting in serious injury or death. She roosted in trees, of course, because that's what an Owl was expected to do, but excessive elevation was nerve-wracking. Having solid ground beneath her talons was crucial to her equanimity. At any rate, flying was problematic. She was no longer a featherweight.

Kawphonious tilted sharply. Owl peered down into the gray abyss and saw a smear of green. What was this—color? She was pretty much color blind, seeing only graduated shades of white, gray, and black. Why was she now seeing colors? And how did she even know how to recognize colors when she saw them? Her eyes were shaped like tubes, built to only see the "colors" of the night.

She hadn't ever traveled much beyond the Slough. Venturing outside her hunting territory wasn't a smart move; other Owls and predators attacked her. Eating locally was best, even when prey was scarce. Fortunately, Coyote had provided her with enough White Field Mice to ensure that she didn't waste away.

Owl was airsick. Tightening the grip of her talons, she leaned forward and vomited, releasing a steaming slurry of fur and bones. She felt hollowed out and lightheaded, her throat burning from acrid digestive juices.

Taking a deep breath, Owl reviewed her knowledge of Kawphonious, the Giant Raven who had guided the first animals to Come Along Slough. He still visited his old stomping grounds, wearing the midnight mist like a veil of invisibility, but Owl had excellent depth perception, and even on moonless nights, she easily spotted Kawphonious ghosting the Slough, his phantasmal presence gliding above the cattails or through the understory of cottonwoods. In his windy wake, every stem and leafy limb shivered and glittered, releasing a barely audible *"ahhhhhhhh."* Swamp gas sometimes created the spooky illusion of a gray fire burning on the surface of the water. This eerie phenomenon alarmed the other animals, but Owl knew it was the atmospheric afterglow of the Ancient One's passage.

Once, Owl had spied a small, egg-shaped object in the shadowy crotch of a dead cottonwood. Kaphonious pecked his way out into the daylight, presenting a tangled angularity of beak, wing, and talon. The freshly-hatched Kawphonious was grizzled and long in the beak, his legendary largeness reduced to a timeworn tatterdemalion of feathers and bones. He was much too small to be called a Giant Raven, yet his imperious glare more than compensated for his lack of size.

Owl had hawked up a casting and waddled over. "Hello. May I be of service?"

Kawphonious ignored her. Had she said something wrong? Perhaps he was hard of hearing. Owl didn't want to shout; that would be rude. She averted her eyes, then snuck a peek back at him. He was gone, but a tidy pile of ivory-white Raven crap signified the Ancient One's brief visitation.

Now Owl struggled to bring her attention back to her current predicament. Kawphonious was cutting a dizzy spiral down to a vast body of gray water. Owl squinted, trying to spot a familiar landmark, but everything below was terra incognita. The gray water stretched toward the horizon and merged with gray sky. Was this another Slough? If so, she had never seen one so large.

Kawphonious landed on the sandy shoreline with a hard thud. Owl tumbled off and flopped onto her face. Righting herself, a soft breeze riffled her feathers. Small waves lapped the shore. She shivered and lurched sideways, her head spinning. The Giant Raven stood nearby, observing her. Owl saw a massif of black feathers, a giant beak, and a pair of savage yellow eyes. Yellow? She was seeing color again.

"Where are we?" she demanded.

The giant beak opened. An avalanche of hot vomit drenched Owl in half-digested bones and feathers. She shook herself off, staggered, and fell. Gaining her feet, she flapped her wings, sputtering, and looking up, she was astonished to see Kawphonious was now a blurry black dot dissolving into the gray underbelly of the sky. She was stranded.

She needed to wash herself off. The waves hit the shore and fanned out into a hissing white foam, but easing out into the frigid water, she wetted her feathers. A wave splashed up into her face. Brrrrr! She tasted salt. The frothing water nearly swept her off her feet. Lurching back to shore, she flapped her wings and shivered, her beak clacking. The salty water hadn't washed away enough carrion stink. She couldn't stand the smell of herself.

Owl locked her wide yellow eyes on the hazy horizon, the veil of cold gray light intensifying her desolation. The thigh muscles in her stubby legs cramped up. She wanted to take flight, but her morbid fear of heights kept her grounded. Anyway, her weight prevented her from becoming airborne. She'd hop around like a Bullfrog with a bellyful of swamp mud. She squawked in exasperation. How would she ever find her way home?

She waddled along the shoreline, staying alert, her body lurching heavily through wet sand. Scanning the shoreline ahead, she spied a large tree. Owl stopped and squinted at the tree's lustrous wealth of greens, blues, reds, and oranges. The profusion of splashy colors scorched her eyeballs. The tree's foliage resembled a full display of Bird plumage. In fact, they looked like Maggie the Lorikeet's feathers!

As Owl puzzled over this, a vision abruptly flared into view. She saw Hummingbird scooping up nectar from a red penstemon and depositing it on Maggie's tongue. Her forked tongue touched the brushy tip of the Lorikeet's tongue. Owl didn't like seeing this. Two Birds touching tongues like that was ... disturbing.

Owl shook off this vision but kept thinking about Maggie, the upstart Lorikeet from Down Under. What a yakker! And her pushy personality wasn't anything to squawk about, but her well-endowed body was worth several squawks. The vibrant blue of her head! Her red beak! The green of her thighs and rump! All those appetizing colors brought Owl's digestive juices to full boil. Her hunger for the Lorikeet had embarrassed her. With great effort, Owl choked back an urge to rip her apart on the spot. Nobody had suspected how she felt, though. Owl didn't like revealing her basic instincts to the other animals, fearing it would falsify her dignified demeanor. To this end, Owl always tried to wear a thin mask of stoicism. Unfortunately, this didn't work very well. The mask often slipped off her face, exposing her character to public scrutiny.

Witnesses had described the Lorikeet's violent death. Scratchit had pounced on Maggie, biting down on her neck. Then Coyote appeared. He snatched Maggie from Scratchit's jaws, bolted into the woods, and ate her, beak and all. Only a spatter of blood and a few green tail feathers marked the passing of Come Along Slough's life coach.

As usual, Coyote had satisfied his appetite. Disregarding the USA's eating quotas, he specialized in extrajudicial killing, using intimidation and guile to escape the consequences of his actions. But Scratchit had suffered immediate consequences. Enraged by the murder of her foreign friend, Hummingbird had pecked out the Cat's remaining eye.

Still gazing at the multi-colored tree, Owl stiffened. Next to the trunk, a fat White Field Mouse rested on its haunches, its eyes closed. It had a goofy grin, droopy facial whiskers, a grungy pelt, a sizable potbelly, big ears, and a shaved pate, the exposed scalp an unsightly splotch of pink.

Coyote's White Field Mice were always delivered dead, but this one was alive, its hairless tail twitching. No matter. She would bite off its little bald head, then gulp down the goods.

She approached warily, affecting a nonchalant air as if out for an afternoon stroll, and stopped approximately three wing lengths from her target. The White Field Mouse didn't open its eyes or stop grinning, but lifting a pink paw, it motioned for Owl to approach. It was an impatient "hurry up" gesture. Owl stepped within pouncing distance.

The White Field Mouse opened its eyes, which were bright pink. "I'm Timothy the Rat," he said. "My preferred pronouns are he/him."

Owl took a step back, her beak opening and shutting. "You're a … uh … Rat? Not an extra-large Field Mouse?"

Timothy bared his incisors. Two uppers, two lowers. He screeched, his pink eyes bulging out. "I'm a Rat. A White Rat. You got something against white fur?"

Owl retreated. "I never discriminate. I eat all colors."

"The consumption of White Rats will rot out your brain," said Timothy. "It's a bloody mouthful of toxic chemicals." He tugged on his whiskers and made a face. "Yuck! Somebody bust a dookie on you?"

Owl glared down at White Mouse's shaved pate. "'Bust a dookie'?"

"You stink."

Owl spread her wings, preparing to close her talons

around Timothy. "The first bite might hurt, but after you lose your head, you'll feel nothing."

Timothy wrinkled his snout. "You know about your serious eating disorder, right?"

"Huh?"

"You have a bad case of gluttony."

"Having no wish to starve myself, I occasionally snack between meals."

"Here's some friendly advice. Slim down your waistline before it ruptures. Use portion control. Don't go back for seconds and thirds. And switch to a plant-based diet. Don't eat anything with a face."

"Carnivores don't eat clover."

"To get your gluttony-be-gone weight loss plan off to a good start, let's meditate."

Owl extended a talon. "I don't meditate. I only masticate."

"Meditation isn't for sissies, but humor me, okay? Let me do my thing."

Owl retracted her talon. "Meditate fast. I'm on the hunger-be-gone plan."

Timothy exposed his incisors, closed his eyes, and parked his upturned paws on his lap. "Imagine the sound of one wing flapping."

"Are you finished?"

Timothy's mouth formed a wobbly O shape. "Ommm-mmmmmmmmmmm…"

He sounded as if he had a Bottle Fly stuck in his throat, and as Owl listened to this guttural buzz, she shuddered. Her vision went blurry. She shook her head, flapped her wings, and flexed her talons, trying to steady herself. She stared up at the tree's colorful leaves. More than ever, the foliage resembled luminous Lorikeet feathers. As she mulled this over, the tree trunk abruptly formed itself into two legs with talons. A blue head and red beak appeared. Owl caught a strong fruity fragrance. The tree had morphed into a giant Lorikeet! Dead Maggie was now a larger-than-life Maggie. She was at least ten times Owl's size. She leaned down and fixed her big red eyes on Owl.

Her voice rang out clear and melodious. "Fancy meeting you here, Owl."

23 THE BEAVER BLUES

In the early evening, the USA convened to discuss how to cope with the dismal state of the Slough. Beaver wasn't available anymore to slap his tail and call the meeting to order. Nutria had offered to replace Beaver, but his Ratlike tail lacked sufficient splashing power.

The Slough was now nearly dry. The Squibs had drained the water to an all-time low, exposing discarded appliances, truck tires, auto parts, plastic buckets, and spools of rusty cable. On hot days, tangled clumps of pondweed and lily pads stewed in the muck.

Gathering around a cottonwood, the animals gawked at the corpses that the Squibs had nailed to the lower trunk. Beaver and his buddies had been skinned, their tails cut off, their skulls crushed. Nearly every Beaver on Come Along Slough had been trapped and slaughtered. The Fly-infested bodies nailed to the cottonwood trunk seemed a stern message to the USA from the Squibs: NO BEAVER DAMS ALLOWED!

Hummingbird hovered above the other animals, her wings whirring. "Beaver gave his life fighting the war on low water. Like Owl, he's a war hero."

"Now we have two war heroes," said Mole. "One's dead, and the other's just plain nuts."

Close to the shoreline, Carp flopped around in a muddy pool. "Even when it was empty, Owl had a good head on her shoulders."

"Does anybody have a clue what Owl's thinking about right now?" Mole asked.

"She's contemplating," said Coyote.

Scrub Jay hopped around on a stump, squawking with laughter. "That old Bird's busted brain can't contemplate nothing."

Everyone gazed up at Owl. She sat motionless on a cottonwood branch, her large yellow eyes blank, an uncracked acorn in her beak. She'd been there day and night, rain or shine. She appeared frozen in place.

Coyote sat apart from the other animals as Elrod the Stoat raked Lice from his tail. Elrod was a member of the USA again, but on probationary status. At an earlier meeting, Coyote had successfully argued that Elrod's post-traumatic slaughter disorder had flared up, inducing a temporary state of insanity.

"He's my personal groomer now," Coyote explained. "I can hold him accountable for his actions. You could even say that I'm his . . . life coach. "

"His PTSD is a load of hooey," said Muskrat. "He's just a bloodthirsty Weasel."

Coyote stared hard at her. "Do you have so much anger in your heart," he asked, "that you have no empathy for his pain and suffering?"

"He ate Madame Rabbit! Where's the empathy for her pain and suffering?"

"Elrod is a wounded warrior who deserves special consideration. That's clear to everyone, except you."

Squirrel had supported Coyote. "Elrod's more screwed up than ever. He keeps threatening to kill Muskrat for banishing him. If we show him more empathy, maybe we can stop him from doing anything rash."

"It's Musk-RAT," said Coyote. "Not Muskrat. The emphasis is on the last syllable."

At the meeting now, the animals were griping again about the low water. Everybody had a complaint, but nobody knew how to solve the problem.

Coyote yawned extra wide. "Elrod and I must hunt for our dinner soon, so let's bring our deliberations to a close."

"I'm the secretary-general," said Raccoon. "*I* will decide when the USA's business is concluded."

Coyote yawned again. "Oh, I'm sorry. Please proceed, but can you speak up? My stomach is growling so loudly I can hardly hear you."

The upper cottonwood branches shook with the harsh cries of Red-Tailed Hawk, Osprey, and Bald Eagle. Flicker nervously pecked Termites from a rotting log, and Squirrel gnawed on a hazelnut. Mole pushed mounds of dirt back and forth. Near the shoreline, Western Pond Turtle perched on a muddy log, retracted her head, then poked it back out.

Raccoon stood on her hind legs, spread her paws, and hissed for attention. "Our grief for Beaver cuts deep into our hearts," she said, "but now we must admit the ugly truth. Beaver's dam-building project was a big fat fiasco."

Elrod flicked a Louse off Coyote's tail. "A big fat fiasco? Why are you hating on Beaver?"

Coyote nipped Elrod's ear. "Get back to work! The Lice are lunching on my tail!"

Elrod snarled. "Nobody cares what I think."

Crow flew down from the cottonwood and cocked his head at Raccoon. "When things go kablooey, you go screwy!"

Hummingbird zigzagged between cottonwood branches. She alighted on a stem of Slough grass and spoke. "Maggie could've helped us solve our problems, but Scratchit murdered her."

Elrod snickered. "At least all that good meat didn't go to waste."

Hummingbird let out a loud chirp. "I hate you, Elrod!"

Heron ventured closer to shore. Standing knee-deep in Slough muck, he uttered a loud *grrrrak!*

Kingfisher hovered close to Heron's head. "You're absolutely right! Absolutely!"

"I'm not finished yet, Kingfisher. Don't interrupt me."

"Oh, sorry."

Heron cleared his throat. "Beaver is dead."

"We know that already," said Raccoon, motioning at the cottonwood. "What else can you tell us that we already know?"

"You're a nincompoop," said Heron.

"An absolute nincompoop," said Kingfisher.

Raccoon clutched her tail. "Heron, I know you're a big grump who hates to hang out with others, but unless you have a helpful proposal, please let us nincompoops get back to work. Many heads are always better than one."

"That's what I'm trying to tell all you nincompoops," said Heron. "One good head beats many bad heads any day. Put a buncha smart animals into a group, and they turn stupid. It's a fact. Building dams was a group decision—a very stupid group decision—yet many animals went along with it."

"But didn't you also vote for Beaver's dams?"

"I caught the stupid bug from all of you nincompoops." Heron cast an eye at Kingfisher.

"You're absolutely right!" Kingfisher quickly cried. "Absolutely!"

Raccoon looked deflated. "I was a Beaver-believer," she said, hanging her head. "I failed—but we all failed, didn't we? A majority of us voted for those dams. We must share blame equally, right?"

"It was hardly a majority," said Muskrat. "Coyote tricked Squib Dog into casting the tiebreaker."

Squib Dog barked as if bitten. "I got tricked? Sheesh."

Crow flapped his wings at Raccoon. "Here's the skinny, Miss Minnie. Your every idea gives me bad diarrhea. Being Coyote's fool makes you his tool."

Scrub Jay squawked from overhead. "We want Owl back in charge!"

"I agree! I agree!" Mole shouted.

Raccoon chewed on her tail, her ears flattened, as if waiting for a thunderstorm to pass over.

Squib Dog barked and everyone fell silent as he nudged Scratchit Cat forward. She moved cautiously, her eyes puckered over with scar tissue.

"Me and Miss Kitty got a bone to pick with the USA," Squib Dog said.

"Go ahead and pile on," Raccoon sighed. "Everyone else is."

Squib Dog sneezed. "On cold nights," he said, "my Squibs let me sleep in the crawl space beneath the house. But them Beaver dams flooded everything. Now my cubbyhole is full of mold."

Scratchit Cat moved in front of Squib Dog and turned

her blind gaze toward Raccoon. "My comfy Cat bed is all icky and stinky-wet. So disgusting. I feel like a dirty animal."

"You *are* a dirty animal!" Hummingbird cried. "And a murderer!"

"I hear you," said Scratchit Cat, "but I can't see you."

"I blinded you once," snapped Hummingbird. "Too bad I can't blind you twice!"

"Oh, don't get so huffy with me," said Scratchit. "You lost your girlfriend, but I lost my eye! Anyway, I didn't eat Maggie; Coyote did. He stole her from me. Isn't possession nine-tenths of the law—the Natural Law of Animals? Is there no justice for the blind?"

"I just want my crawl space back," said Squib Dog. "As a voting member of the USA, I got my natural rights. Even Larry says so."

Coyote sneered. "You and Larry got no natural rights, 'cause Dogs ain't natural."

The animals laughed. Raccoon laughed the hardest, puffing out her chest and swishing her tail, relieved that somebody else was being picked on.

After the laughter had faded, she spoke. "Beaver's dam plan had some minor flaws," she conceded, "but I now have a new and better proposal to Save Our Slough. I propose that—"

"I propose that you resign because you have no spine," Crow interrupted.

Red-Tailed Hawk and Osprey screeched agreement.

Raccoon faced the raucous assembly and cleared her throat. "As I was saying, I propose we build more dams— dams that will raise the water just enough so that the Squibs won't notice."

"Beaver and his buddies are dead," said Muskrat. "Who's gonna build your new dams?"

"We'll import some foreign Beavers," said Raccoon, "from beyond the Slough. It's my borrow-a-Beaver plan.

After these foreign Beavers build our dams, we can send them packing—or keep them around in the less desirable parts of the Slough in case we need their services again."

Coyote laughed. "You been chewing ragweed? Not even foreign Beavers are that stupid. Why should they help us? What's in it for them?"

"Well," said Raccoon, "Beavers like to keep their teeth sharp, don't they?"

A few animals gazed up at Owl, hoping that she might add her voice to the debate. They gasped. Owl still held the acorn in her beak, but she had finally cracked it open.

"Hurray!" Mole shouted. "Owl is back in charge!"

24 THE CHOSEN ONE

HALLUCINATIONS HAD CLAWED APART Owl's brain. Nothing made sense to her anymore. Now she was staring up at a very large Lorikeet, her feathers a riot of color.

"I thought Coyote ate you," she said.

Maggie laughed. "Why bring up dead history?"

I have a confession to make."

"I'm listening."

Owl averted her eyes. "I was going to eat you, but Coyote beat me to it."

"You planned to gobble me down, beak, wings, and all?"

Owl shifted her weight. "Why bring up dead history?"

"Guess what, Owl? Here's your chance to have a second go at it. Do you prefer dark meat? Or white meat?"

"I am hungry, so if . . ."

"Close your bloody beak. I'm only teasing."

Owl gazed at the prismatic splendor of Maggie's feathers. "Are you real? I only ask because the unreality of this reality keeps tying me in bloody knots."

"I'm as real as you want me to be," Maggie chirped.

"How did you get so . . . large?"

She brought her head closer to Owl. "Large? Small?

Keeping a firm grip on form identity is a slippery affair. It's like sniggling for Eels."

"I need a ride home. Will you fly me back to Come Along Slough?"

"I'm your hallucination—not your transportation. But I do have a very important message for you." She extended an enormous wing toward the water. "Take a look."

Owl's eyes widened, her breath catching in her throat. The vast expanse of gray water had vanished. She saw instead an oily glob of sunlight oozing across a small body of water. Cottonwoods along the shoreline creaked and swayed as a gust of wind delivered the scent of mud and rotting vegetation.

"Am I hallucinating Come Along Slough?" she asked.

"You are lost," said Maggie, "but a trustworthy hallucination can guide you home."

"A trustworthy hallucination? That's a contradiction in terms."

"See anything else out there, Owl?"

Owl trained her eyes on the shimmering water. Detecting movement, she squawked. Was it a mirage? Or . . . She had trouble getting the words out. "Is that ... a Squib?"

"A female Squib," said Maggie. "A young one. I'd guess she's around eleven or twelve."

Owl shifted her weight and grumbled. "Even half-sized Squibs represent a security threat to the USA."

"Give her a second look."

Owl saw the Squib Girl's brown legs and arms protruding from a ragged garment. Her straight black hair hung past her shoulders. Her eyes were also black. Owl was puzzled.

"Is she walking on water?"

"She's standing on a flotation device. It's called a raft. Do you see it?"

She saw her perching on some catawampus contraption that bobbed on the water like driftwood. Using a pole, she moved herself closer to shore, and as she shifted her weight, the raft tilted, water sloshing over her bare feet. Squib Girl fixed her eyes on Owl and raised one hand. She wagged it slowly.

Alarmed, Owl lifted a talon. "Is she going to attack me?"

"Stand down. She's just saying hello to you."

"Can she speak?"

"No. She's also deaf."

"Deaf and dumb?"

"Calling her that is very disrespectful."

"She's shaking her hand at me. That's also very disrespectful."

"She's signaling that she can help you—and the other animals."

"Squibs don't help us. They hurt us. And kill us."

"A catastrophic flood will soon destroy Come Along Slough."

Owl flapped her wings. "Are you sure?"

"Trust me on this. I see the future like yesterday. Without Squib Girl's help, every animal will drown."

As Maggie spoke, Squib Girl vanished from view. Owl sighed, disappointed to see only a bleak tablet of gray water. "What else does your future yesterday tell you about this big flood?"

Now Maggie sighed. "Many animals will die. Squib Girl will help those that survive. You have been chosen to help her."

"Chosen?"

"Yes, you *are* the Chosen One."

"I never chose to be the Chosen One."

"Try to be a good sport about it, okay? You and Squib Girl will help the survivors find a place of safety."

"I refuse to collaborate with a Squib."

"Being dead doesn't prevent me from being your life coach. I know what's best for you. You must collaborate with Squib Girl."

"I just want to go home and forget about all this."

"You'll be home sooner than you think, but sad to say, you will also die sooner than you think."

Owl gulped hard. "Will I hallucinate dying—or die for real?"

"As you already know, 'real' is a very relative term."

"Enough of your double-talking snuffbumble! Uh, how do I die?"

"Starvation."

"I can't starve! I love to eat! In fact, somebody recently told me I suffered from gluttony."

"That was Timothy the Rat. Upon your return to Come Along Slough, you will follow his advice: Eat nothing with a face."

"Argggggh! No more White Field Mice? That's the worst kind of death sentence I can imagine!"

"You're such a big sourpuss! Cheer up! After you die, you will enter the Bardo."

"Can I eat meat there?"

"No meals are available there. The Bardo is a dream state between life and rebirth. After losing your life, you lose all your illusions."

"In other words, it's hallucination hell."

"Don't worry, Owl. I'll show you around the Bardo. We'll see all the sights, meet some colorful characters, and hang out at a few fruit bars."

"I thought there wasn't any food there."

"Liquid snacks are allowed. We'll tour the Down Under together, just you and me, a coupla old Birds on holiday. How's that sound?"

"Like I'm trapped in a zoo cage inside a zoo cage with no exit in sight."

"Goodbye," Maggie said. "See you soon. Ta-ta!" She spread her wings and closed her eyes. She erupted in a geyser of flames.

Owl staggered away from the hot glare of greens, blues, reds, and oranges. She squawked softly and waddled along the beach, the afterimages of the bright lights glowing behind her eyes like embers from a dying fire. After several paces, she was winded. She heard tittering. Then squeaking. Looking down, she saw the tiny White Mice again. They were clinging to her talons. "Go away!" she shouted. "Begone! Scram!"

In unison, they squeaked at her: *"LONI SWEETENS HOOCH!"*

Owl shuddered. "What?"

The White Mice squeaked again: *"LOONIES HOT WENCHES!"*

Owl was baffled. "I … don't understand your nonsense."

Inhaling deeply, the White Mice released an ear-piercing shriek: "OWL IS THE CHOSEN ONE!"

25 RIVER OTTER MEETS SQUIB GIRL

River Otter was happy he could swim above the muck. The Squibs had inexplicably pumped a large quantity of water back into the Slough. The water was pretty iffy, yet it was deeper and cleaner than usual. No telling what had prompted this gift. A gift was a gift. He was ready to swim the day away.

After snacking on Crawdads, Freshwater Clams, and Carp, he slid down a muddy bank into the Slough, making a satisfying splash. Garbage and gobbets of Squib sewage floated around him, but the reassuring pressure of water on his pelt felt fantastic. Full-body wetness was the real deal. Water was great fun—even filthy water. He just wished his River Otter friends were here.

On occasion, Nutria joined River Otter for mud-sliding frolics, but the husky, slow-witted creature was a tiresome companion and never had anything interesting to say. He just chewed on willow branches and twitched his Ratlike tail. Nutria was a poor conversationalist, and his humor was … pretty simple.

"Hey, Otter," he'd say, water squirting from his pudgy

nostrils. "We *otter* go find the *otter* Otters. Get it? *Otter otters?*" Then he'd snuffle and fart.

The Slough had water again, but River Otter felt a little off, even a tad dreary. Spoiling playtime with cheerless contemplation ran afoul of his principles, yet he couldn't help it. The Slough's despoiled state deflated his buoyant spirits. He tried avoiding politics, but since he was a voting member of the USA, getting tangled up into thorny issues was unavoidable. Preferring the go-along-to-get-along philosophy of life, River Otter groomed his public image of plucky positivity. Staying on the sunny side of the Slough worked best for him. Petty squabbling offended his good nature. Power and prestige might be fine for others, but not for him.

More than ever, the Slough seethed with conflict. The diminishing food supply brought out everybody's nasty side. The USA was a shaky house of twigs. The slightest tremor might topple it, reducing the status quo to shambles. As the water level went up and down without warning, the animals suffered. They squabbled and shouted insults. To make matters worse, Owl had gone nuts. Coyote and Elrod were taking advantage of the chaos, sowing the seeds of conflict throughout the Slough.

Swimming in troubled waters, River Otter maintained his equanimity. Staying calm was a point of pride. It was useless to kvetch, to make threats or think bad thoughts about others. What a waste of energy!

He felt he had only one character flaw: he liked to tease the other animals. Especially Coyote. He couldn't help it. That much-too-clever carnivore was really full of himself. River Otter loved to poke fun at him. A dangerous thing to do, but he always ensured he had a quick escape route to the water.

He loved the soothing, silky flow and ripple of water. Loved the little whirlpools and waves his body made in it.

Water gave him extended holidays from gravity. It protected him from predators. On land, he was slow and stumble-footed, but in water, he was a magician of motion. Water was his world.

But clean water had become scarce. Even in the Big River not far from the Slough, Squib-befouled water had caused the fishing to fail. River Otter was lucky to catch any Squawfish, Salmon, Suckers, or Bullheads. He ate Perch and Carp, but even these bony Fish now had a bitter metallic flavor. Eating too many of them burned his throat and made him pant like a sick Dog.

Beaver's dam-building project had backfired. Beaver and River Otter had once shared a passion for swimmable water. River Otter missed his upbeat, tail-slapping companion. Building dams had been a reckless act, but River Otter had loved Beaver for his courage, optimism, and egalitarian values.

The water level was high right now, but how long would it be before the Squibs drained the Slough again? The nose-twisting chunks of Squib junk cluttering the shoreline saddened him. River Otter had to remain positive. He just had to.

He'd seen Squibs lurking around lately, some on foot. Others operated vehicles and big machines. What was that about? Why couldn't the Squibs leave the Slough alone? Hadn't they done enough damage already?

River Otter had another concern. Recently, he'd seen a Squib Girl on the Slough, balancing herself on a wobbly wooden platform, a floating heap of scrap wood and metal barrels, a curious thingamabob fastened together with stringy thingamajigs. The Squib Girl used a pole to push herself through the thick mats of algae. The raggedy clothing she wore contrasted with her smooth brown skin, long black hair, and black eyes. Seeing River Otter, the Squib Girl had showed her teeth. They were a little crooked, but not in an unpleasant way. Despite his better instincts, he'd shown his own teeth. It was important to be courteous —even to Squibs. Not wishing to push his luck, he swam swiftly away from her.

Glancing back, he had seen her watching him. Then she raised her hand. He submerged, and using his best stealth techniques, he followed her to the far end of the Slough next to a large drainage ditch, where the water was shallow and muddy. The Squib Girl berthed her wooden contraption, hopped onto shore, and walked up a path through a blackberry thicket toward a copse of cottonwoods. He followed her, keeping a careful eye out for feral Dogs or animal traps. He was defenseless on land, but his curiosity was stronger than his caution.

He saw her walk into the Squib homeless camp. He crouched low in the grass and watched the Squib Girl walking past tents, campfires, and mounds of trash. Losing sight of her, he scurried back toward the water. He kept thinking about the Squib Girl's uplifted hand. Had she been trying to communicate with him?

Close to the Slough's shoreline, River Otter had encountered a Dog. He was eating something. River Otter stopped and said hello. He introduced himself.

"I'm Larry," the Dog told him. "You hungry?"

Larry treated River Otter to an open can of Sardines. They were crazy delicious. Larry was smart, very funny, and a great conversationalist. Best of all, he complimented River Otter for having such an upbeat outlook on life.

"I don't see how you do it," he said. "From an evolutionary standpoint, it's hard for us animals to stay positive. Fear is hardwired into our brains. Somebody always wants to harm us."

River Otter found the camp depressing. Too many sad and angry Squibs. He'd asked Larry about them.

"The casualties of late-stage Capitalism," he said, but didn't elaborate.

Otter told Larry about his encounter with Squib Girl. "I think she was trying to talk to me."

"I know her face," said Larry. "She mostly keeps to herself. Some Squibs around here call her 'Cute'n'Mute,' which is just plain mean."

"Why do they call her that?"

"She can't speak. Can't hear. She talks with her hands."

"Could I talk to her with my paws?"

Larry thought it over for a moment. "Obviously, Slough Speak won't work. To exchange thoughts with Squib Girl, you must speak Umwelt."

River Otter sniffed the air, as if picking up an unfamiliar scent. "Could you teach me to speak this . . . Umwelt?"

"You can't speak it. It's a silent language based on empathy—not words."

"I'm not sure I follow you."

"Talking with your paws isn't much better than Slough Speak. It's a very crude form of communication. You and Squib Girl belong to different species. If you wish to share her reality, to understand how she thinks and feels, you must learn Umwelt."

"But how do I learn it? Where do I start?"

"Start with Swimming. Swim with Squib Girl. Like you, she loves the water."

As he swam in the Slough now, River Otter wasn't feeling the Umwelt. He hated feeling so mopey and low-spirited. Flipping onto his back, he swam leisurely toward the far shore, trying to rehydrate his good cheer. Three moons past, he'd chatted with several female Otters. He'd taken a liking to one of them, and shortly thereafter rubbed noses with her. Very thrilling! He and his new acquaintance had taken turns scampering after each other. Then they tumbled around in the grass before wriggling down a muddy bank. The sex act, when it finally occurred, lasted a long time. It was a total no-holds-barred free-for-all. He and his mate rocked, slithered, and rolled. They yipped, growled, squealed, and whistled, really going at it. A good time had by both.

River Otter mated with lots of females. His uncouth male friends called females Bitches or Sows, while females called his friends Dogs or Boars. For River Otter, this wasn't very classy. He also disliked hearing "cutie patooties" or "cuddle butts." Poking fun at himself, he told the females he was Big Daddy Yum-Yum. That really cracked them up. Eating, sleeping, swimming, mud sliding, and frequent sex—what a perfect life!

River Otter had fathered lots of pups but disliked taking care of them. He did what he could to help out, but up and down the Slough, he was known more as a serial philanderer than a stay-at-home dad. Unfortunately, ready-to-mate females were getting scarce. A life without females was worse than a Slough without water. Recently, he'd gotten into a fight with another male over an available female. He hated fighting. Sharing was much better than fighting. Fighting over food was sometimes necessary, but fighting over mating privi-leges? Scarcity of resources put everyone on edge, causing Otters to lash out at each other. It was so self-defeating!

Catching the scent of danger, he went on full alert. His eyes were weak, but his sense of smell was excellent. Coyote soon trotted into sight, moving down to the shore. Even with poor vision, River Otter discerned a yellow substance drip-ping from Coyote's jaws.

River Otter glided back from the shore. "What are you up to, Coyote?"

"Ah, River Otter," Coyote crooned, narrowing his eyes. "Your slippery little self seems to be shadowing my footsteps."

"You got egg on your face," said River Otter. "Yellow is a perfect color for you. It reflects your character."

Coyote licked his nose. "Mama Mallard kindly donated her eggs."

"Did you kill Mama Mallard?"

Coyote stopped licking his nose. "Food is scarce. Even so, I manage to live within my means."

River Otter had heard this line before. "You always violate the USA's kill quotas."

Coyote yawned. "You expect me to starve?"

"You never starve. You eat anything that moves."

"I'm having trouble hearing you. Come closer and we won't have to shout."

River Otter didn't budge. "You remind me of a Squib. You just take and take and don't care who you hurt."

"The USA has it all wrong. Government regulation depresses the meat market and robs me of my right to feed myself. The market must be allowed to seek its own level, free of outside interference. A paws-off policy works best for everyone."

River Otter moved further from shore. "In other words, you stuff your gut while the rest of us starve."

"You make me sound like a carnivore without a conscience."

"We won't survive without cooperation."

"Cooperation is the creed of the weak. Domination is the doctrine of the strong."

River Otter shook his head. "That's the doctrine of the stupid."

Coyote yawned. "My, my. You've got yourself all worked up. Grrrr! Go get 'em, Fido!"

River Otter decided to go for the jugular. "Is it true what the animals are saying about you behind your back?"

Coyote stopped yawning. "Saying what?"

"That you poop out your brains and talk to Old Man Coyote. Everyone thinks you've gone stark raving mad."

Coyote growled. "This water won't always keep you safe, River Otter. When the Slough goes dry again, you will swim in your own spit, and I will come looking for you."

River Otter heard a loud noise. Squib Dog broke a path through the brambles, racing hard toward the shoreline. He skidded to a stop next to Coyote, panting hard.

"Larry just served me up bad news! We're screwed! Totally screwed!"

"Get back," said Coyote. "You're slobbering on me."

River Otter risked swimming closer to shore. Coyote had been slightly nicer to Squib Dog as of late. Hummingbird had explained Coyote's change of attitude.

"Squib Dog hangs out with Larry," she said. "Coyote doesn't like anyone else playing with his favorite chew toy. He's still mean to Squib Dog, of course, but not as mean as he could be."

Now River Otter heard a yelp. Coyote had nipped Squib Dog's ear.

"Ouch! Don't do that!"

Coyote curled his lip. "You're in a hot lather. Has Little Larry been barking his head off about the Big Bada Boom again?"

"Larry only barks facts."

"Larry has more fleas that facts."

"Geez, Coyote, will ya lay off him for a bit? I'm trying to tell you why we're screwed."

River Otter splashed the water. "Hey! I want to hear your news—even if Coyote doesn't."

Squib Dog looked up, noticing River Otter for the first time. "Larry says the Squibs are screwing the Slough big time."

"Please excuse my rude reference to your missing

Canine parts," Coyote told Squib Dog, "but Little Larry likes to tickle your testicles."

"He's not that kinda Dog."

"Don't let him bait you," said River Otter. "Please tell me more, Squib Dog."

"It's something bad. Real bad."

Coyote laughed. "Real bad? I'm real scared."

Squib Dog furrowed his brow and whined. "The Squibs are turning the Slough into … an industrial sanctuary."

"Those are big words," said River Otter. "What do they mean?"

Coyote laughed. "Little Larry uses big words to keep Squib Dog on a tight leash and make him heel. He tried the same thing with me, but I put him in his place."

"Big words sometimes express big ideas," said River Otter.

"Then go hang out with Little Larry so he can hound you to death with his hooey and hogwash. He'll bamboozle you about the Big Bada Boom, too."

"The Big Bada Boom isn't hooey and hogwash," said Squib Dog. "And neither is the industrial sanctuary."

River Otter shuddered. "Larry knows more than we do. He's the smartest animal on the Slough."

"He's not that smart," said Coyote. "I've had to teach him a thing or two. I feel sorry for him, though. He foams at the mouth and acts crazy."

Squib Dog growled at Coyote. "I hear somebody's been pinching off a loaf and shouting at his sloppy plops. That's what I call crazy."

River Otter kept a straight face. "Sloppy plops? Old Man Coyote has a pet name?"

"Sometimes it's 'poopsie-whoopsie'."

River Otter and Squib Dog laughed.

Coyote wasn't laughing. He clamped his jaws and trotted off at a brisk pace.

Squib Dog watched Coyote making his way along the shoreline. Then he faced River Otter. "This industrial sanctuary is nothing to laugh about. The Squibs plan to bury the Slough and pave it over."

River Otter swam to the shoreline. "That's terrible!"

Squib Dog hung his head. "The homeless camp goes first. Then the Slough."

"No water!" River Otter cried.

"It's much worse than that. My home's getting demolished."

"Will your Squibs find you a new home?"

"They don't have jobs. They'll be homeless, too."

"We must inform the USA immediately about this," said River Otter. "If we work together, we can stop this industrial sanctuary."

"Larry says we'll get squashed no matter what we do," Squib Dog interrupted. "It's something called the power of . . . eminent domain."

"This is no time for big words—or negative thoughts. Try to stay positive!"

Crow sailed in over the Slough and landed close. "Mind if I join this private party? Two can't be a crowd 'til three makes it loud."

"Good day to you, Crow," said River Otter. "Do you know about the industrial sanctuary?"

"What does it rhyme with?"

"Gloom and doom."

"Gloom and doom is a tune I can croon all afternoon."

"Aw, forget it," said Squib Dog and left.

"Nice talking to you, Crow," said River Otter, "but I need to go for a long swim."

"I got death breath or something?"

"Please don't take it personally."

"I take everything personally."

River Otter swam off to a deeper part of the Slough

and sank to the bottom, holding his breath for as long as possible. He felt heartsick. How could his wonderful water disappear? Swimming slowly through the murk, he imagined himself as a thread of sunlight, his body weaving itself into the shining fabric of the world.

Coming up for air, he saw Squib Girl again. She stood on her floating platform. She lifted a hand. River Otter hesitated, then lifted a paw. His heart raced. Hand and paw signals—the first Squib-Otter conversation ever.

"Wow!" he shouted. "Umwelt, here I come!

26 COYOTE SNEAKS AWAY FROM THE SLOUGH

Coyote ran for his life. He'd stolen food scraps from the homeless camp, and now a pack of feral Dogs was on his tail. Larry had ordered these ruffians to attack him. That really hurt. Wasn't Larry his friend? Or kinda his friend? Sure, he'd said a few harsh things about that pipsqueak, but didn't Larry know that getting critical feedback from a more accomplished carnivore would improve his game?

The Dogs in pursuit were big brutes. Coyote hadn't stolen much of value, so what was their problem? The Squibs had killed a Chicken and gutted it, and he'd seized some of the slops. Finders, keepers. No big deal. Except it was. The Dogs chased Coyote around the Slough and through the brambles. He couldn't shake them. Getting winded, he dropped the Chicken guts, and his pursuers pounced on the food and fought over it. From cover, Coyote watched the victors devour his food. He hated Larry more than ever.

Hiding in the brush, he kept his head low, panting. He was still hungry, but his prospects were dim and slim. The word was out on him. Everyone knew he was after an easy meal and not much else. While hunting, he'd forbidden

Elrod to tag along with him. The little Stoat cramped his style. He was too high-strung, and all his constant griping scared away the game.

Coyote suspected that his days on the Slough were numbered. Many of the animals didn't seem to respect or fear him anymore. He kept getting sidewinding comments about how many animals he'd eaten. The USA delegates viewed him with increasing suspicion and didn't always cave to his will. Just for the sheer pleasure of it, he'd flaunted his power and stirred up trouble, then sat back and enjoyed the squabbling. He'd easily manipulated Owl and Raccoon, but his influence over those hapless secretary-generals had waned. Owl had always been a useful idiot; now she was a useless one. And Raccoon? She was too dumb for words. Coyote was bored and frustrated. Time to skedaddle—but before he did that, he needed some advice from Old Man Coyote.

When it was safe, Coyote left his cover and took a whopping dump, depositing the steaming remains of his last meal on a moldy slice of cheese pizza that some Squib had discarded. Talking to his feces was somewhat awkward, but apparently this was the only way to get face time with OMC. Other animals had caught him in the act and spread slanderous stories that he was a shit-eater. Even River Otter was ridiculing him.

Let them laugh. OMC had been lodged in his head like a brain turd. Flushing him out into the open air gave Coyote great relief.

He spoke to his feces. "I'm in a terrible fix. I need help. I can't find enough to eat, and everyone hates me."

He trotted back and forth, waiting for a response. His feces grew cold, yet Old Man Coyote said nothing. Dropping another load wasn't feasible; he was running on empty. Coyote collapsed next to an old truck tire overgrown with weeds, feeling faint, and pondered his next move. Talking to his pile of half-digested bones and bloody wads of fur wasn't working.

Coyote had a gut hunch that OMC was a real Coyote—one with physical substance, like a tree or a rock. He pictured him as grizzled and stiff in the joints, but with an erect tail and sharp teeth. OMC most likely lived in a mountain valley next to a lake, a bountiful abode where he gutted wild game and mated with countless female Coyotes.

Coyote now realized why his feces were giving him the silent treatment. It was so obvious. OMC had already granted permission to visit him. Instead of dragging his paws here at the Slough, Coyote should go touch snouts with the *real* OMC.

While nursing him as a pup, his mother had told Coyote about OMC. For her own reasons, she preferred calling him "First Coyote." His mother claimed that a little something of First Coyote was in each mouthful of her milk. She told him stories about how First Coyote was a talented trickster —and teacher. Coyote's favorite ones were "Old Man Coyote Steals Grizzly Bear's Salmon," "Old Man Coyote Drowns the Beaver Sisters," and "Old Man Coyote Shows Badger How to Knock Up His Wife."

Now he recalled another story: "First Coyote Talks to His Feces."

Coyote was shocked. "Why would he want to do something like that?"

"First Coyote made many mistakes," she explained. "His feces gave him wise advice on how to make things right, but because he was so arrogant and proud, he often rejected their suggestions."

In the pre-Squib world, she explained, First Coyote had taught the other animals survival skills. At times, life was cruel, capricious, and deadly. Only the clever and ruthless prevailed. First Coyote's lessons were brutal. Playing tricks on animals, he broke their bones, tore their flesh, and burned down their homes. In this manner, he taught every creature how the world worked—or didn't.

"If you fail to learn his lessons," his mother had warned him, "First Coyote will punish you very severely."

"What will he do?"

"He might kill you."

"He isn't our friend?"

"No."

He pestered his mother for more details. What did OMC look like? Where did he live? Did he have a favorite mate?

One day, she gave up a tidbit of information. "First Coyote is a Horndog. He humps anything on four legs."

His mother had sounded bitter, but why? As he eyeballed his feces, the answer struck him so hard that his head bone buzzed. First Coyote had to be … his father! His absentee father! Why hadn't his mother told him this? First Coyote aka OMC was one of those love-'em-and-leave-'em Coyotes. But why hadn't he ever acknowledged his son?

Coyote leaned close to the bloody lump of his excrement. "Hello, Father. Wherever you are, I will soon find you. Ready or not, here I come!"

As he departed the Slough, he spotted Elrod prowling the shoreline for Duck eggs. Looking up from a demolished nest, Elrod squealed a greeting. Coyote sighed and trotted over.

"Wassup?" he asked.

"Where are you going in such a big hurry?"

"On a long journey."

Elrod stood on his hind legs, mouth quivering. "When … will you be back?"

Coyote didn't meet his eyes. "Hard to say."

"I want to go with you."

"Sorry, but I travel solo."

"Don't desert me, Coyote. Please! The two of us have

stripped the Slough clean of Rabbits and other game. Now I'm getting blamed for it. I gotta lay low 'til it's safe to kill again."

"Where I'm going isn't Stoat-friendly."

"Neither is the Slough."

"Be strong, Elrod."

Elrod narrowed his eyes. "It's not like you to cut and run. What's going on? Tell me."

Coyote saw Crow perching on a cottonwood limb. How long had that blasted pest been there? What had he heard? He faced Elrod again. "You'll do fine without me."

Elrod scowled. "You been acting awful weird lately, shouting at your poop and all that. Everybody's whispering about how you've lost it. Scrub Jay claims you're even crazier than Owl."

"Goodbye, Elrod."

"You look shook-up, Coyote. Did your Big Bone Daddy rip you a new one?"

"What?"

"That's what Crow calls Old Man Coyote."

Coyote broke into a run. He didn't know where he was going, but he couldn't get there fast enough He cast a glance back at the Slough and saw the Squib Girl on the water. She was watching him! He ran faster.

27 CROW'S SHINY OBJECT

CROW PERCHED ON A TELEPHONE WIRE. It was raining, and he was soaked to his gizzard. He hated rain. It dulled the gloss of his spiffy black feathers. All day, he'd dropped wet walnuts on the road below, hoping to crack them open. But the walnuts remained intact. A few soggy shells had peeled off to no advantage. He'd wasted time and energy, and now he was in a dark mood.

The previous day, Raccoon had raided his favorite plum tree and stripped it clean of ripe fruit. Crow had complained loudly, but Raccoon had just shaken her ass at him. Crow didn't ask for much, but he demanded respect. He rarely received it. Only River Otter showed him a small degree of respect.

Crow spent lots of time by himself, but not by choice. Unlike Heron, he was a social creature, but the other Crows always gave him the cold shoulder. He wanted to caw with the Corvids, to be part of a full-throated murder of Crows, to perform aerial somersaults above the Slough, and to mob Red-Tailed Hawk, Osprey, and Bald Eagle. Unfortunately, in Crow society, spouting poetry was a grievous offense—a symptom of a severe personality disorder. He was somebody to be shunned.

Not long ago, in an effort to gain favor among his brethren, Crow had resigned as the unofficial poet laureate of Come Along Slough. It hadn't worked. First off, nobody had ever appointed him poet laureate; he'd appointed himself. The other Crows held him in contempt more than ever, refusing to forgive him for his crimes of rhyming. They mocked him, calling him "Joe Blow the Slow Crow."

His sister was particularly cruel. "Your poetry has left a permanent stain of shame on our family name."

Hostility hounded him sans mercy. He deserved better. Versifying was exhausting, especially when celebrating the color of his feathers. Coming up with respectable rhymes for "black" fritzed out his brain. *Attack, crack, payback, whack, smack…* Each word felt like a Cat scratch on the inside of his skull.

Though Crow had relinquished being poet laureate of Come Along Slough, he was still a USA delegate and had to represent the interests of his kith and kin. Despite their intense dislike of the Slough's governing body, the other Crows had voted unanimously for him to hold high office. This private joke of theirs gave them all a good squawk. In their opinion, the USA deserved a clueless cluckbucket like Crow.

Crow had ignored their snickers, hoping his elected office would provide an appreciative audience for his poetry. It hadn't. Reciting verse at USA meetings, he was mostly ignored. Such indifference stuck in his craw like a fish bone.

Only River Otter had commented favorably about his poetry. "You rhyme nicely," he said, "but your rhythm's a bit wonky."

Maintaining his game face, Crow reminded himself that any kind of attention was better than none. Anyway, he'd heard that a poet was never honored in his own time. Being reviled was his lot in life.

Yearning to gain more popularity, Crow had decided to soften his hard edges and adopt a more positive attitude about life, like River Otter, who had many friends. Hoping to make at least one friend, Crow began to emulate Otter's upbeat personality. Striving to say nice things about other animals, he practiced positivity whenever possible. He complimented Scrub Jay's for his "melodious squawk" and praised Hummingbird's "dainty beak." They both had given him a disgusted look, as if he'd farted in their faces.

His positivity hadn't worked on Cormorant, either. Landing on the half-submerged log where she perched, Crow had cawed out a casual compliment.

"I really admire your fishing skills," he said, fighting back the temptation to rhyme "admire" with "liar."

Cormorant had closed her eyes and spread her wings wide to dry. Crow repeated his words more loudly, but she just dived into the water.

Crow had tried Squirrel next. "I love your nut collection," he said.

"Stay away from my nest!" Squirrel shouted. "You gobbled down Robin's hatchlings! Now you want to eat my nuts!"

This was a cheap shot. Yes, Crow had snagged Robin's hatchlings, but the USA had preauthorized his raids on designated nests. The USA's mind-boggling eat-and-be-eaten quota system operated upon "consumable surplus." Robin produced several batches of hatchlings a year, and Crow was within his rights to eat his allotted share of them. Trying to follow the rules, he only raided USA-approved Robin nests. He wasn't a scofflaw like Coyote or Elrod. He was a law-abiding Crow, but still got treated like Rat dung.

Reluctantly, he'd concluded that being positive wasn't any better than getting a sharp stick up his ass. His gloomy outlook on life came more naturally. Seeing the darker side of everything resonated with his suspicion that the universe was hostile to his poetic aspirations.

Maggie the Lorikeet had really twisted him up. She was even more positive than River Otter. And so funny! So crazy and carefree! Many of the animals—especially Humming-bird—had loved her irreverent spirit. But wasn't he also irreverent? Why wasn't he ever praised for the ingenuity of his poetic put-downs? Maggie was dead, but he still wanted to skewer her with a pointed poem. Even now, the memory of her colorful plumage infuriated him. Nobody ever complimented the beauty of his black feathers. So unfair. He wasn't a glob of pinfeathers and pine pitch, but the quintessence of gorgeous black.

Coyote taunted him, saying black was the absence of color. This was a lie. Standing in the sun, Crow had extended one wing and admired its ebony sheen. His majestic black feathers revealed a shifting mosaic of startle-ments. Sunlight confirmed his blackness, yet it also teased out a subtle array of colors. Crows saw more colors than many other animals. Rotating his wing slowly, he detected a palette of eye-pleasing delights. Flecks of green. A splat-tering of yellows and reds. A few winks of orange. The blush of violet. Then a shimmering wave of indigo surfaced from undertones of charcoal. Wowie-zowie! He was a Crow of many colors.

He'd shared this astonishing discovery with the USA. Cawing for attention, he'd extended his wing and rotated it to catch the brilliance of the noonday sun. The other animals laughed, claiming to see nothing except what Mole called "a blinding blotch of black."

Crow wondered why he'd bothered to put more polish on his personality. Why try to make himself into a better Crow? Wasn't he pretty much perfect already? Well, not quite perfect. Not until he found a mate. He yearned to make baby Crows. But to acquire a mate, he needed to gin up his sex appeal. Female Crows didn't think he was sexy, though—just creepy. He dropped walnuts onto the pavement and plucked out the sweet meats for them, yet every female still turned a cold shoulder to him.

Neither did his poetry impress. "You won't hem or haw or caw for your ma and pa," he recited to one, "when you cry, 'Egads! Just look at Crow's gonads!'"

His peculiar body odor was also off-putting. He didn't smell like a Crow. His non-Crow essence gave off alarming whiffs of Beaver musk with a strong note of wet Dog. And he had Lice. Crow pecked at his feathers to no avail. He was infested with vermin.

Crow knew he'd be a great dad. Doing his share of chick-rearing, he'd teach his offspring how to drop walnuts, steal shiny objects, and rhyme "black" with "tamarack." Crows mated for life, cuddling up and coupling up, but now he seemed fated to remain a bachelor with zero prospects for procreating. He'd grow old and feeble, keeling into the Slough like a rotten cottonwood, an unconsummated Crow moldering into oblivion.

It had stopped raining. Crow gave up dropping wet walnuts. The clouds parted, and he felt the sun hot on his back. He flew up to his favorite cottonwood snag that towered above the Slough, where a stiff breeze dried his feathers. From this lofty perch, he felt supreme and serene as he observed the world below. Sometimes, Eagle or Red-Tailed Hawk contested this perch, but today, he had it all to himself. From his elevated vantage point, Crow inhaled clean air, saw great distances, and brooded about all the things in his life that made him miserable.

Nothing escaped Crow's attention. From this commanding height, he had a sharp eye for the tumultuous but tedious routines of daily life. The animals spent most of their time eating. Eat, eat, eat—that's all they did, day in and day out. They nibbled, gnawed, and chewed. They killed, ripped, and swallowed. They scavenged or stole. Then they slept until it was time to restart their routines. That was life on the Slough.

Crow had often observed Coyote and Elrod the Stoat. They were always up to no good, wantonly violating the USA's kill quota. He never tattled on them. If the USA couldn't enforce the law, Crow wasn't going to do it for them. In principle, everyone agreed that greed wasn't good, blah, blah, blah. Because the Squibs had stripped the Slough of resources, nature's balance of death and life had to be maintained artificially, blah, blah, blah. Food was scarce, blah, blah, blah. Coyote and Elrod were criminals, but Crow knew they would never be punished, which confirmed his core belief that the natural world was permeated with toxic levels of injustice.

A short time ago, Crow had witnessed Coyote slinking along the shoreline. Flying down to a lower branch, Crow saw him speaking to Elrod, who appeared upset. Eavesdropping on them, Crow learned that Coyote was leaving Come Along Slough. This was very good news. Crow hated many animals, but he hated Coyote most of all.

Coyote had broken off the conversation and run. Crow followed him, flying from tree to tree, but Coyote soon slipped out of sight as he entered a Squib neighborhood. Why was he leaving his home? Crow didn't care. He hoped he never came back.

As Crow perched on his snag, he felt something stab his eyes—a bright light. He squawked and almost toppled from his perch. Gripping the branch, he shook his head. He was dizzy, his eyes smarting. Something or somebody had attacked him. His vision slowly cleared, though he still saw yellow spots. He searched for his attacker.

Far below, he noticed a young female Squib floating on the water. On Come Along Slough, stories had spread about her. River Otter called her Squib Girl.

She stood on a slipshod flotation device of wood and metal barrels, and in her open hand, she held something shiny. Now he suspected what had stung his eyes. Was a sun Snake coiled up in her palm—one that spit hot venom into his eyeballs?

Crow usually kept a good distance from Squibs, but this one appeared small and harmless. He decided to fly down and investigate. Before approaching her, he analyzed the situation. Squib Girl held something dangerous. If he weren't careful, her sun Snake could blind him.

He quickly reviewed his knowledge of Squibs. They were dangerous, yet their behavior and activities fascinated him. He'd closely observed them and listened to their windy speech, which required them to twitch their lips, twist their tongues, and spit. They also snarled, gurgled, yawped, and wheezed. Crow had learned a few of their words. He could say, "Hello, Joe," "Shut up!" and "Back off, bitch!" He'd recently learned, "Don't shoot! Don't shoot!" and "I'm gonna put a cap up your ass!"

Given the opportunity, Crow often stole shiny things from them. It might be an ornament, a silver coin, a scrap of foil. Everything he stole, he hid inside a small crack high up in his cottonwood snag. He  plugged this crack with moss and mud. When depositing a shiny new treasure, he pecked out the moss and mud, secured his new acquisition, and stoppered the crack with fresh materials. His crack was packed. Soon, he'd need to find a new hiding spot. Crow stayed vigilant, ensuring that no other Crow ever tried to rob him of his treasures. Scrub Jay was also a big thief. So were Flicker and Downy Woodpecker.

When flying beyond the Slough, he frequently observed Rats scrambling over a gigantic Squib trash dump that glittered like thousands of tiny suns. Upon closer scrutiny, Crow had discovered that scrap metal and broken glass reflected the sun's fierce light. Crow suspected that Squib girl wasn't holding a sun Snake in her hand; it was most likely a piece of glass or metal that she was turning every which way to torment him. He wanted to steal this shiny object from her, so he could hold it in his beak and blast Raccoon whenever she climbed his plum tree. Red-Tailed Hawk was fair game, too. Crow imagined firing shards of sunlight into the sky, blinding those haughty nest-robbers, causing them to fall to the earth or crash into trees. Best of all, the firepower of his shiny object would impress the female Crows. They'd mark him as somebody who could be counted on to protect a clutch of eggs. He'd have his choice of mates.

Looking down at Squib Girl, Crow craved the shiny thing in her hand. He'd absorbed scads of useful Squib knowledge. Squibs were smart—dangerously smart. They hurt animals. In fact, they hurt everything they touched. But they had great power. Crow wanted a piece of that power. He had so many scores to settle. It was time for some payback.

Crow knew he had to plan his theft carefully. He couldn't just swoop down and steal what he wanted—way too risky. He was so big, and her hand was so small. If he didn't snatch it up on the first pass, he'd most likely not get another chance. He had to use his brains.

He had a brilliant idea. He wouldn't steal; he'd trade. That was it! He'd trade one of his precious treasures for Squib Girl's shiny thing. Crow had never done anything so audacious before, but risking his neck for this reward outweighed the danger.

Crow hurriedly pecked out the mud and moss from the cottonwood crack, and after careful consideration, he extracted a small, round white stone. When he'd stolen this pretty object, it had been part of a whole string of round white stones. He'd snatched it off an outside table. Many Squibs had screamed at him, but Crow flew off with the goods. The string of white stones had been hard to grasp, and when Crow flew across the Slough, the string broke. He lost all his pretty white stones except one. Picking up the solitary survivor with his beak now, he extended his wing and brought the object close to it, admiring the contrast of its creamy white beauty against the marvelous black of his feathers. Yes, this white stone would be a fair trade for Squib Girl's shiny thing.

Crow left his perch and flew above Squib Girl several times, circling the Slough in a nonchalant manner, but he kept his wits sharp. He didn't want to get picked off by Red-Tailed Hawk or Bald Eagle. Even if he evaded airborne assassination, he might drop his precious round white stone into the water.

Squib Girl directed her shiny thing at him again, and he turned his head quickly, avoiding the fiery blast. Crow remained cautious. As he circled the Slough, Squib Girl kept flashing light at him. Did she want to capture him? He'd heard tales about captured Crows. Squibs kept them in cages and fed them stale bread and peanuts. Crow's wing muscles cramped up at the thought. To manage his stress, he silently recited some relaxation rhymes. *Oh, yabba dabba doo, what should Crow do? Here's what he will do! He'll swirl and whirl, then rendezvous with Squib Girl on Come Along Slough.*

Crow tightened his circle, evaluating his options, and sailed closer to the water. Squib Girl stopped shining the light at him. Instead, she lifted one hand and waved it at him. Crow nearly splashed down into the Slough. No Squib had ever gestured at him like that before. They'd used their hands to toss rocks, sticks, and dirt clods at him, but Squibs never waved. Was this a hostile gesture? Crow was going to find out. Stifling his fear, he swooped down to where she stood.

Landing on the slick plank, he skidded and slewed toward the water, but righted himself and adjusted for the rocking motion of whatever he was floating on. Keeping his precious white stone cradled in his beak, he gave Squib Girl a suspicious look. She didn't move. If necessary, he had enough space and time to escape. Taking a few tentative hops, he maintained a safe distance and cocked one dark eye at her. She wore some baggy rags that covered her thin brown legs down to the knees. Stretching her lips, she exposed her teeth. Crow had seen Squibs show their teeth before. It was nerve-wracking. Was it a threat? At least she had black hair; he approved of the color.

Very slowly, Squib Girl set the shiny object on the planks and backed away, still showing her teeth. Crow hopped forward, then backward, trying to determine whether she planned to trick him. Finally, he hopped close enough to Squib Girl's shiny object to see it clearly. He felt a little let down. It was just a piece of … glass. He peered at it more closely.

Yikes! It was like a Squib window—the kind that Sparrow had crashed into and broken his neck. Yet it wasn't exactly a window. The glass had eyes—Crow eyes! Was another Crow staring at him? Some black-breasted thief out to steal his pretty round white stone? Furious, he lunged forward and pecked at the glass, then quickly hopped backward. He cawed a warning at this intruder Crow. The round white stone fell to the raft boards. Crow snatched it up and glanced at Squib Girl. She hadn't moved. He remained on full alert.

Why hadn't the other Crow jumped out of the glass and attacked him? Probably too scared. He concentrated again on how to make the trade. This Squib glass could capture animals; it was much more valuable than his round white stone. He couldn't believe his good luck. Clearly, Squibs were terrible at trading. Crow was cagey enough to know he'd better make the trade fast before Squib Girl changed her mind.

He looked into the glass again. Aaaagh! What kind of magic glass was this? He wasn't looking at another crow; he was looking at himself! He'd seen his reflection in water before, but never so clearly. Gadzooks! He was one handsome Crow. His swarthy good looks, combined with his new treasure, would improve his prospects with the females. He'd be first in line for mating privileges. Keeping an eye on Squib Girl, he placed the round white stone next to the looking glass and wedged it into a crack between the planks so it wouldn't roll away. Cocking his head at her, he felt obligated to say something, just to seal the deal.

"Hello, Joe," he said. "Don't shoot! Don't shoot!"

Squib Girl didn't answer. Instead, she made signs with both hands. Her fingers danced, swiveling in all directions. Then she linked two fingers together and pressed them to her chest, nodding her head.

Crow cawed softly, communicating bafflement. He decided to try more Squib words. "Back off, bitch!" he said. He repeated this phrase, but with greater volume. "BACK OFF, BITCH!"

Squib Girl raised a hand and waggled it.

Crow didn't want to dilly-dally any longer. He was in a perilous situation here. With difficultly, he got a solid grip on the looking glass and lifted it with his beak. He glanced at Squib Girl. He wanted to caw some kind of parting sentiment, such as "Thanks, sucker!" But since his new treasure poked out like a second beak, doing this was problematic. He turned slowly and spread his wings to fly away.

At that moment, River Otter surfaced from the water. "Hey, Crow," he called, "how low can your mojo go?"

Startled by River Otter's unexpected appearance, Crow hopped sideways and opened his beak, cawing with rage. The looking glass hit the edge of a plank and fell into the water. It was gone.

Crow pivoted toward River Otter. More Squib words abruptly came to mind. "I'm gonna put a cap up your ass!"

Crow heard another splash and turned. Squib Girl had dived into the Slough and disappeared. This was another shock: River Otter had gotten in his face, he'd lost his treasure, and now Squib girl had jumped into the water. He didn't know what to think.

"No need to go nuts on me," said River Otter. "Relax." He slithered onto the raft, stretched out in the sun, and belched. "Whatever you lost, Squib Girl will find it. She swims almost as good as me."

Crow shook his wings, still agitated. "You like her?"

"She likes me," River Otter said, "and so I like her back. Larry the Dog says we share Umwelt."

"But she's a Squib. Animals and Squibs never share anything."

"I try to keep an open mind and not judge individuals based upon their species."

"Can you talk to her?"

River Otter laughed. "Nobody talks to Squibs. Not even Squib Dog. Anyway, it doesn't matter. She can't talk any kind of talk. Her words stay stuck in her head. She barely even makes sounds. Talks with her hands instead, and if I pay close attention, I sometimes sorta get what she's saying."

"What does she say?" asked Crow.

"She's alone. No family of any kind. Thing is, she can't talk or hear. Never jumps at loud sounds. Sometimes I squeal at her, but she doesn't react. Poor thing. Must be tough."

At this moment, Squib girl resurfaced and swam to the side of the raft opposite Crow and River Otter, her hair slick with algae. She wriggled Otter-like onto the raft and stood, her garment streaming water. Smiling at Crow, she opened her hand to reveal his lost treasure. She knelt and set it next to Crow's round white stone. Then she straightened and backed away. Once more, she locked two fingers together and brought them close to her chest. Crow watched her, speechless, his mind reeling.

"Don't get wiggle-waggle about this," River Otter told him. "Squib Girl wants to be your friend. Best I can tell, you need all the friends you can get."

"Squibs aren't my friends," Crow managed to say, keeping an eye on his recovered treasure.

"To me, she's more River Otter than Squib. Who knows? Maybe she's got some Crow in her, too."

"You trying to insult me?"

"She's a great friend. We chase Carp and try to see who can stay underwater the longest. Too bad you don't swim. It wouldn't hurt you to take a bath. Even a splash bath. Just saying."

Crow ignored River's Otter's playful jibe about his personal hygiene. At any rate, Squib Girl didn't appear to represent any kind of immediate threat. Why had she retrieved his shiny looking glass? That had been an act of kindness. Crow wasn't used to kindness.

He studied her more closely. The sunlight reflecting off her wet skin glowed like hot glass. She had large black eyes. Not much fat showed between her brown skin and bones. Perhaps she didn't have enough to eat. Crow sympathized. Food was scarce for everybody.

"She must want something from us," Crow said to River Otter. "Squibs always want something."

"She wants to warn us," said River Otter. "It's the same thing Squib Dog warned us about."

"What's that?"

River Otter sobbed and pounded his paws on the raft. "It's not fair, Crow. It's just not fair!"

"What's not fair?"

"Squib Girl lives in that homeless camp. But it's getting wiped out. Bad Squibs are chasing off the good Squibs. It just sucks, Crow. It just sucks, sucks, *sucks*!"

"Who cares about homeless Squibs? No skin off my beak."

"You don't get it, do you, Crow? It's not just the homeless camp. They're gonna destroy the Slough, too! It's a fact. They're gonna smash up all our homes and disappear our water." River Otter kept sobbing.

Crow looked away and hopped toward his treasure. He snatched up the looking glass and eyed Squib Girl. Her arms hung loose at her sides, her hands not moving. Seeing the tears splashing onto her muddy feet, Crow forgot all about his new shiny thing.

28 COYOTE SEARCHES FOR HIS FATHER

Coyote had begun to have second thoughts about leaving Come Along Slough. Getting to the mountains was a grueling gauntlet of torments as he cut a zigzag path through countless Squib settlements. Dogs attacked him. Squibs fired guns at him. Crossing busy highways, he dodged speeding vehicles.

Wild game was nonexistent. He raided garbage cans and caught Rats and feral Cats. Mostly, he survived on roadkill. Whenever possible, he grabbed a few winks in alleyways or storm culverts before skulking like a gray ghost through moonlit streets.

He spoke to his feces, hoping to glean tidbits of advice from OMC about the correct traveling route. He got squat in return. His hunger was taking its toll. He was so hollowed out now that he hadn't pooped for days. Surviving on his scattered wits alone was the worst kind of feeling.

Reaching the foothills at dawn, Coyote was famished, but as he entered a dying pine forest, he spied the distant, dusky hulk of the mountains. What a welcome sight! His heartbeat accelerated. On those lofty heights, Old Man

Coyote—his father—was surely awaiting his arrival. Coyote would ferret out the right rendezvous spot and howl out his brains with joy.

After lapping water from a muddy creek, he inspected the sickly pine trees. They were dropping their yellow needles, and on the discolored bark, he saw telltale Beetle marks. Once-stately green trees had become pest-infested cadavers. Beetles and Squibs—both were tree killers.

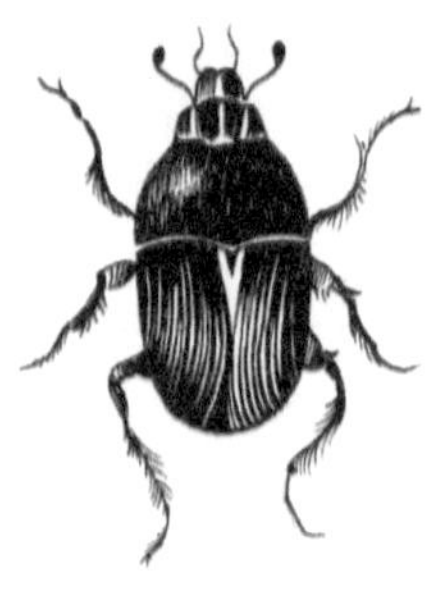

At idle times, he'd deigned to chat with Beetles—Blister Beetles, Dung Beetles, Bark Beetles, all of them going about their Beetle business. He was curious about how they viewed their place in the world, but apparently sorting out the edible from the inedible occupied all their time and energy. Listening to them grated on Coyote's nerves. The clickety-clack of appendages and mandibles. Their chittering voices. Beetles were clannish and dull as dirt, expressing no existential rage over their lot as bottom feeders. Railing against life's shortcomings never occupied their time. Beetles, Ants, Termites, Millipedes, Crickets, Spiders, Worms, Grubs—teeming hordes of squirming and skittering nobodies lived and died beneath Coyote's paws. More than ever, he felt grateful that he was an apex predator.

Coyote had eaten Beetles. They were crunchy, bitter, and full of yellow-green glop. He'd gagged them up. What had he expected from creatures that devoured Mouse droppings, Rabbit guts, and Squib garbage? They also cannibalized their own dead. Doing nature's dirty work, they converted stinky stuff into non-stinky stuff. For the moment, he put aside his disdain for the dirt scroungers and parasites. He was faint from hunger. A Beetle or two would tide him over until he could eat higher up on the food chain, but searching the dying trees for an easy snack, he found nothing. Apparently, the Bark Beetles had moved on to a healthy forest.

It was safer now to travel by day. Climbing into the mountains, he gained elevation quickly, resting often to gaze down into the maw of the valley. Smoke partially cloaked the landscape, but a river slithered through a tight cross-hatch of roads, grassy fields, and Squib settlements. The land below was vast. The Slough was somewhere out there in that vastness, a tiny wet spot upon the thin skin of the world.

Now that he was in the mountains, Coyote expected to encounter a variety of wild animals. Communicating with them might be difficult, since they probably didn't know Slough Speak. He preferred speaking pure Coyote—his native language—but not many animals knew it. Fortunately, his mother had taught him a polyglot tongue called Scat-Chat, which enabled different species of wild animals to understand one another. Like Slough Speak, this language was a tongue-punishing mingle-mangle of grunts, squeals, hisses, and growls. Speaking Scat-Chat would offer more opportunity to trick potential prey into thinking he was friendly.

As he rested atop a boulder, Coyote recalled Squib Dog's alarming message about the industrial sanctuary. What if he couldn't find OMC and had to return home? Would the Slough be buried in an avalanche of mud and rocks, the animals fleeing to parts unknown? He'd figure out some way to survive, though. He always did. But now, his stomach had shrunk to the size of Muskrat's eyeball. If he didn't find sufficient nourishment soon, he'd drop dead, the Beetles quickly chewing him down to tiny Coyote crumbs.

Panting hard, he climbed higher and saw a range of mountains, their slopes denuded of trees. Everything green had been hacked down and pulverized. A few spindly trees, like survivors of a storm, huddled on shattered ridgetops. Coyote's eyes swept over the gutted carcass of the land. The forest had been butchered and hauled off to market. Only slash remained.

For two days, he trotted through mountains stripped naked of trees. Delirious from hunger, he ate a few Spiders and Springtails. He chewed Bear grass. He even gummed some devil's club, its thorns cutting up the inside of his mouth. Such slim fare kept him going. Following a path among skeletal snags, he slept fitfully in piles of slash or in the shelter of a muddy gully. Every whoosh of wind through the dead branches made him jump. The land seemed alive with the ghosts of the dead forest.

Coyote knew that the body existed—'til it didn't. But his Coyote remains would live on in animals, plants, and rocks, in the rain, wind, and clouds. The Squibs had worked this land hard, killing its life and spirit. If he died here, would he crumble like a fallen leaf and disappear into the dark beginning of things?

On the third day, he entered a small uncut forest, the mature trees tall and fragrant, the ground cool and spongy beneath his bleeding paws. Many trees had strips of colored plastic tied around their trunks. He saw a metal plate nailed to one tree. He sniffed it, the stench of Squib strong, and squinted at the black marks on the metal. Turning his head in different directions, he tried to puzzle out the markings, but they meant nothing to him. Coyote understood a few Squib words, but he couldn't understand Squib symbols. All he knew was that wherever Squibs made marks on things, they were up to no good.

Going deeper into the forest, he drank from a small mossy creek, then searched for food, his eyes tracking the shadows. He smelled fresh blood, and his tail perked up. A slaughtered Doe lay only a few paces away, its throat ripped open, its death-startled eyes catching a shaft of sunlight. Then Coyote saw a very large gray Dog. It was hunched over the Doe, chewing on a steaming pile of entrails. The big Dog was making loud slurping sounds and appeared oblivious to Coyote's presence. Coyote gawked at the sag and heave of the Dog's huge black testicles. Wow! Impressive!

Coyote trembled, salivating at the sight of available food, but was too weak to fight this big Dog for the Doe. It was best to act humble. He'd adopt the soft and slow approach first. Fighting required more energy than he currently possessed. After he'd filled his gut on fresh meat, he'd send this Squib Dog packing.

Approaching slowly, he grinned submissively, then whined, communicating his nonthreatening intentions. The Dog lifted his head, stood swiftly, and regarded Coyote. Gore streaked his chest and snout. He bared his fangs, a ridge of fur rippling from neck to tail.

Coyote laid back his ears. "Greetings, Squib Dog," he said, mouthing out the syllables of Scat-Chat. "Would you mind sharing your surplus Deer with a ravenous stranger?"

The big Dog growled, fixing his bright yellow-green eyes on him. "What did you just call me?"

"Squib Dog?" said Coyote.

"I am Wolf, you brainless idiot."

Coyote froze in place, his jaw hanging open. He'd never seen a Wolf, but his mother had told him stories about them. Larger than Coyotes, they were ferocious. No other carnivore dared challenge their hunting territory. Running in packs, they were ruthless killers. Only Squibs threatened them, hunting them almost to extinction. But some of these fierce creatures had survived, keeping their wild natures intact.

"Sorry," Coyote mumbled. "My mistake."

Wolf exposed his fangs. "I know who you are. You are Coyote—a very mangy-looking Coyote."

Coyote nodded. "I am Coyote, but I'm not mangy."

"I hate Coyotes. They're sneak-around thieves, always stealing food from their betters. I kill them but don't eat them. Only Buzzards can stomach something that's rotten down to the core."

Coyote retreated a few paces. He had to distract this carnivore fast. "You alone, Wolf? Where's your pack?"

"Dead."

"How?"

"Squibs."

"I feel your pain. The Squibs also attack my own kind."

Wolf snorted. "For once, the Squibs are doing something right."

Coyote knew it was prudent to retreat, but the heady reek of a fresh kill encouraged him to stand his ground.

"I am a stranger to these parts, Brother Wolf."

"I'm not your brother."

"Nor am I your enemy."

Wolf's yellow-green eyes bore down on Coyote. "Listen and listen good, shit face. You're not getting a scrap of my food, so scram before I rip your head off."

Coyote trotted a short distance away and spun around. "I'm looking for Old Man Coyote. Have you seen him?"

This question appeared to perplex Wolf. "Who's that? Your grandpa?"

"A vicious Wolf killer. He'll swallow you down in one bite and won't even leave your balls for the Buzzards."

Wolf snarled. "You think you're clever, but you're not!"

"LOOK OUT!" Coyote cried. "OLD MAN COYOTE'S RIGHT BEHIND YOU!"

Wolf wasn't fooled. He lunged toward Coyote, his large paws pounding the ground.

Coyote sprinted up the slope with Wolf snapping at his

heels. Wolf soon left off the chase and returned to the Doe. Coyote considered circling back and snagging a few scraps but rejected this idea. Wolf wouldn't leave behind even a cloven hoof or rib bone.

Exiting the small forest, Coyote crossed another clearcut cluttered with piles of rocks and logging slash. He nibbled on tree bark and tried to bag a few Ground Squirrels, but they were too quick for him. He stalked a fat Marmot, but it whistled, warning its companions before ducking down into the rocks. Finally, he settled on his haunches and panted.

Suddenly, Coyote heard a rustling in the underbrush. He waited, not moving, his eyes sharp. A small brown creature finally emerged and wobbled slowly towards him. Its lumpy body was coated with spines, and it had a short tail. Coyote didn't recognize this odd little animal, but it was meat on four feet. The creature stopped to chew on a twig, ignoring Coyote. This was going to be an easy meal.

"Why, hello, little feller," he said.

The creature lifted its head and squinted. "Who's talking? I can smell you, but I can't see you too good."

"I am Coyote. What's your name?"

"Porcupine."

He'd heard that name before, but where? The Slough had no Porcupines. Maybe his mother had told him about them. Regardless, meat was meat.

"Allow me to come closer," Coyote said. "Your nose shouldn't have to do all the seeing for you."

"Don't make any sudden moves," said Porcupine. "I'm kinda twitchy."

"I know many Porcupines. They're my friends. My close friends."

"I have no close friends."

"Then I shall be your first."

He bolted toward Porcupine. At his approach, Porcupine

swiveled around, presenting his tail. Coyote pounced and pinned the creature in place. He sank his teeth into its rump —and yelped, then howled. He lurched away, shaking his head, his face on fire.

"My apologies," said Porcupine, "but it's advisable if you don't stick around any longer."

Coyote's snout, ears, and forepaws bristled with quills. In a frenzy, he ran in erratic circles, howling. The pain nearly paralyzed him. He lunged and twisted, rolled on the ground, and scraped his head and paws against a tree stump. Nothing helped. Gradually, his howls became strangulated whimpers. He limped a short distance away, crawled onto a boulder pile, and flopped down, his face still on fire. The pain wouldn't go away.

He cried out for his dead mother. "Why didn't you ever tell me Old Man Coyote is my father?" he sobbed.

As the night closed in around him, Coyote grew weaker. He began to hallucinate. Owl stood next to him, her eyes large and vacant, her musty feathers smelling of forest, earth, and blood.

"I'm curious," Coyote asked, "why do you have three eyelids? Isn't one enough?"

"One blinks away dirt," Owl explained, "one helps me spot prey, and the third cleans my seeing tubes."

"'Seeing tubes'?"

"I don't have eyes; I have seeing tubes. When I'm on the hunt, my tubular vision helps me to accurately judge distance, height, and weight."

"I'm very, very hungry," said Coyote. "Do you have any of those … White Field Mice to spare?"

Owl screeched at him. With her beak, she plucked a quill from Coyote's face.

"Ouch!"

She jabbed the quill back into his face, twisting it deeper.

"Ouch! Ouch! *Ouch!*"

Owl flew off into the night. Coyote came back to his senses, quickly realizing Owl was a figment of his imagination. She hadn't pulled out the Porcupine quill, then jabbed it back in—he had! With his own paws! Was he trying to kill himself?

Abruptly, a freezing rain arrived, drenching Coyote and driving the cold into his bones. Shivering, he lifted his bleeding head and searched for shelter. Hearing a sound, he caught the sight of something shadowy moving across the rocks and heard pebbles bouncing down the incline. An animal was coming toward him—perhaps something edible.

"Who goes there?" he asked, squinting into the darkness.

No answer.

Rain pelted his face. "Friend or foe?"

Through the downpour, a pair of disembodied eyes glowed like green fire. He heard a soft purr, then a wet gurgle.

"I am Coyote. My face is full of Porcupine quills, but I'm nobody to mess with. Please go away before I hurt you."

He heard a low, throaty growl.

"Who are you?!" Coyote demanded.

The creature's soft yet menacing voice floated toward him. "Mountain Lion."

Coyote had never seen a Mountain Lion. Its green eyes grew larger.

"You shouldn't be prowling around in this stormy weather," Coyote said. "Why aren't you home, staying warm and dry?"

The answer came quickly. "I'm hunting for food. I have three very hungry cubs to feed. Mommy must find something yummy for their tummies."

Coyote heard the purring again. It vibrated through his bones. He began looking for an escape route.

"Were you sleeping, my juicy little darling?" asked Mountain Lion. "Did Mommy wake you?"

"I was already wide awake."

"You must be tired. Let Mommy give you a good night kiss."

Coyote ran, tearing lickety-split down a rocky slope. Mountain Lion followed, but she seemed in no hurry, stalking him in an easy and teasing manner. Glancing back, Coyote saw her shadow rippling across the rocks.

"Mommy is searching for you," she called out to him. "Come out, come out, wherever you are!"

Rain slashed at Coyote's head. Porcupine's quills jabbed his face. Stopping, he heard her voice again.

"Mommy will sing you her sleepy-bye song, little yum-yum. She'll make all your pain go bye-bye. Mmmmmmm…"

Coyote ran faster.

"Mommy's sweet snookums smells good. Mmmmmmm…"

Coyote skidded to a stop and peered over a cliff edge. In the darkness, he couldn't see much. The cliff didn't appear too awfully steep, but he wasn't confident he could climb down without losing purchase. He had to try, though. Coyote edged one paw over the precipice. Rocks broke loose and tumbled from sight, cracking and snapping branches far below. Coyote backed away, his heart thudding.

Without warning, Mountain Lion struck him from behind, her claws gripping his hindquarters. Both of them tumbled over the cliff. Rain and wind whipped past them. Tree boughs lashed their bodies, flinging them out and away from the slope. They hit the bottom together, Coyote on top. Mountain Lion's body cushioned the impact. Coyote didn't move, the breath knocked out of him. Then he heard a sound, like water gurgling up from rocks. It was Mountain Lion.

Coyote couldn't see well, but he smelled fresh blood. With one paw, he prodded Mountain Lion. She was a hot, wet lump. Was she dead? Or just temporarily knocked-out? Coyote didn't wait to find out. He ran. Climbing out of a canyon, he careened blindly in every direction, expecting Mountain Lion to ambush him. By dawn, he finally felt safe. Quills still festooned his face, blood oozing from his cheeks. He was still starving to death.

29 THE CHOSEN ONE
SPEAKS

RACCOON LOOKED MISERABLE. For reasons known only to herself, she'd insisted that the USA delegates call her "Jane the Raccoon." As a result, she received a resounding vote of no confidence. Now she was out of a job.

She hadn't taken her ouster well. Chewing on her tail had mutilated the signature symmetry of the black and brown rings, creating unsightly bald patches. "It's not fair!" she cried. "Why am I a scapegoat for everything that's not my fault?"

"Sorry, Jane," said Carp. "The USA is all about the blame game—not the name game."

Flapping his wings, Crow ridiculed Raccoon: "It looks like Jane the Vain's gone down the drain."

Muskrat was quickly reelected to the office of secretary-general. Nobody else wanted the job, but she still felt honored.

"Thank you, thank you," she gushed. "I will work very hard to reestablish a climate of trust—and to rigorously enforce the USA's eating quotas."

"Don't start calling yourself Marsha the Muskrat," Mole warned.

Everyone laughed except Raccoon.

Muskrat took a deep breath and whispered a phrase she used to bolster her confidence: *"It's my time to shine, it's my time to shine."* She was more ready than ever to reassume the solemn burden of public service. She knew her plodding manner aggravated the other animals, causing them to make unkind remarks about her shortcomings, but she felt confident that her thick skin would shelter her from verbal abuse. Steady-as-she goes diligence to duty was her strong suit. Given time and opportunity, she would stabilize the USA's wobbly governmental structure and demonstrate that making the Slough great again didn't require waging war on water or going belly up to a trickster like Coyote.

She glanced at the dark sky. Rain was coming. To call the USA delegates to order, she instructed Nutria to jump off a log into the Slough. Nutria made a theatrical splash, which lacked the dignity of Beaver whacking his tail on the water, but in due course, the animals fell silent, awaiting the new secretary-general's opening remarks.

Muskat propped her head up on the brow of the muddy shore, projecting a sober visage, and prepared to address the sparse ranks of the assembly. She still wished her voice weren't so squeaky.

"We have many important topics on today's agenda," she squeaked, "but first, I ask your indulgence to—"

"I call for a no confidence vote on Muskrat!" Raccoon shouted, rearing up on her hind legs and waving her paws. "She's incompetent!"

"Aw, give her a fair chance to flop on her face," said Squirrel.

Other animals chuffed, squawked, squeaked, quacked, and snorted, expressing similar sentiments.

Muskrat exposed her two orange incisors and spoke more loudly than usual. "Before Raccoon interrupted me, I was trying to—"

"Speak with less squeak and more gruffness," Scrub Jay suggested. "You're putting me to sleep."

Elrod snickered. "She makes me saw logs all day long."

Muskrat couldn't mask her exasperation at seeing Elrod at the meeting. How did this insolent Rabbit-killer always manage to worm his way back into the USA? Now here he was again, taunting her and trying to make her lose self-control and lash out at him. Elrod liked to elicit sympathy by playing the victim, but she wasn't going to fall into that trap.

"Please continue, Sister Muskrat," said Squib Dog. "I want to hear what you have to say."

Muskrat cast a look of gratitude his way and gave it another try. "I propose we appoint Owl as my … vice secretary-general."

"Didja say 'Mice'?" asked Mole. "You wanna make a Mouse secretary-general?"

Muskrat's tail stiffened. Her nose twitched. "No, no. I said 'vice,' not 'mice.' Making Owl my vice secretary-general means she's second-in-command. If something bad should happen to me," she added, cocking an admonishing eyebrow at Elrod, "Owl would take my place until my replacement is elected."

"You can't put a brain-dead Owl in charge of anything without first calling for a proper vote," said Squirrel.

"I'm sorry, but the Slough's dire circumstances dictate that I make an executive decision," she said.

"Dictate?" asked Squirrel. "Does that mean you're a dictator?"

Muskrat ignored this remark. "We need continuity of leadership. We're facing many existential emergencies, and any disruption in the governance of the USA puts everyone in peril."

Owl was in no shape to hold any kind of office, of course. She was way too daft for that, but her name still had enough magisterial clout to command respect. Muskrat needed Owl as much as Raccoon had. No secretary-general could stand alone against this loudmouthed mob of malcontents. Silencing the fusspots and faultfinders required a silent partner.

"Making an executive decision like this is the death of our democracy," said Scrub Jay. "Are you trying to create a dictatorship of the downtrodden?"

Muskrat wrinkled her brow. "Downtrodden? Are you suggesting that Owl's downtrodden?"

"No—but you definitely are."

The other animals laughed. Elrod laughed the loudest.

Muskrat gargled a mouthful of water, spat it out, and brought a more persuasive argument into play. "Owl is a USA patriot and a war hero who's absolutely committed to safeguarding our democratic traditions."

The animals gazed at Owl, who sat on a nearby shit-bespattered cottonwood branch, her body rigid, her eyes vacant. She'd lost a lot of weight, and her feathers now hung loose on her bones. She was more skeleton than Bird.

"With all due respect to our war hero," said Scrub Jay, "having a no tummy stuffed dummy as second-in-command doesn't inspire confidence." Scrub Jay hopped onto the limb where Owl was perched and rapped his beak on her noggin. Owl's wide yellow eyes retained their glassy vacancy. "Nobody's home," he said. "It's like an echo chamber in there. Plain to see she's off her nut."

No doubt about it. Owl was crazy. Round-the-moon-and-back-again Cuckoo Bird crazy. Everyone had grown accustomed to her sporadic gibbering, followed by long silences. She sometimes screeched about tiny White Field Mice. The animals blamed her derangement on Coyote. These nonsense utterances were obviously caused by the suspect food he had provided her.

Hummingbird hovered in front of Owl. "Speak to us," she begged. "Tell us what's on your mind. Do you want to be Muskrat's vice secretary-general?"

Owl muttered something.

Hummingbird hovered closer. "What? I couldn't hear you. What do you want?"

Owl spoke. "MEAT! I WANT MEAT!"

Hummingbird retreated. "Just meat? Nothing else?"

Owl opened her beak wider. "Call me the … Chosen One."

Muskrat spoke quickly. "Okay, that settles this issue. Owl just chose herself to be my vice secretary-general."

Owl groaned, her emaciated body convulsing. She appeared to be choking on something, her beak gaping, but nothing came out except "Urp!" and "Grrrrrrrrkkkkkk!"

"Hooray for Owl!" Hummingbird shouted. "She has reclaimed her brain!"

Owl made another sound. "Aaaaaaggghhhhh!"

"What is it, Owl?" Hummingbird asked.

"Unkaunkaunka! Gluuuuuuk!"

"We're listening! Speak to us!"

"I am the Chosen One!"

"Yes," Hummingbird cried. "You are the Chosen One!"

"Aaaaaaggghhhhh!"

Hummingbird buzzed circles around Owl's head. "Keep talking, Owl. What else do you have to say? Come on, everyone! Let's help Owl out. Tell her she's the Chosen One!" She began to chant, "Chosen One! Chosen One! Chosen One!"

As if in thrall to a spell, the animals chanted with her. "CHOSEN ONE! CHOSEN ONE! CHOSEN ONE!" Only Muskrat remained silent.

"WE SHALL FIGHT ON THE LAND!" Owl screeched. "WE SHALL FIGHT IN THE AIR AND IN THE WATER!"

She toppled from her perch, hitting the ground like a wad of wet leaves.

Hummingbird hovered overhead. Scrub Jay and Crow hopped around Owl, cocking their heads. Squirrel and Elrod crowded in for a closer look.

"She's dead!" Elrod shouted.

"First Maggie, and now Owl!" Hummingbird sobbed. "All our best Birds keep dying before their time. Who will be next?"

Elrod flexed his neck muscles. "She doesn't have much meat on her bones, but it'd be a shame to waste it. I call first dibs."

"Get back," warned Hummingbird, "or I'll impale your rotten little heart!"

More animals gathered. Nobody spoke. Owl's eyes looked like sheets of black ice. Overhead, thunderclouds gathered.

Muskrat scampered up from the shoreline, stopping short of the milling throng, and cleared her throat. "As secretary-general," she said, "I hereby decree that we will honor our war hero with an official USA funeral."

"Squeak louder!" demanded Scrub Jay. "I can't hear you."

30 OLD MAN COYOTE

FOR DAYS, Coyote stumbled through the mountains, mumbling deliriously, his snout bristling with Porcupine quills. His hunger was intolerable. He chewed moss and pinecones. Licked Carpenter Ants off a log. Swallowed Six-Spotted Spider. Took a bite of Banana Slug—gak! Self-pity overtook him. If he died alone in the wilderness, nobody would mourn his passing or commemorate his legendary cunning. No tearful eulogies, no posthumous honorifics of any kind. He would be the nobody who never was.

Coyote recalled Squirrel, Crow, Muskrat, Raccoon, Hummingbird, Heron, River Otter, Squib Dog, Elrod, and all the other animals he detested. He knew their names, their smells, their speech, but couldn't visualize what they looked like anymore. Shutting his eyes, he conjured a claw, a beak, a wing, an eyeball, but no faces or bodies materialized in their entirety. He spoke names. *"E-l-r-o-d. R-a-c-c-o-o-n."* He spoke his own name: *"C-o-y-o-t-e."* A stranger's name. Who was Coyote? Did such a creature even exist?

Whimpering, he followed a narrow creek threading its way through the scrub brush. He spoke to it. "Hello, my little bubbly buddy," he crooned. "Can you help me? I am so thirsty and hungry."

He drank water and searched for Fish. Even a Fingerling would be a feast at this point. Snapping at a Water Slider, he slipped and fell into a shallow side pool. He shook himself dry, chewed more moss, and flushed out a Wood Thrush, but he was too weak to make a play for it.

Coyote rested often, his legs shaking, his vision blurry. He pined for his easy meals at the Slough. Rabbits, Moles, Muskrats. Ducks, Snakes, Mourning Doves. He'd sampled the whole lot. On occasion, he'd even bagged a Fawn or a yearling. He also raided the Squibs, carrying off their Chickens, baby Goats, Piglets, and house pets, but Maggie had been his greatest prize, a scrumptious mouthful of tender delights. Other animals on the Slough often went hungry, but by hook or by crook, he hardly ever wanted for food. He took whatever he wanted whenever he wanted it.

"I'm so sorry," he moaned, "for all the horrible things I've done!"

Coyote shook his head as if receiving a hard blow. Why had he blurted out something so idiotic? What was he sorry about? Nothing! It was just his hunger talking. He gnawed moss off a log and staggered down the canyon.

Near dark, he entered a forested valley, the air still and warm, and spied a small lake. In the fading light, its serene slate-gray water beckoned him. Maybe he could catch Fish here. It was worth a try. He quickened his pace, then stopped, startled at the sight of a peculiar structure. A Squib house? Maybe, maybe. He crouched down and examined it for hidden dangers, such as claw traps or a pack of Squib Dogs. This grimy white structure was shaped like a large pointy-headed toadstool, with wooden poles poking out the top.

He saw smoke, then he smelled roasted meat. Coyote trembled. His eyes watered. He whined, his nostrils flaring. Summoning his remaining strength, he cut a cautious path toward the tantalizing smell, then ran.

Coyote skidded to a stop. Another Coyote was limping toward him. Male? Female? He considered his options. He could run, which was the least risky, or he could stay put and take his chances. If this were a female Coyote, he could assert his dominance and mount her. But what was he thinking? He lacked the vigor for that kind of surprise attack.

Narrowing his eyes, he determined that the Coyote was a male. With each step, his wrinkled nut sack swung side to side, as if he were flaunting his junk.

Then he saw something that astonished him. This Coyote was walking erect on his hind legs! In one paw, he gripped a walking stick. Coyote berated himself for not noticing this right off. A Coyote walking on two legs? How did he keep his balance? Looking more closely, he saw a grizzled snout, crumpled ears, and a crooked gray tail. Coyote smiled. Walking on two legs exposed vital organs. A strategic blunder. It would be easy to rip out Grandpa's guts.

Coyote raised a paw in greeting. "Hello. I have traveled a great distance in search of a special someone."

Stopping a few paces away, the old Coyote grinned, exposing discolored teeth. His yellow-brown eyes glinted like broken glass. "Who are you searching for?" he asked, his voice gruff and unwelcoming.

"Old Man Coyote."

"Well, you have found me," he said with a throaty chuckle. "Congratulations."

Coyote gasped, his eyes bulging. "It's really you?"

"Yes, it's me."

"You're really Old Man Coyote? Really, really him?"

"It's really, really me."

"I blew my bowels inside out looking for you! I pulled out all the stops!"

OMC nodded, his eyes twinkling. "You sound very clever." He pointed a paw at Coyote's nose. "So, you met Porcupine?"

"Yes, but we soon parted ways."

"What gifts have you brought me?"

Coyote's heart thumped hard against his breastbone. "Gifts?"

"As a gesture of respect, my visitors always give me something of great value. You must do the same. If you don't give me a proper gift, I will kill you."

Coyote's heart thumped harder. Old Man Coyote was probably just joshing with him. "Would you consider me as your gift?"

Leaning on his cane, OMC studied him for a long moment. "How much of yourself can you give me?"

Coyote hesitated. "Uh, hard to say. Right now, there's not much of me left to give. I haven't eaten for days."

"I've forgotten my manners," said OMC. "After your difficult journey, you must really be famished."

Food at last! He felt a rush of affection for OMC, squelching an urge to tell him that his long-lost son stood in front of him—on four legs rather than two. He must eat first and recharge himself. A father-son reunion would come after that.

"I could do with a little bite of something," he said.

OMC tapped his walking stick on a rock. "A little bite? Or a big bite?"

"A big bite. The bigger, the better."

"Excellent. A bigger bite it is. Please follow me."

Catching a strong whiff of roasted meat, Coyote woofed with joy, and to keep his mind off his hunger, he speculated on why OMC walked on his hind legs. How weird was that?

Maybe some kind of terrible injury or birth defect had forced him to become a biped.

After following a rocky trail downhill, they stopped before the odd-looking structure that Coyote had seen earlier. Fabricated from animal hides, it was decorated with symbols. Coyote saw creatures with big heads, big teeth, big claws. Some had jagged wings and twisty-looking snouts.

"This is my humble lodge," OMC said. "Please come inside and make yourself comfortable."

OMC pulled back the flap, and as they entered, Coyote felt the crunch of bones underfoot. A small fire sputtered on the dirt floor, casting spidery shadows across the walls.

OMC leaned down, cricking his knees slightly, and whispered into his ear. "What do you smell?"

Coyote smelled OMC's breath. Bad Buzzard breath. Maybe his father preferred roadkill to fresh game.

"I smell meat," he lied. "Delicious meat."

"You smell meat, but can you see meat?"

Coyote inspected the shadows. He caught the scent of damp soil and moldy vegetation. Not very appetizing.

OMC straightened and pointed his cane at a reed basket. "Perhaps your meat is over there, just waiting for your first bite."

Coyote stared at the basket, wanting to shred it and devour its contents. But not wishing Old Man Coyote to think him uncouth, he vowed that he wouldn't rip and gulp. He'd nibble and swallow, showcasing the good manners his mother had taught him. After satisfying his appetite, he'd belch, crack his joints, settle back, and jaw with OMC on a variety of practical topics. What was a fail-safe method for hamstringing a big Buck? Or quickly snapping the necks of Rabbits and Muskrats? Were Canada Goose eggs more nutritious than Heron eggs? What was the best way to ask a female for a quick hump? Lounging next to the cozy lodge fire, Coyote would spring the big surprise. He'd shout, "Father! Your son has found you!"

Coyote approached the basket, and drooling heavily, he used his paw to nudge open the lid. The smell of moldering vegetables grew stronger. Poking his snout into the dark interior, he tried not to drive the Porcupine quills any deeper into his face. He heard a soft rattle, then a loud one. Curious, he probed more deeply. Then he felt a sharp pain as something bit his neck. Coyote yipped and staggered backward. He heard OMC's harsh laughter.

"Ha ha ha! That was your first big bite. Was it enough? If not, Rattlesnake will serve up seconds."

Coyote thrashed around on the dirt floor, howling. "Father! Why have you done this to your son!"

OMC whacked Coyote with his walking stick. "You miserable, misbegotten fool, I'm not your father! I am your teacher! You have many lessons to learn, so pay attention! It's time for class to start."

OMC kept whacking him. "Fire, snowflake, and flower!" he shouted, every word came with a hard whack on Coyote's head or backside. "Beetle, Butterfly, and Worm! Fang, claw, blood, bone, and eyeball! Run! Swim! Fly! Crawl! Nobody remembers you! Nobody knows your name!"

Eventual Porky, I figger ev'ry critter's heart's in the right place.

—*POGO*, WALT KELLEY

31 THE FUNERAL

A HEAVY RAINSTORM had formed muddy rivulets beneath the thin canopy of cottonwoods. Close to the shoreline, Muskrat hunkered down in the muck, enduring the plop and spatter of raindrops on her head. She felt miffed. Wasn't she the secretary-general? Yet not one animal had asked her advice for planning Owl's funeral, nor even suggested that she deliver the eulogy.

Nearby, Nutria was flopping around in the mud. "Muskrat!" he called. "Wanna go for a swim? Hey, hey, whadaya say?"

"Maybe later."

"Aww, come on. We could dive and see who can hold their breath the longest."

"Go away," she muttered.

Nutria waddled off into a stand of yellow flag irises, and Muskrat returned her attention to the spot where other members of the USA were fussing over Owl's body. Nibbling on a cattail, she squinted at several large Birds struggling to stay aloft in the downpour. They landed and formed a circle around the corpse. She saw Red-Tailed Hawk, Bald Eagle, and Osprey. Standing shoulder to shoulder, they flexed their wings, casting haughty looks at the Songbirds descending from overhanging branches. Curious to see what would happen next, Muskrat finished off her cattail and snagged a second one.

The Birds braced themselves against the punishing fusillade of raindrops, and working together, they hoisted Owl, the smaller ones supporting her body from below, the larger ones latching talons onto her limp wings and tail feathers. Owl's head flopped to the side. Muskrat glimpsed her distinctive half-dome shape, the facial disc, and the symmetrical ruff of feathers. Gaining altitude above the Slough, Owl's body hung in the gloom like a ghost. A whirlwind of wings swept away the rain as the retinue of Birds became a single-minded organism, its assemblage of muscles, bones, and feathers straining to keep its unwieldly load aloft.

Owl's funeral procession progressed across the water. The other animals gathered along the shoreline, chanting softly, their throaty murmur almost inaudible to Muskrat's ears. "Chosen One! Chosen One! Chosen One!"

The storm's intensity increased, stripping the leaves off the cottonwoods. Muskrat ignored the pelting rain, keeping her gaze upon the slow twist and wobble of Owl's body. She expected the entire funeral procession to crash-land into the water. The Birds stopped in the middle of the Slough, hovering in place.

Muskrat caught sight of Squib Girl. She stood on her flotation device, barefoot and bone thin, the rain matting her hip-length hair, her large eyes the color of burnt wood.

Then Muskrat gasped, shocked to see Squib Girl's slender brown arms stretching out toward the Birds to accept the delivery of Owl's body. Along the shoreline, the animals kept chanting.

"CHOSEN ONE! CHOSEN ONE! CHOSEN ONE!"

Even Muskrat chanted. She couldn't help herself; she was spellbound. Then she fell silent, embarrassed that her emotions had overthrown her judgment. Giving Owl's body to Squib Girl was a gross violation of the Natural Law of Animals. Whether living or dead, no wild animal should ever suffer the touch of a Squib. Owl's corpse had been defiled! Outrageous! Why hadn't anybody asked her about the advisability of giving up Owl to this … Girl?

Squib Girl was no stranger to the Slough, of course. Since the violent removal of the homeless camp, she lived alone on what River Otter called a "raft." Nobody was sure how she survived, yet she went with the ebb and flow of life on Come Along Slough, and because she appeared nonthreatening, most animals had adjusted to her presence. But in Muskrat's opinion, Squib Girl was still a Squib.

After the homeless camp had been demolished, the steady expansion of the industrial sanctuary was plain to see. It would soon devour the Slough. Knowing her world was going to disappear, Muskrat's love for the Slough grew stronger. In these cattail-strewn waters, she and her siblings had been born pink, bald, and blind. Now she was the last surviving member of her family, and if the Slough perished, she would perish with it.

She saw River Otter swimming toward her. Amazingly, he had figured out how to communicate with Squib Girl. Perhaps he could explain why she now had Owl in her clutches.

He swam up next to Muskrat, settling his belly down into the mud, and sighed. He still kept his distance from the contentious USA meetings, preferring to float on his back and think his happy thoughts, adhering proudly to his "no Flies on me" attitude in regard to community affairs. As he crouched next to her now, he seemed uncharacteristically preoccupied with something.

"Hello, River Otter," she said.

Twitching his whiskers, he gave her his customary "glad to see you" grin. "Back atcha, Muskrat."

"You look a little down. Everything okay?"

His grin vanished. "Owl's brain rotted out like a soggy log."

Muskrat nodded slowly. "Happens to us all, sooner or later."

"She died just when we needed her most, but dead or alive, Owl is still in my dreams."

"Oh? You dream about her?"

He nodded. "All the time. In one dream, tiny White Mice were crawling over Owl's body, squeaking and singing. Pretty wild, huh?"

"Singing Mice?"

River Otter shrugged. "Others also dream about Owl."

"Who?"

"It's kinda weird to talk about, but I think Owl has talon-picked a few of us in the USA to be dream-talkers. Crow, Raccoon, and Squirrel. Even Elrod. Not everyone wants to admit it, though. They're afraid that the other animals will laugh at them."

Hearing Elrod's name rankled Muskrat. If that vicious little Stoat dream-talked with Owl, why couldn't she? Once again, she felt excluded from the group. She snapped off another bite of cattail. "Owl is dead. The dead don't dream —or talk. And we can't talk with them."

River Otter scrunched up his face, formulating his words. "Water can be liquid, ice, or fog. Death and life are like that. They're always changing into something surprising. Get what I'm saying?"

Muskrat gave him a sour look. "No."

River Otter nudged her with his nose. "I toldja my dream. Tell me yours."

Muskrat hesitated. "I only have nightmares. In one of them, the Slough was an—"

"Industrial sanctuary?"

"Don't finish my sentences for me, okay?"

"Oh, sorry for Otter-splaining. Please continue."

"I saw big fires. And heard animals screaming."

"What else?"

Muskrat searched River Otter's face for signs of incredulity. She wasn't used to anyone wanting to hear what she had to say. "The Squibs caught me and killed me. Then…"

"Yes?"

"Darkness."

"Nothing else?"

"My body turned into a cloud of cattail fluff. It was very strange. Felt like I was part of everything all at once."

"Ah," said River Otter. "The individual you changed into the universal you!"

Muskrat shot him a perplexed look. "That's a little rich for my blood."

Flipping onto his back, River Otter used his paws to scrub mud off his face. "My dreams paralyze me with wonder."

"Otter, I keep wondering about something."

"Yeah?"

"Owl lost her mind because those White Field Mice obviously had something bad in them. But I don't get why she starved herself to death."

"A real mystery," he agreed. "Some of the Raptors provided her with meat, but she refused it. Toward the end, she just chewed on sticks and pine cones."

Muskrat sighed. "Eating was her greatest pleasure in life."

River Otter stuck his tongue out to catch the raindrops. "Owl gave us dream-talkers an urgent message. We have to skedaddle before a big flood drowns us."

Muskrat belched and sniffed the air. She grimaced, embarrassed by her bad cattail breath. "Owl went full whackadoodle on us. Now she's dead. So are her dreams."

River Otter wriggled closer. "Squib Girl also knows about the flood. She isn't a dream-talker, but she talks with her hands. If Squib Girl joins the USA, she can help us escape the flood."

Muskrat almost barfed up her cattails. "A Squib in the USA? I will never, never, *never* sanction such a shameful sacrilege!"

River Otter nodded. "If the majority of the delegates vote for her, you got small say in the matter."

Sheet lightning sent a wave of fire across the Slough. Muskrat ducked low, then poked up her head and scanned the expanse of water. Where was Squib Girl? She and her raft were gone—along with Owl's body.

River Otter gave her a grave look. "Squib Girl will guide us to safety."

"So says a dead Owl?"

"Owl is the Chosen One. She sees what we can't."

32 A FACE FROM THE PAST

THE USA GATHERED for an emergency meeting, its ranks thinner than ever. Hunger, loss of habitat, and the prediction of a catastrophic flood topped the agenda. Many animals hadn't bothered to show up, convinced that Come Along Slough had come to the end of its days.

Muskrat sulked in the cattails, nursing her resentments and keeping an eye on Elrod's movements. If she offered opinions on critical issues, nobody listened to her. Secretary-general in name only, she had no incentive to showcase her statecraft. The sting of irrelevance was painful.

No one oversaw the meeting. Spit flew in all directions as the attending delegates wrangled about the Slough's impending demise. Attempting to purge the venom of fear from their systems, they hurled accusations and insults at each other.

Carp, Western Pond Turtle, and Heron raged about the loss of water. All the Birds, Raptors, and Songbirds bemoaned the loss of trees. Mole fretted about the availability of Earthworms, 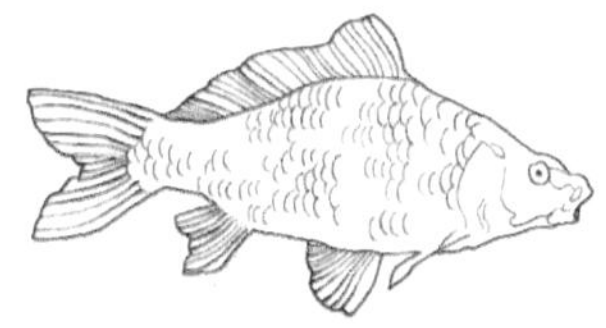

Grubs, and diggable dirt. Dung Beetle and Carpenter Ant also had legitimate complaints, but as usual, their weak voices were disregarded.

Owl's confederacy of dream-talkers had warned that a big flood would remove Come Along Slough from the face of the known world.

"First this industrial sanctuary buries us alive," Squirrel moaned, "then we drown. Talk about overkill."

"If I get buried," said Elrod, "I can dig my way out. If everything liquefies, I'll go full aquatic."

Raccoon grasped her tail and raised it above her head, indicating that she wished to speak. The other animals cast dismissive glances at her but fell silent and listened. "This flood will also destroy the industrial sanctuary," she said. "The USA can claim it as a decisive victory over the Squibs."

"Hooray for our side," scoffed Scrub Jay. "Even in death, we still prevail."

"I hope a flood provides more water for me to swim in," said Carp.

It's plain to see what the Squibs are up to," said Mole, "but I don't see no flood happening. What if all this dream-talker stuff is a buncha fluff and phooey about nothing? All due respect to Owl, but …"

A few animals agreed with Mole. The prediction of a big flood seemed too fantastical to be credible, but the industrial sanctuary had the blunt force of reality. Everyone was suffering. Houses and other structures had been razed, trees toppled, the land bulldozed bald. Squibs in orange hats swarmed over mounds of mud and rocks, slashing vegetation and pounding wooden stakes into the ground.

The homeless camp neighboring Come Along Slough had been eliminated fast. One night, the animals heard screams, sobs, and curses, then sirens and gunshots. Flames rose from the far end of the Slough. The animals sheltered in place, hearts pounding. At dawn, River Otter and Squib Dog had investigated the homeless camp site, finding only a wasteland of smoke, ashes, and garbage.

"I barked and barked for Larry," Squib Dog reported. "But he didn't bark back."

As the meeting continued, River Otter swam closer to shore. He gave Carp a speculative glance before addressing the assembly. "I'm very happy to report that Squib Girl is safe. The water is higher again. She still lives on her raft.

"I saw that rickety thing," said Carp. "It's just a floating Squib shack."

"She scavenged some extra materials," River Otter explained. "Her raft is bigger now."

"Why does she need a bigger raft?" asked Raccoon.

"Right now, only she and Owl's body are on board, but when the flood comes, her raft must have enough room for the survivors."

"I'm sick and tired of hearing about this flood," said Scrub Jay. "For all we know, it's just a big scare story."

Mole piped up. "Why is this Squib Girl still holding Owl captive?"

"It's nothing like that," said River Otter. "They just keep each other company."

Mole didn't look convinced. "Why would Owl want to keep company with a Squib?"

Squib Girl's possession of Owl's body had disturbed many delegates. The Birds had delivered Owl's corpse to her raft, never explaining their reasons. Nobody talked—not Red-Tailed Hawk, Bald Eagle, or Osprey, not Sparrow, Finch, Swallow, or Black-Capped Chickadee. What did Squib Girl plan to do with Owl's putrefied body? Maybe River Otter knew, but he offered no information.

Squib Dog barked for attention. "I'm glad her and Owl have a home. Being homeless is the worst kind of feeling."

"Stop your sniveling, Bowser brains," Squirrel chittered.

"Do you think you're the only animal with a hard-luck story?"

Squib Dog scratched his ear with a hind leg. "I'm just saying it's hard work staying alive. Me and Miss Kitty got abandoned by our owners. I scavenge food from garbage cans and share it with Miss Kitty 'cause she's blind and can't hunt."

Nearby, Scratchit crouched next to a clump of thistles. At every Bird chirp or tweet, she flinched and flattened her ears. If she dared to move, Red-Winged Blackbird dive-bombed her.

"Isn't this Squib Girl a member of the USA now?" asked Western Pond Turtle.

Mole poked her head up from the dirt. "We haven't officially voted on it. Some of us have moral scruples about admitting a Squib to the USA."

"Moles have moral scruples?" asked Scrub Jay.

Mole ducked down into his mound, only his snout protruding. "My moral scruples aren't any of your business."

"If Squib Girl joins the USA," Raccoon asked, "who is her constituency? Does she represent other Squibs?"

"She represents only herself," River Otter said. "She can't speak or hear, of course, but she uses sign language to communicate. Nobody can understand her except me."

"Well, aren't you special," said Elrod.

"If Maggie were alive," Hummingbird said, "I'm sure she would counsel us to keep an open mind about the Squibs."

Elrod snickered. "She is alive. The great Mushroom Maggie got reborn as one of them Mouse Dicks."

Hummingbird performed a few J-shaped dives, then came to an abrupt halt just above him. "Scratchit murdered Maggie and Coyote ate her. She never had the chance to rip the demons of negativity from your little black heart."

Elrod jumped as if kicked in the butt. "Maggie made your own little heart go pitter-patter, didn't she? Now she's just one of Coyote's poopsicles. Better wise up, pollen puss. The same could happen to you."

Hummingbird flew up into the treetops and released a series of trills, buzzes, and high-pitched chirps.

"We go at each other like a pack of rabid Dogs," Heron grumbled.

"I'm not rabid," said Squib Dog. "I'm current with my shots."

"Then you must have Hookworms. Maybe that's why you keep dragging your ass across the dirt."

Heron was going through a rough patch. Kingfisher had gotten sick and died, and now Heron was even grumpier than usual. He missed having somebody around to absolutely agree with him.

Raccoon stood on her hind legs, clasping her patchy tail. Being booted from her job had left a deep emotional wound. "If Owl trusts Squib Girl, so should we. As one of the talon-selected dream-talkers, I'd like to say that— "

"I'm a dream-talker, too," said Elrod, "but I don't go around blabbing about it like a brainless fool."

"We are in full crisis mode," Raccoon continued. "To confront our frightful emergencies, we need inspirational leadership. Therefore, I propose we remove Muskrat from office and reinstall me as secretary-general."

"You still calling yourself Jane?" asked Heron.

"Why do you ask?"

"That name stinks like a dead Fish."

Raccoon gnawed her tail. "You really despise me, don't you?"

"Absolutely."

Raccoon looked around the assembly, seeking support, but found none. "What's so wrong about calling myself Jane the Raccoon? Nobody calls Elrod just plain Stoat or

Weasel. Why does that Rabbit-killer get a name and I don't!"

Elrod flashed his fangs. "Careful, sweetheart. You don't wanna trigger my PTSD."

Squib Dog barked loudly. "Let's focus on the important stuff. Larry's still missing and I'm worried sick about him."

"Coyote's also missing," said Elrod. "How come you're not worried sick about somebody that matters?"

Squib Dog snorted. "I hear something spooked him, so he cut and ran like a scared Rabbit."

"Coyote just needed some alone time!"

Squib Dog scratched his ear again. "Alone time? Did he want to talk to his dinky stinky without an audience?"

From her muddy spot in the cattails, Muskrat let out a weak squeak. "Oh, would you two please give it a rest?"

Squirrel emerged from a root wad. "We're all scared, Muskrat. Awful things are happening to us."

River Otter clambered onto a rotten cottonwood log not too far from Muskrat and stood erect. Whenever he wanted to express his thoughts, he could chirp, grunt, or hiss. He could also whistle, which he did now, alerting everyone that he had something important to say.

"I propose that we officially vote Squib Girl into the United Slough of Animals," he said.

Crow hopped down from a cottonwood limb. "I agree. She's easy to fool. I traded her for a shiny thing. All she got in exchange was a round white rock."

Red-Tailed Hawk squawked from the topmost cottonwood branch. "You're using that shiny thing of yours to blind me!"

"He blinded me, too," said Heron. "Makes it hard to gig Frogs."

Crow hopped in a circle. "I try to stay civil while you fools snivel your drivel, but every stool I drop still looks just like you and you."

Scrub Jay squawked. "Will somebody remind me again how this little hand-talking Squib can help us?"

"We can't survive the flood without her," said River Otter.

"If a flood comes, I'll just fly up into a tree and wait it out. But I keep wondering about something. How come you and Squib Girl are so chummy?"

River Otter kept his composure. "We like each other's company. She talks to me with her hands. I talk to her with my paws. And we enjoy swimming together."

A gurgle rose from Elrod's throat. "You swim with her?"

"Swimming is very therapeutic. It's what Maggie would call liquid meditation. Anyway, lots of us love to swim. Nutria, Carp, Western Pond Turtle, Muskrat. Now that I think of it, Elrod, even you don't mind wetting your fur when you're scarfing Duck eggs on the sly."

Saliva fizzed between Elrod's fangs. "Why are you taking a big crap on my good name? I thought you were too goody-goody for that, but you're just like everybody else!"

River Otter held up his paws. "No harm, no foul. To help us win the war on the Rats, we admitted Squib Dog and Scratchit Cat to the USA. They're kinda like half-Squibs, but we gave them the vote. Therefore, I think we should invite Squib Girl to join us. "

"I didn't vote for no lousy house pets," said Elrod. "They're not real animals like us. Neither is Squib Girl."

"You couldn't vote for anybody back then," Raccoon reminded him. "You were a general in the Grand Army of Rats. You were trying to kill us."

"Elrod's just barking out his butt," said Squib Dog. "Me and Miss Kitty didn't get any kind of free ride. We earned our votes fair and square, thank you very much. But if this Squib Girl will play toss and fetch with me, she's got my vote."

"We need Squib Girl," said River Otter. "And her raft. A

hard rain's gonna fall. I can't make it any simpler than that. Let's vote for Squib Girl to join the USA."

"You've gone sweet on her," said Carp, swimming toward the safety of deeper water. "Your vote shouldn't count."

River Otter took a deep breath. "Let's keep our eye on the prize, okay? We must escape. Soon. Otherwise, we'll all die."

"Escape to where?" asked Mole.

"Owl calls it Second Chance Slough."

"Will we get a second chance there?"

River Otter shrugged. "A second chance sounds much better than no chance, doesn't it?"

Squib Dog groaned. "This flood is a death blow from the Big Bada Boom. Larry warned me about it. Coyote ridiculed him, but Larry was a prophet."

"Live prophets tell lies," said Elrod, "but dead ones don't."

"Larry's not dead! And he isn't a liar!"

Muskrat moved from her cattail cover into full view. Elrod was showing his fangs but she didn't flinch. "I have a question for River Otter," she squeaked. "Is Squib Girl's raft large enough to save *all* the animals of Come Along Slough?"

River Otter took a long moment before answering. "There's hardly enough room for the current members of the USA."

"We're going to abandon our constituents? The ones we've sworn to protect and serve?"

River Otter hung his head. "If we try to save everybody, we save nobody."

Muskrat reached back and snapped off a cattail. "So you're saying that we're the chosen ones of the Chosen One?"

River Otter shuddered. "It hurts my heart, Muskrat, but we must leave behind our kith and kin."

"As the chosen ones, have we chosen to do the right thing?"

River Otter still didn't meet her eye. "Life goes on—by any means possible."

"That might be true," said Muskrat, "but why do we get to decide what kind of life goes on?"

A rustling sound in the underbrush alarmed them.

"The Squibs are coming!" Elrod shrieked. "We're all gonna die!"

A branch snapped. A thin gray shadow appeared.

"Everybody chill out!" Elrod shouted. "It's Coyote!"

"He looks half-dead," said Mole.

Coyote limped toward them, his tail drooping, several bald patches showing along his lean flanks. He looked … old. He halted and lifted his gray head. "I have returned home," he announced.

"Nobody missed you," said Squirrel. "Go away."

"Ditto that," said Raccoon.

Elrod scrambled over to Coyote, stood on his hind legs, and squinted at him. "Is it really you, Coyote? You don't look like yourself no more. You been run over by a truck or something? What happened to you?"

Coyote moaned. "Old Man Coyote happened."

Elrod snickered. "I bet you were just crunching a grumpy. Or maybe your hot sloppies ripped you a new one."

Coyote gazed at the Slough, his eyes cloudy. "Old Man Coyote was real enough to starve me and beat me. He set me on fire, dunked me in an icy lake, and drowned me. He brought me back to life and drowned me again. I never knew whether I was dead or alive. That's how real he was."

"This Old Man Coyote must be a big asshole."

Coyote groaned. "I thought he was my father, but I was wrong."

"Then who was he?"

"A cruel teacher, but I learned his lessons well."

"Didja learn anything worthwhile?"

"To avoid Rattlesnakes."

"Sheesh. You're really harshing on yourself. How come?"

Coyote grimaced as he shifted his weight. "I wish to apologize to you, Elrod."

"Stop it, okay? You're really weirding me out."

"I took advantage of your weak intellect. For that, I am truly sorry."

"Uh-oh," Mole told Elrod, "Coyote's still taking advantage of your weak intellect."

River Otter whistled loudly. Heads turned. Everyone saw him pointing one muddy paw at the Slough.

"Look!" Raccoon squealed. "Look! Look!"

Close to the shoreline, Squib Girl stood on her raft. A flimsy crossbeam bisected a wooden post affixed to the aft. Owl's skeleton hung from the crossbeam, her extended wing bones tethered in place. A few remnant feathers fluttered in the breeze. The skull listed to one side, as if Owl were enjoying an afternoon nap.

Some animals began to chant. "Chosen One! Chosen One! Chosen One!"

33 STARVATION ISLAND

The murky silhouette of land came into sight. Squib Dog paddled harder, keeping his head above the floodwater as Scratchit Cat clung to his back, her claws clasping his neck. Waves of wind-driven rain swept over his head. All day, he'd carried stranded animals to Starvation Island. Exhausted and hungry, he was losing patience with Scratchit. He'd just coaxed her down from a tree, where the floodwaters had trapped her. Now she was pasted flat against his back.

"Swim faster," she demanded. "I'm getting wet."

"Let's swap spots," Squib Dog said. "How about I ride on your back for a while?"

"Sorry, but I don't swim."

"Do the Cat paddle. Or the Kitty crawl."

"I said, I don't swim. I didn't say I *can't* swim."

"So, you can swim?"

"I have some emotional issues related to water."

Squib Dog wished Larry could help him with these rescue missions, but he was still missing. Squib Dog had had several dreams about him. More waking hallucinations than dreams. Larry kept popping up in unexpected places and disappearing. He never stuck around for long. Was Larry dead? Squib Dog didn't want to think about it too much, but he sure missed his friend.

He spoke to Scratchit. "Since you can swim, it'd sure be swell if you could spell me for a bit."

She dug her claws in deeper. "Not gonna happen. I hate water. Before you knew me, I had … a litter of kittens."

"Aww, how sweet. You were a mama! How many baby Pussy Cats didja pop out?"

"Eight. My Squibs drowned them. They hadn't even opened their eyes yet. That's why I hate water."

"Oh. Gosh. Sorry."

"Please keep swimming."

For weeks, a heavy rain had fallen nonstop. Solid things became spongy and slumped from sight. Water liquefied the land, the days and nights dissolving into a netherworld where no sun lit up the forest floor, and no moon silvered the meadow. The flood had caused the Slough to double, then triple in size. Spilling over its historic boundaries, it had swamped the surrounding neighborhoods and merged with the Big River to the north, submerging the land in a vast mass of oceanic gray that churned and roared over everything in its path. The Squibs fled to higher ground, abandoning homes and workplaces.

Many of Come Along Slough's animals had drowned in their dens, burrows, cubbyholes, and nests. Western Pond Turtle, Carp, and Nutria swam up a side channel, seeking less turbulent waters. Red-Tailed Hawk, Osprey, and Bald Eagle clung to the treetops, hunching their shoulders against the lashing rain. Hummingbird, Flicker, and Red-Winged Blackbird sought shelter in the crevices and hollows of snags or logs but were soon flooded out. Squib Dog had rescued those that he could. The survivors congregated on a small shoulder of land still above the floodwaters. Food was scarce there. Muskrat had named it Starvation Island.

This island was a gigantic Squib landfill. It looked like a

lopsided volcano, its bulging flanks venting cloudlets of sulfurous smoke. Yet it hosted dense growths of weeds, shrubs, and trees that rooted themselves in subterranean slabs of garbage. Squib Dog had helped bury hundreds of Rats here. Dead Rat Island seemed a more fitting name than Starvation Island.

Regardless, the island had saved dozens of lives—at least for the moment. The surviving animals shivered in the cold there, the ground a churn of sticky black pudding. Strong winds had sheared off limbs and toppled trees.

Fighting the turbulent current, Squib Dog swallowed water and gagged, but kept his eyes on Starvation Island.

"Are we there yet?" asked Scratchit.

"Hang on. Just a little bit longer."

"I'm soaked."

"I'm completely dry."

"Ha ha. Very funny."

"I'm kinda curious about something."

"Curious? You're not a Cat. A Dog can't be curious about anything."

"Didja ever have more Kittens? After the first ones got drowned?"

"No."

"Squibs get you fixed or something?"

"I refused to mate anymore. Why have more offspring if they just get drowned?"

"Whoa. That musta been rough. Not mating, I mean."

"Not as rough as losing my babies."

"For me, mating was a special kinda fun. Then my Squibs whacked off my nuts. Talk about rough. Don't you miss mating—all that scratching, hissing, and yowling?"

"When a female Cat says no, she means it."

"We've both been through the ringer," said Squib Dog. "We're trauma-bonded. Larry taught me all about that."

He squinted at Starvation Island, searching for a safe

spot to crawl ashore. He recalled a line from a song he'd heard Squib children singing: *"Ding-dong, Pussy's in the well!"* He swam harder, more determined than ever to save Scratchit from drowning.

Once, before the creation of the Industrial Sanctuary, Squib Dog had gone to Starvation Island with Larry. It hadn't been an island then, of course; it was just a landfill reeking of things that only a Dog's nose could appreciate.

"This place has its own tectonics," Larry had explained. "Subterranean layers of garbage collide. They grind against each other and release enough nutrients to support this stunted forest of cottonwoods, pin oaks, ash, ailanthus, red alder, and cedar. The Squibs can't ever get it through their thick heads that Mother Nature bats last."

As usual, Squib Dog hadn't understood all of Larry's big words, but he had enjoyed exploring this Dog-unfriendly jungle with his friend. Larry had studied up on plants. He identified tangled thickets of hawkweed, loosestrife, and spiny cockleburs that hugged the twisted tree trunks. Blackberry vines and English ivy were entwined in the forest canopy. Chunks of concrete, broken glass, bricks, and rusty machine parts were jumbled up in the understory. They had left the landfill limping, their paws punctured and bleeding.

Squib Dog caught a wind-driven wave and hit the shore hard. Gasping for breath, he worked his way up through a mingle-mangle of tree branches, plastic bags, broken bottles, fishing tackle, steel cables, and rebar. Gaining higher ground, he collapsed onto a water-soaked mattress pooching up from a hummock of shattered glass and spent shell casings.

"I am one soggy Dog," he said.

Scratchit jumped off and shook out her fur. She raised a paw and licked it. "What a dump," she said.

Squib Dog laughed. "You're lucky you're blind."

They still had to climb higher, but Squib Dog felt too

exhausted to carry Scratchit on his back. If he'd had his druthers, he'd transport her by the scruff of her neck, but Scratchit would have none of that. Dog slobber disgusted her.

"We gotta keep going," he told Scratchit. "Can you walk for a bit?"

Scratchit shook off her fur. "You lead. I'll follow your scent trail."

He was tired of being her seeing-eye Dog. When he guided her, Scratchit insisted upon verbal directions. "Go left" or "go right" worked just fine for her. "Stop," "turn around," and "duck" also worked. Sometimes, he made mistakes, failing to warn her when Birds swooped down to attack her head. She blamed Squib Dog for every bump, bruise, scratch, or patch of missing fur.

In the heavy downpour, they climbed slowly up the muddy slope, Squib Dog barking out commands to Scratchit. Torrents of water plowed-up rocks and garbage, creating a series of small avalanches. Scratchit flattened her body and released a long yowl.

"I'm not taking another step," she moaned. "I want to die!"

"We're almost there. Then you can die."

"Leave me alone! I hate you!"

"You hate me? Why?"

"Because you're trying to save me!"

Squib Dog seized Scratchit by the scruff of her neck and carried her uphill.

"Put me down!" she screeched. She tried scratching him but couldn't twist her body around into an effective attack position.

With a mouthful of Cat fur, Squib Dog pushed ahead. Branches swatted his face, the thick sludge on the slope sucking at his paws. He stumbled several times, dragging Scratchit through the slop, but he kept going until he arrived at a level space where the thin canopy of trees provided partial protection from the storm. Even this high up, the roar of the floodwater was loud. He dropped Scratchit next to a bush. She crawled into the foliage, flattened her body, and growled.

Squib Dog spotted the survivors. The animals were huddled together for warmth. Nobody greeted him. In the branches above, a bedraggled company of Birds kept silent watch. A dreary, unsociable bunch, but Squib Dog didn't blame anyone for feeling under the weather. The animals had lost everything—homes, friends, families, and food. He wasn't any different from them, except he was too busy helping others to moan about the sorry state of everything.

Muskrat came forward, her black tail dripping water. Squib Dog was pleased that she was still the USA's secretary-general. Given all the abuse she'd endured, he was surprised she'd hadn't just called it quits, but during the current disaster, she'd shown the gumption to do the thankless job of coordinating the logistics of disaster relief. He admired her for that.

"Good work," she told Squib Dog. "Is that everybody now?"

He wagged his crooked tail. "Everybody I could find."

He wanted her to pat him on the head and say, "Good boy," instead of "Good work." Whenever he pleased them, his Squibs had patted his head. A friendly hand felt much better than an angry fist.

"On behalf of the USA," said Muskrat, "let me congratulate you on your selfless service. You must be hungry."

Squib Dog's tongue flopped out. "I could eat the south end of a Skunk and come back for seconds."

She laughed. "Better a Skunk than a Porcupine. Coyote told me he tried eating one. It didn't end well for him."

"Did Squib Girl deliver more food?"

"Yes. Her raft arrived this morning. It was a real mob scene. Everyone's close to starving."

Squib Dog had no idea how Squib Girl obtained bread, sunflower seeds, dried fruits, and root vegetables. She even delivered gunny sacks of meat scraps, bones, and fish guts, which Elrod and Coyote quickly dispatched. Muskrat wanted the food stockpiled at the island's summit, where it could be rationed out. But dragging the food uphill from Squib Girl's raft was a slow show. Everyone kept stopping to gorge themselves on the goods. Very little food made it to the top.

Squib Dog glanced at a scattered, picked-over pile of vittles. While he was out rescuing animals, the others had been stuffing themselves.

"Please eat," Muskrat told him. "We'll be leaving soon."

Squib Dog whined. "I just got here."

"The water keeps rising. Squib Girl will take us aboard her raft."

"Larry hasn't showed yet, has he?"

Muskrat shook her head. "Sorry."

"Dang."

"I hate to tell you this, but River Otter learned from Squib Girl that the Dogs at the homeless camp got shot."

Squib Dog whined again. "Larry was way too smart to get himself shot."

"Go eat. You need to keep up your energy."

He approached the food pile, avoiding the muddle of carrots, celery, and turnips. Sniffing and pawing at a slice of moldy white bread, he discovered a small chunk of cold fat beneath it. He wolfed it down. The bread, too. Looking up, he saw Elrod smirking at him. He stood next to Coyote, who was napping. Squib Dog felt the hair on his back stand up.

"You on a d-d-diet?" Elrod asked. "You're just p-p-picking at your food."

Since Coyote's return to Come Along Slough, Elrod had

developed a bad stutter. Squib Dog figured it had something to do with what Larry called a "crisis of confidence." It could happen to anybody.

"Not much left that'll stick to my ribs, Brother Elrod."

"I f-f-forgive you."

"For what? For not getting my fair share of the grub?"

"For f-f-failing to defend me. Because of your incom-p-p-pee-tence, I got banished from the Slough."

Squib Dog turned away from Elrod and gazed at the other animals in the general area: Crow, Hummingbird, Nutria, Squirrel, Mole, Scrub Jay, and Raccoon. More animals lingered further off. Some chittered, snuffled, or growled, but most were silent. All in all, a sullen group. Nobody looked very alert. Squib Dog felt grateful for his meager leftovers.

He had carried many of these animals to Starvation Island. He resented that Hummingbird, Scrub Jay, and Crow had hitched a ride on his back instead of flying. At least they didn't weigh much. He had also hauled Coyote and Elrod to safety. They swam just as well as he did, yet both claimed they had bad "swimmer's cramps." Squib Dog wasn't going to hold a grudge against anybody who took advantage of him, though. Helping to keep a few noses above water was all the thanks he needed.

Searching for something else to eat, he looked up. Larry stood a few paces off, wagging his bald tail. Squib Dog wagged back. Larry hadn't changed; he still had kinky white fur and bulging green eyes. Squib Dog looked left and right. Nobody else seemed to notice Larry except him.

Larry gave him a knowing wink. "This Big Bada Boom is a real Toad-choker."

"It's raining devils and pitchforks," Squib Dog agreed.

Larry yelped and flopped around on the ground, his mouth foaming, his legs rigid. "Run!" he gasped. "Run!"

Squib Dog ran in circles around him. "Run where?" He bumped into Elrod.

"Hey! Watch where you're g-g-going!"

"Larry told me to run!"

"Larry's d-d-d-dead, numb n-n-nuts. Or haven't you heard?"

34 THE FEATHER CEREMONY

Muskrat cleared her throat and addressed the assembled group, her squeaky voice competing with the wind howling through the canopy.

"Squib Girl will meet us on the leeward side of the island," she said. "She and River Otter will help us board her raft."

"Why can't we just stay here and wait out the storm?" asked Nutria.

Muskrat stared up into the trees. "The flood is ripping the island apart."

"Any f-f-food on the raft?" Elrod asked.

"Squib Girl has scavenged enough to last us a few days."

"Better b-b-be some meat. I hate v-v-v-v-vegetables."

"Beggars can't be choosers," said Squib Dog.

Elrod snarled at him. "At least I don't t-t-talk to dead Dogs!"

Squib Dog ambled over to Elrod, cocked his hind leg, and let loose a stream of hot urine. "Oops! Sorry. Thought you were a rotten tree stump."

Elrod screeched and shook himself dry. "You d-d-d-did that on purpose!"

Coyote had been napping, but Elrod's outraged cries woke him. One eye snapped open. His snout wrinkled up. "Ugh. What smells so bad?"

"Squib Dog p-p-pissed on me!" Elrod shouted.

"Pipe down," said Coyote. "I'm trying to sleep."

Muskrat squeaked for attention. "To calm our nerves for the ordeal ahead, we must conduct a special ceremony."

"My nerves won't ever calm down," said Raccoon, "until I feel safe."

Muskrat sighed. "Squib Dog, will you please do the honors?"

He trotted over to the hollowed-out base of a red cedar and retrieved a feather. Holding it gently in his jaws, he delivered it to Muskrat. The feather hadn't weathered well. It was frayed, the quill frail and limp like a snippet of straw.

Muskrat cradled the feather in her paws, gazing reverently at its tattered patterns of gray and tan. "This is one of Owl's tail feathers," she explained.

Lightning flashed through the canopy, brightening the dark spaces below. Trees groaned and branches cracked. Thunder shook the ground. Black water bubbled up. Muskrat kept talking.

"We will pass Owl's feather around, and when you hold it, you will share your feelings about—"

"G-g-g-give it to me first," said Elrod, who was hunched down into a brown furry ball, his teeth chattering. "I-I-I-I got lots of f-f-feelings."

"No!" said Coyote. "I will speak first."

Coyote was fully awake now. He stood in a pocket of gloom, gaunt and gray, his eyes hooded. Limping over to Muskrat, he took the feather from her, then dropped it on the ground.

"I can't speak with a feather in my mouth," he explained. "My apologies."

Muskrat backed away. "Just say whatever you wish to get off your chest."

River Otter scampered out from the underbrush. "We got to leave!" he shouted. "Now! A humongous mountain of water is headed our way!"

"You can't speak," said Muskrat, "'til Coyote gives you the feather."

"Squib Girls says the dams have busted open!"

Nutria waddled up to River Otter. "Dams? Like Beaver dams?"

A black geyser erupted nearby. Water surged around the trees, sweeping up the debris. Then the ground vomited a huge clot of decomposed Rats. They surged across the ground as if still alive.

"Eeeeeeeeeeek!" Elrod screeched. "Run for your lives!"

"Don't panic!" Muskrat squeaked. "We will exit toward the raft in an orderly manner."

Blinded by the rain, the animals sprinted, scampered, and skidded downhill. Elrod ran the fastest. The Birds beat their wings, trying to gain the advantage of flight, but the downpour drove them to ground, forcing them to hop and skip along with the land animals. Even Hummingbird couldn't stay airborne.

River Otter zig-zagged up and down the hill, urging everyone forward. "Stay together!" he shouted. "We're almost there!"

With no canopy to protect the animals, the storm's full force slammed into them. The ground cracked open and spewed a gaseous stench.

Squib Dog helped where he could, picking up the fallen and barking words of encouragement. Then he skidded to a stop. He'd forgotten Scratchit!

35 THE RAFT

Squib Dog fought his way uphill against torrents of muddy water and dead Rats. Every step was punishing, but he found Scratchit wedged beneath a log. She turned her puckered eye sockets toward him, mewling like a lost Kitten.

"If I get on that raft," she moaned, "I'll drown!"

"Get on my back!" Squib Dog commanded.

He lowered himself next to her, mud squishing out from beneath his haunches. Scratchit hesitated. Then she climbed slowly onto his back, her chin quivering against his neck. Squib Dog bolted down the hill, Scratchit flopping from side to side, but she dug in her claws and held fast.

At the bottom, Squib Dog found the raft. The other animals were already aboard. It was a smaller group. Not everyone had made it.

Squib Dog saw Owl—at least, what was left of her: talons, a rib cage, and a large boney beak attached to a skull. Her skeleton gyrated in the wind, rattling against the pole and crossbeam. A few animals hunkered below the bones, chanting.

"Chosen One! Chosen One! Chosen One!"

Squib Girl had fastened several slipshod structures

together, creating a Caterpillar raft. Rope lashed the segments together. The raft rolled and bucked in the turbulent water like flotsam. At the center of the main raft, boxes were stacked and secured with netting. Several ropes were looped and knotted around a slab of concrete and rebar that jutted out from the shore, preventing the raft from being swept away.

Squib Dog hesitated at the shoreline. Wind roared over the island, snapping trees and heaving them downhill. To board the raft, he'd have to swim with Scratchit on his back. He wasn't sure whether he had enough strength left for that now.

"Put me down," she said. "I want to die!"

A bolt of joy shot through Squib Dog. He saw Larry standing at the corner of the raft! Bracing his legs to maintain balance, Larry wagged his little bald tail.

"Jump, Squib Dog!" he barked. "Jump!"

Squib Dog jumped, Scratchit hugging his back. Spanning the water, he landed on the pitching deck. His legs buckled. He slid and spun, cracking his head hard against the corner of a wood box. Scratchit flew off his back.

Squib Dog lifted his head, his vision blurry. His head was bleeding. He saw Squib Girl's thin brown body in the raging water. She was swimming toward land, the water yanking at her white garment. Flopping onto the shore, she crawled forward, her hands grasping for purchase. She untied the ropes but the wind blew her back into the water, her hair a flag of black. River Otter swam next to her, his teeth grasping her white garment. He rose and fell as he tugged and pushed Squib Girl. Soon, she wriggled back on board and River Otter followed as the flood took full possession of the raft.

Gaining his feet on the pitching deck, Squib Dog searched for Scratchit. He found her cringing between two wooden boxes.

"You hurt?" he asked.

She didn't answer.

Water roared around the raft. A rumble rose from the deep. Squib Dog dropped to the boards, cowering, his fur mushing up against Scratchit's.

River Otter scampered back and forth. "Hold tight everybody! Things are getting ugly!"

Squib Dog felt the ticklish rasp of a tongue on his face.

"You're bleeding like a Pig," said Scratchit. "I'm trying to clean you up."

The raft rose quickly, as if flying up into the sky. Then a huge wave crashed onto the raft and pushed it underwater. Darkness. The raft resurfaced, spinning faster and faster. Squib Dog felt Scratchit's claws on his neck.

"I really do hate water," she moaned.

Yet another wave pounded the raft. Darkness. Squib Dog swallowed water. The raft rose again, and he gasped for air, hacking up a string of bloody phlegm. Something snaked past his nose. A rope! At night, his Squibs had roped him up outside in the rain and cold after neighbors complained that he'd knocked over their garbage cans. He hated the feel of a rope on his neck. Dogs were meant to run free! But now he clamped his jaws on the rope. It was his only lifeline.

36 BONE SOUP

JUST AFTER DAWN, Squib Dog woke cold and groggy. His muscles and bones ached. His head was spinning. He spat something out—a chunk of rope. He looked around, his neck bones cracking.

The storm had wrenched off parts of the raft, its rickety remains creaking in the slow lift and roll of each swell. Up and down the raft went, its nauseating motion tugging at his guts. The wind and rain had stopped, but the low gray sky promised no sun. Water stretched in all directions. No land in sight—just big water and big sky. The raft was small. He was smaller.

He caught a heady whiff of salt. Was this the ocean? Sure smelled like it. His Squibs had taken him to the ocean once. He'd been just a Pup. He'd romped on the beach, snagged seaweed, chased Seagulls, and crunched Crab shells. Wet sand and spindrift clogged his nostrils. What great fun! His Squibs had tossed a stick into the surf, commanding him to fetch it. The breaking waves knocked him silly, but his Squibs laughed and tossed the stick again. Going after it, he had gone under and come close to drowning.

He looked around the raft, searching for Larry. His friend's words still echoed inside his head. *"Jump, Squib Dog! Jump!"*

During the night, he'd dreamt that he and Larry were trotting together around Come Along Slough, the midsummer sun bearing down on their heads, the air thick with the smell of rotting algae, warm mud, and motor oil.

"You're a good boy," Larry told him.

Squib Dog beamed. "Thanks for making me into a better Dog than I was ever meant to be."

They discussed sundry subjects such as supply-side economics, the Big Bada Boom, the bone-deep delight of rolling on dead animals—and sex.

"I miss my balls," Squib Dog said.

"Even without them," said Larry, "you still have a pair."

"Being all balls and no brains had its upside. Thinking is hard work."

"If you have a big heart and a big soul, who needs big balls—or a big brain?"

Squib Dog stopped and faced his friend. "Living without a home is hard. I don't miss my Squibs, but I miss being warm and having a juicy soup bone to gnaw on."

"Do you miss anything else?" asked Larry.

Squib Dog pondered for a moment. "I miss belonging to someone who cares what happens to me. That should be part of a Dog's Bill of Rights."

A cold, wet nose against his ear startled Squib Dog. It was River Otter.

"How you feeling?" he asked.

Squib Dog yawned. "I got Nightcrawlers on the brain."

River Otter scratched his belly and belched. "Not me. I just got Fish breath."

"I'm parched. I need to wet my whistle."

"Look around. Water's everywhere. Drink your fill."

River Otter chuckled. "I was joking. You can't drink salt-water—but there's some fresh water that Girl collected."

"Girl? You mean Squib Girl?"

"We don't call her that anymore. She's earned the right to be called Girl."

"I almost forgot to ask. Is Scratchit okay?"

River Otter frowned. "Sorry. She was swept overboard. She wasn't the only one. I did my best, but I couldn't save everybody."

Squib Dog whimpered as he recalled the curative rasp of Scratchit's tongue on his head wound. "Me and Miss Pussy didn't always see eye to eye, but we kept each other company, and during hard times, we pulled in the same direction."

River Otter patted his shoulder. "I really appreciate how you always try to see the best in everybody."

Squib Dog looked around the raft. "Larry was here. I saw him."

River Otter's brow furrowed. "I haven't seen him. Sorry."

"So many animals have died. Where did they all go?"

"It's a real puzzle," said River Otter. "Here today, gone tomorrow. It's like somebody's playing a joke on us, huh?"

"I'm not laughing. How can Scratchit and Larry just stop ... existing?"

"You need to eat something. If you don't eat, *you'll* also stop existing."

Squib Dog pointed a shaky paw at a stout wooden pole that supported a rectangular patchwork of rags. Catching a breeze, it billowed out. "What's that?"

"We got one clever Girl aboard," River Otter explained. "She pieced that thing together herself. Calls it a 'mainsail.' Now the raft moves at a pretty good clip. She steers the raft with some kind of weird-looking thingamajig called a 'rudder.' We got taken for a wild ride, but critters like us were born to weather storms."

"You helped . . . Girl swim back to the raft. She was drowning."

River Otter smiled. "Take a good gander at her. Ain't she something gorgeous?"

She stood at the edge of the raft, her head tilted back, eyes closed, arms outstretched. Water laved her feet, the morning breeze weaving her hair around her shoulders. As he watched her, Squib Dog wondered whether Girl wanted a four-legged companion—a faithful Dog who would stay close by her side and protect her from danger. He'd talk to her with his paws and beg her to rub his belly. He gave River Otter a suspicious glance. Had Mr. Positive beaten him to claiming rights? Was he Girl's pet? He fought off an urge to scent mark the space around her, just to let River Otter know he had claiming rights.

"You and Girl seem joined at the hip," he said.

River Otter chirped, amused by this statement. "Like I toldja, she talks with her hands. I talk with my paws. She swims, I swim. We're perfect pals. Two peas in a pod!"

Squib Dog was unsure what "two peas in a pod" meant, but maybe Girl wouldn't mind having *two* pets. It was possible. He squinted at the expanse of water. "We close to Second Chance Slough yet?"

River Otter waggled his head. "What's your hurry, friend? This water's terrific! Been swimming around in it all morning. Snagged some weird-looking thing with tentacles. No bones. Very, very tasty. Wanna join me for a quick wake-up dip?"

"Naw. I already swum off twenty Dog lives. I got none to spare."

Squib Dog watched River Otter slide into the water. Struggling to his feet, he took a few steps, his head pounding, and looked around the raft. He wasn't the only one feeling rocky. Muskrat, Nutria, Crow, Coyote, and Raccoon sat apart, keeping company with themselves while staring listlessly at the heaving plateau of green water. The other survivors huddled elsewhere, their fur and feathers forming muddy clumps of misery.

At the far end of the raft, Squib Dog saw Owl's skeleton. It dangled from the crossbeam, rattling and clicking in the morning breeze. The leg bones were missing. Swallows darted past the skull, their bodies streaks of iridescent blue.

Something whirred close to his face. He flinched. It was Hummingbird. She hovered in front of him, her pepper-speck eyes blazing.

"I saw Owl!" she told him. "I saw Owl!"

Squib Dog tilted his head toward the skeleton. "She's pretty hard to miss."

"I saw her for real!"

"You one of them dream-talkers?"

"I didn't dream-talk with her. During the big storm, I found a crack in her skull large enough for me to squeeze through. I huddled inside her head. It kept me warm and snug. Then a flash of lightning almost blinded me. That's when I saw the Down Under."

"Inside Owl's head?"

"I saw Australia, silly. Maggie's home. Saw it in living color. She and Owl were flying through this lush forest full of flowers and Birds."

"Did Owl say anything to you?"

"Yes. She said if we don't starve, die of thirst, or get killed by hostile animals, we'll eventually make it to Australia."

Squib Dog sighed. "For us, the Down Under might be an impossible dream."

Hummingbird pivoted her body, her wings still whirring, and stared out at the water. "I miss all our dead friends."

"Even Scratchit?"

"She wasn't my friend."

Squib Dog lowered his head. "I miss Larry."

"He helped you build a better brain. Before then, you didn't sound too … Well, you weren't exactly the brightest Pup in the litter. No offense intended."

"None taken."

Squib Dog limped away and stood next to Girl. Her eyes were on the sky. A ragged white garment exposed her chestnut brown legs, arms, and one shoulder. He was close enough to feel her body heat and smell the dried salt on her skin, yet she didn't even give him a glance. He felt deflated.

Other animals gathered behind him: Raccoon, Squirrel, Elrod, and Muskrat. Nutria lagged behind, chewing on something he had dragged up from the water. Scrub Jay, Crow, and Osprey perched on the tattered mainsail. Hummingbird hovered above Girl's head. River Otter climbed onto the raft, water coursing from his pelt. Nobody spoke.

Coyote joined the group last, wincing with each step, his eyes dull yellow. A breeze raised a thin ridge of gray fur along his backbone. Everyone watched him, including Girl.

Muskrat broke the silence. "That storm stole away Owl's

feather," she said, "but Coyote still wants to share his thoughts."

Coyote eased himself slowly down onto his haunches and scanned the water. "I have some bad news," he said. "I regret to inform everyone that Second Chance Slough doesn't exist. It has never existed."

The animals gasped.

"I was h-h-hoping to eat some Second Chance R-Rabbits," said Elrod.

River Otter's paws communicated Coyote's words to Girl. Her face showed no emotion.

Coyote kept talking. "From the graveyard of Owl's brain, a fog rose like corpse gas, making it easy for phantasms of false hope to prey upon your vulnerability."

"What's a phantasm?" asked Nutria.

"It's like an air bubble," Squib Dog explained. "It pops into sight, then disappears."

"Second Chance Slough is an air bubble?" asked Squirrel.

Coyote nodded. "Air bubbles on the brain."

Squirrel groaned. "Now I'm really depressed."

Hummingbird buzzed past Coyote's head. "You think you're so clever, but you're a liar and a trickster!"

"I'm a liar and a trickster by nature," Coyote admitted, "but it's also part of my nature to tell stories—true stories."

Muskrat approached Coyote. "You've already told enough bad stories. Isn't it about time for you to tell us a good story?"

"Old Man Coyote told me that. He beat my brains bloody before I finally figured out what in the hell he was getting at."

"He probably just taught you how to tell bigger lies," said Scrub Jay. "Second Chance Slough has to exist. It just has to!"

"Wishful thinking," said Coyote, "is a big mouthful of cattail fluff."

"Then all is lost?" asked Muskrat.

Coyote studied her for a moment. "Perhaps not. But first we must tell ourselves a better story."

"Huh?

Squib Dog whined, frustrated that Girl still hadn't looked at him. Her unnerving black eyes were trained only on Coyote. "My gray matter is all gummed-up," he complained. "Maybe a good story will squash all this danged double talk."

Coyote lifted his paw and pointed at Owl's skeleton. "We already have the bones of a good story."

"You want Owl's bones to tell us a story?" asked Nutria.

Coyote grinned. "We need to flesh out the skeleton and put some meat on those old bones. Then maybe we'll get the story we want to hear."

"Coyote's right," said Elrod. "Let's b-b-b-beef up our story."

"That flood scrubbed the beef clean out of me," Squib Dog groaned.

Squirrel chittered at Coyote. "Since you're such a clever carnivore, tell us a story. Not just a better story. One that's as real as walnuts."

"Then help me make real walnuts. You and everyone else."

"Coyote's using metaphors on us," said Squib Dog. "Bet he learned that's trick from Larry."

"Metaphors?" asked Nutria. "Can I eat them?"

"Metaphors only feed your head," Squib Dog explained. "With pictures."

"Enough of this!" Squirrel screeched. "I just wanna find dry land before I starve!"

"Coyote's asking for our help," said Squib Dog. "He

wants us to help him make soup. Story soup. A good story soup starts with good bones."

Squirrel scurried back and forth on the deck of the raft and stopped. "Too many storytellers will spoil the soup."

"Soup sounds good," said Nutria. "When will it be ready?"

"Larry told me a soup story," said Squib Dog. "Seems this hungry Dog was trying to make soup by boiling this dried-up old bone in a pot of water."

Elrod interrupted him. "Did that Dog piss in the s-s-s-oup?"

"He didn't do nothing of the sort. Different animals kept dropping by, you see, and adding something to the soup. They tossed in carrots, potatoes, turnips, onions, tubers, cattails, dead Mice. Even walnuts. Whatever they had."

"You got it right for once," said Coyote. "I think we're ready to make some soup."

Squib Dog looked at Girl, hoping she might turn her gaze his way and give him an admiring smile. But she only had eyes for Coyote.

The animals fell silent. Coyote cleared his throat and bent his head. He spoke slowly, as if finding his way in the darkness past unseen hazards. "In the beginning, wind, rock, water, and sunlight shaped our world. We had air to breathe, water to drink, food to eat, and a mate to snuggle up with on cold nights." He eased himself back onto his haunches, grimacing. "That's all I got for now. Who's next?"

Girl's hands danced in front of River Otter's face.

"She says Coyote left out an important ingredient," he said.

"He didn't add anything about Kawphonious the Giant Raven," said Hummingbird.

River Otter waved his paws at Girl. Her hands quickly replied.

"Coyote needs to add First Coyote to the soup," he said.

"Last Coyote sounds much better than First Coyote," said Squirrel.

Crow hopped down onto the deck. "Coyote's crock pot is full of tricky talk," he versified. "The pout on his snout leaves no doubt what he's really about."

"We're refugees on Squib Girl's raft," said Muskrat. "Let's honor her wishes about First Coyote."

Many animals muttered their agreement. Crow squawked and flew back to his perch on the mainsail.

Coyote groaned, rose to his feet, and squinted at Girl. Then up at Owl. "Kawphonious was old," he wheezed, "but he wasn't First Coyote old. It was First Coyote who changed the course of rivers, created the mountains, and named the plants and animals."

"He had some kinda magical power?" asked Squirrel.

"Yes, his stories had magic. They made the wind howl, water roar, volcanoes erupt. His stories even had talking animals."

"What about talking Squibs?" asked Raccoon.

"He had no stories to tell about Squibs."

"Was F-F-First Coyote on friendly terms with Stoats?" asked Elrod.

"Did First Coyote name the First Flowers?" asked Hummingbird.

Raccoon held up her tail. "First Raccoon gave me my beautiful rings—not First Coyote."

It was slow work, but the animals contributed whatever they had, every ingredient adding more fat to the story soup.

Girl's hands brought everything to a halt.

River Otter squinted at her, then spoke, his voice tense. "Girl apologizes for the interruption, but she wants us to agree to something that's very important to her."

"I agree to stay alive," said Scrub Jay.

"Just spit it out, River Otter," Raccoon sighed. "What must we agree to?"

River Otter waved his paws again, seeking clarification. He faced the group, his jaw quivering. "She wants our story to tell the future. Our future."

"How can we tell our future without first telling our past?" asked Muskrat.

River Otter looked ill. "She says if we don't create a future, the past will be dead to us."

Muskrat scratched her head. "I guess I'm confused. Can't you just tell us what she's really getting at?"

River Otter gave Girl a glance but didn't move his paws. "She says our future can't have . . . carnivores. The meat eaters of today must become the vegetarians of tomorrow."

"That's a pretty tall order," said Squib Dog.

River Otter nodded agreement. "Even so, she wants the carnivores to switch to a plant-based diet. She feels it's much better for the environment."

Elrod screeched as if snake bitten. "I don't eat plants. End of s-s-s-story."

The other carnivores looked stricken. So did the omnivores. Coyote clenched his jaws and shut his eyes. His tail went limp.

"She's asking us to violate the Natural Law of Animals," said Raccoon.

"If the carnivores here can't eat meat," said Mole, "maybe they'll go extinct. That's fine by me."

"I suppose I could try eating more grass," said Raccoon.

"Tubers ain't meat, right?" asked Nutria.

Hummingbird whirred around Owl's skeleton. "The meat-eaters better not nibble on my flowers."

Squib Dog sat back on his haunches, waved his paws, and stared intently at Girl. "Here's what I'm adding to our soup story: Because Squib Dog was a good Dog and always did what he was told, he stopped eating meat cold Turkey. He ate only vegetables. He found them very . . . uh, succulent. Especially rutabaga and broccoli."

River Otter quickly interpreted his words.

Squib Dog felt the warmth of Girl's hand on his head. She scratched his ears. He whined softly and shivered. His eyes watered-up, and glancing at the clouds, he saw a brighter shade of gray. If the sun broke through the gloom, he'd stretch out and take a long nap. Perhaps he'd dream about Australia.

EPILOGUE: THE MEMORY TREE

The sun had set. Darkness descended. Time for the Festival of RAW to begin! Remembering Ancestors Week was Muskrat's favorite time of the year. It had already started, but she was running late. River Otter often teased her about her habitual tardiness.

"You're always late for everything," he'd tell her. "You'll even show up late when it's time for you to die."

Remembering Ancestors Week was the best kind of fun. Muskrat loved the food and communal merriment. Loved the singing, dancing, and the opportunity to rendezvous with friends and hear stories that had been passed down through the generations.

Her attendance was also a solemn duty. The festival was held in honor of the ancestors. Muskrat was very proud of her own ancestor. Back in the day, Great Mother Muskrat had been the secretary-general of the USA—the United Slough of Animals. During hard times on the Slough, her steadfast devotion to duty had inspired all its members to conserve scarce resources, and during the War on Rats, she led the USA to victory.

The Festival of RAW began on the first new moon— if

the weather allowed it. She felt grateful for the current spell of warm weather. It would make the festival much more enjoyable. The weather was never predictable. Droughts, monsoons, and typhoons. Withering heat and bone-cracking cold. Anything could happen without warning, but tonight was perfect, the sky clear, the air fresh and balmy.

Muskrat scurried through the eucalyptus forest, the eerie nocturnal glitter of Glow Worms adorning every limb. The Glow Worms were burning extra-bright tonight, indicating that these bio-luminescent bug snatchers were on the hunt. Hunger inflamed their elongated guts. After stuffing themselves to satisfaction, they turned down the lights, reverting to a low, steady-as-she goes glow.

Fly-Fox Bat had schooled Muskrat about the Glow Worm, informing her it was the larval form of a fungus-loving Gnat. To capture Mosquitoes, Midges, Hunchback Flies, Scarlet Robins, and Pygmy Possums, the Gnat's larvae hung their long, sticky filaments from beneath the cave-like canopy of the forest. These ghostly blue-green filaments attracted prey. They also offered perfect mood lighting for telling stories about Long-Ago Time.

As she ran, Muskrat sang a song Fly-Fox Bat had taught her:

> *I wish I were a little Glow Worm*
> *Cuz a Glow Worm ain't ever glum*
> *When the sun shines out her bum!*

Muskrat arrived at a small clearing where the other animals had gathered around the campfire. The cozy glow of the red coals created what Hummingbird called "a radiant cloud of remembrance." If Muskrat stared at the coals long enough, the faces of the ancestors floated overhead, their spectral eyes reflecting the hardships and joys of Long-Ago Time.

Muskrat sniffed a communal pile of freshly-gathered fruits, tubers, wild greens, and berries, looking for a suitable snack. Tasting an orange tuckeroo berry, she spat it out. Yuck! Then she spied a juicy cattail. Her favorite food!

Two groups of animals formed an inner and an outer circle. Taking a seat in the inner circle next to River Otter, Muskrat squeaked a greeting through a mouthful of cattail. He was one of her best friends. They spent time together swimming and goofing around in Wallaroo Slough. Her kits and his pups often played water tag while munching on pennywort, swamp lilies, and nardoo.

River Otter put a paw over his snout. "Shhh," he said. "You're late again. Coyote's already started his Long-Ago Time story."

Muskrat saw Coyote. He was a strange one. He often carried on private conversations with himself. Apparently, he had an invisible friend named "Old Man Coyote." This head spook provided advice regarding the political issues of Wallaroo Slough, assuring Coyote that he was the boss of everybody. Right now, Coyote held an Owl feather between paw and chest. Until he passed it on to another animal, he was the designated storyteller. Coyote was long-winded. Muskrat doubted he'd give the feather to anybody else before daybreak.

"I've heard Coyote's voice so often I even hear it droning on in my dreams," she whispered to River Otter.

"Dreamtime always drones on in the Down Under," Otter murmured.

Muskrat gazed around the inner circle of animals. She saw Raccoon, Crow, Squirrel, Dog, Hummingbird, Scrub Jay, Stoat, and a few others. Like her, they were descendants of the ancestors who had claimed this land as their new home.

On the outer circle sat the indigenous animals of these coastal forests, scrublands, swamps, and billabongs. She saw

Kangaroo, Wallaby, Dingo, and Wombat. Koala Bear was also there with Bandicoot, Kookaburra, Wallaroo, and Rainbow Lorikeet. Saltwater Crocodile lounged back in the shadows, his eyes a hard reptilian yellow. Muskrat always avoided swimming near his nest.

The native Down Unders mostly appeared bored, causing Muskrat to bare her chisel-like front teeth. If they weren't enjoying themselves, why did these outer-circle cobbers bother to attend the Festival of RAW?

Coyote's growl kept everyone's attention from flagging.

"As I have told you before," he said, "history begins as tragedy, but ends as fable. With the passage of time, facts never age well. They falter and crumble into myth."

Muskrat grabbed another cattail. It was going to be a long night.

"The memory tree grows the future," Coyote continued. "This tree is the keeper of what we choose to remember. It sinks its roots into the rocky earth and pulls the ghosts of our ancestors up into the sunlight."

"Get on with it, mate!" Kangaroo shouted. "Me and my mob got a boxing match tonight!"

"I'm here to shake a leg—not to hear some balls-up story about a tree," Koala Bear complained.

Coyote wasn't going to let himself be interrupted. "Many, many generations ago, a courageous few of us migrants arrived here on a storm-tossed raft."

"Calling yourselves migrants is no good to Gundy," said Wombat. "You were refugees who come from the far side of the woop woop. You got washed up on our shores like somebody tossed their bikkies. I don't wanna carry on like a pork chop, but why don't you bludgers go back where you belong?"

Muskrat groaned. Why did some of the outer circle animals insist on insulting those of the inner circle? She and her friends were often called "Joe Blakes" and "illywackers."

Coyote leaned over and nibbled a pile of macadamia nuts, quandong fruit, and wattleseeds. Chewing slowly, he gave Wombat a cold stare. "Our ancestors had no desire to leave their homes," he said, "but the Big Bada Boom swept them out to sea. Like many other animals, they were desperate to find a place of safety."

"That's all fair dinkum," said Dingo, "but I'm curious about something. Your teeth ain't made for chewing mangos, now are they? How come you don't eat Rabbits and Rock Rats? You one of them pookie fart banana benders?"

Stoat stood on his hind legs and bared his fangs. "Who you calling a pookie fart banana bender?"

Dog barked for attention. "Everybody just cool out, okay? We're here to tell stories—not to get into a pissing contest. I'm sure Brother Stoat and Brother Dingo agree."

Bandicoot poked a V-shaped face up from the shadows and made her distinctive "whuff-whuff" sound. "I know you got Dingo blood in your veins, Half-Dog, so whose side are you on?"

"Why do I gotta be on anybody's side?"

Muskrat saw Rainbow Lorikeet fly up to perch on a low-hanging eucalyptus bough, her gorgeous plumage clashing with the phantasmal pall of the Glow Worms. Hummingbird joined her, alighting on Rainbow Lorikeet's feathery blue crown.

"G'Day, mates," Rainbow Lorikeet said. "I enjoy a good chinwag, but having a barney is not worth a brass razoo. Makes us sound like two-pot screamers, now don't it? You all sound like a yobbo who's a larkin. Migrants have always been made to feel welcome in the Down Under."

"Gaslighting us like this," Hummingbird added, "aggravates our historical trauma."

Crow flew up and joined them. He fancied himself a poet. Since one of his ancestors was a renowned rhymester, he strived to keep this tradition alive. "Spit it, get rid of it, and put a lid on it," he said. "When we whimper and bicker, the Glow Worm gets sicker and sicker 'til its glimmer grows dimmer!"

"Crikey!" shouted Dingo. "That wanker's got a roo loose in the top paddock!"

"Dingo, don't you have anything constructive to say?" asked Rainbow Lorikeet

"I just wanna know why some of these garden gobblers and grass grazers keep mucking up the whole witchetty grub food chain. Meat-eaters are meant to eat meat! These drongos are like a gum tree full of Galahs!"

Coyote nibbled on another quandong. The red pulpy flesh clung to his snout as he gazed up at the Glow Worms. "In Long-Ago Time, Squib Girl asked us to forsake our natural instincts. In honor of her memory, we eat no meat."

"She was called Girl—not Squib Girl," said Stoat. "Squib was a dirty word back then. Still is—even if the Squibs are beat down for the count."

Coyote bowed his head. "I stand corrected. Girl it is." He clutched the Owl feather to his chest and began his story again. Nobody interrupted him.

Muskrat didn't listen too closely. Like the other inner circle animals, she'd heard the same old story since birth. Girl had saved a few of Come Along Slough's ancestor animals from drowning in the great flood. She took them aboard her raft, and for several hard seasons, high winds and a turbulent sea flung them in all directions. Some animals had drowned or starved to death. The raft made landfall in many different locations. They encountered other animals that inhabited the shorelines, river deltas, and estuaries. The raft's occupants were occasionally offered food and temporary shelter, but resources were scarce everywhere, and they were often attacked and driven back to open sea. Gale force winds eventually blew them far south of the something called "the equator." Girl told them they were in the "roaring forties."

During these stormy times, the raft kept gaining new passengers—climate refugees fleeing the ravages of the Big Bada Boom. Many mated successfully with the raft's surviving occupants, ensuring that the ancestor bloodlines of Come Along Slough didn't die out. Muskrat was glad that Great Mother Muskrat had found a suitable mate. Even Coyote's ancestor had found a good partner. Now his descendants flourished in the Down Under.

Muskrat gave River Otter a nudge.

"Whassup?" he asked, his voice low.

"I've seen Coyote eating meat. Stoat, too."

He nodded. "Everybody has. When they think nobody's looking, they sneak a bite of bone and flesh. They're partial to Black-Footed Tree Rats."

"They're both backsliders," said Muskrat.

"The Natural Law of Animals runs hot in their blood," he said. "It's like they're still stuck in Long-Ago Time."

"Girl would be very disappointed in them."

River Otter's voice choked up. "Girl was our savior. She brought our ancestors to Wallaroo Slough. All she asked in return was for us meat-eaters to curb our appetites."

"Once a meat-eater, always a meat-eater," said Muskrat.

"My ancestor was a fish-eater, but not me."

"I still don't get why Girl sailed away with Squib Dog," said Muskrat. "Why didn't she stay here with us?"

River Otter shrugged. "I never met her, of course, but I miss her like a soul mate."

"She really couldn't talk or hear?"

"They say she used her hands to communicate with my ancestor."

"I'm glad she didn't end up all alone," Muskrat squeaked. "She had Squib Dog for company. And a few of Owl's weather-beaten bones. The Long-Ago stories tell us that Owl was very wise. That's hard to believe. The Down Under's Barking Owls and Boobooks sound kinda dumb to me."

River Otter lowered his voice to a whisper. "Those stories say that Squib Dog couldn't mate."

Muskrat's face grew hot. "Yeah, that's right. His, uh . . . thingamabobs got cut off."

River Otter laughed. "Good thing Girl left behind a male Dog with his thingamabobs in working order. Didn't take him long to hook up with a few female Dingoes and keep the Bowser bloodline going strong. Just imagine Wallaroo Slough without Dogs."

They fell silent for a moment, thinking things over. Finally, Muskrat whispered into River Otter's ear. "Some of these outer circle animals are so rude and mean. Why can't they act nicer toward us?"

River Otter chuckled. "Great Grandpa Otter told my mother that our ancestors were also rude and mean. Animals probably act the same way everywhere."

Muskrat squeaked with indignation. "I'm sure Great Mother Muskrat urged the USA delegates to treat each other with the utmost respect and kindness."

"Hey, sitting here too long is giving me a bad tail bone ache. Let's go take a dip in Wallaroo Slough."

"We can't. It's not very polite to leave in the middle of Coyote's story."

"We'll return when the music and dancing starts, okay? I know a good spot. It's got lots of cattails. And even better, Saltwater Croc can't see us there."

Muskrat nuzzled his fur. "You are a true friend, River Otter."

"I'll race you there."

"Give me a head start. You're lots faster than me."

And they were off.

ACKNOWLEDGMENTS

No writer can survive without the sharp eye of an editor. "The road to hell is paved with adverbs," said Stephen King. Mark Twain advised, "When you catch an adjective, kill it." I also agree with Oscar Wilde: "A poet can survive everything but a misprint."

I wish to thank Robin Fuller, my editor. She yanked out the invasive weeds that choked my garden of prose. Any remaining weeds are due to my inattention to detail. Many thanks to Alicia Robb and Josie Stapleton for reading a rough draft of this novel. They both made many excellent suggestions, schooling me on how not to dehumanize the animals I wish to humanize.

I'm also indebted to Nancy Henry for her decisive, no-holds-barred critiques about theme, voice, and tone. Better than anyone else I know, she understands the torments and pitfalls of the writing process. Literature runs in her veins.

I was very fortunate to have the artistic legerdemain of Hilary Glass, who has a great empathy for animals. I am extremely grateful for her heartfelt and expert illustrations.

And special thanks to the indefatigable Judy Blankenship and Anne McClard, publishers (and editors, too!) of Aristata Press in Portland, Oregon. They've supported the writing of this book in every way possible.

Lastly, I wish to thank all the wild animals who live around (and in) my house for giving me constant feedback about plot, setting, and character. As the true authors of this book, they cleverly commandeered a human to tell their story.

ABOUT THE AUTHOR

Bruce Campbell lives in Portland, Oregon, where he operates a small urban farm close to a golf course recently rewilded into a nature park. He has worked as a high school environmental science teacher and traveled extensively throughout the world. He co-authored an environmental memoir entitled *This Rough Magic: At Home on the Columbia Slough* with his partner Nancy Henry. Bruce has published short stories in Timberline Review, Fabula Press, and the Tishman Review. He won awards in the Kay Snow Writing Contest, and placed in the San Francisco Writing Contest and the Tucson Festival of Arts.

ALSO BY BRUCE CAMPBELL

This Rough Magic: At Home on the Columbia Slough, by Nancy Henry and Bruce Campbell, illustrated by Amanda Williams, August 2023.

OTHER ARISTATA PRESS TITLES

LEAVINGS: Memoir of a 1920s Hollywood Love Child, by Megan McClard, 2022

Díganle a mi madre que estoy en el paraíso: Memorias de una prisionera política en El Salvador, Edited by Judy Blankenship and Andrew Wilson, 2022.

Butterfly Dreams: a Novel, by Anne McClard, September 2023.

Women Caught in the Crossfire: One Woman's Quest for Peace in South Sudan, by Abuk Jervis Makuac and Susan Lynn Clark, October 2023.

Raising Owen: an Extra-ordinary Memoir on Motherhood, by Suzanne Lezotte, October 2023.

NEW TITLES

Echoes of the Lost Boys of Sudan, by Susan Clark and James Disco, July 2024.

Margaux and the Vicious Circle, by Anne McClard, September 2024.

Aristata Press is non-profit organization. We depend on charitable contributions and volunteers to keep the lights on. We are a tax exempt–501(c)(3)–organization (EIN 92-0281706), which means that your contributions are tax deductible. Contributions that we receive will go directly to supporting the publications of deserving literary works by authors that for one reason or another would be unlikely to find a home in the for-profit publishing sector.

Please visit us at: https://aristatapress.com